PRAISE FOR

BARBARA N. MCLENNAN

——— THE WEALTH OF VIRGINIA ———

McLennan's (The Wealth of Jamestown, 2013) historical novel depicts America at a tenuous stage in its early history, when wealth, violence and political unease were all starting to swell.

Sarah Harrison Blair is the sort of historical figure who demands fictional interpretation. Married to one of the founders of the College of William & Mary, the (as characterized in McLennan's novel) loathsome James Blair, Sarah has the business acumen and independent streak to rival any of Colonial America's male adventurers. She is neither shy with a pistol nor afraid to work alongside the laborers in her family's tobacco fields, if that's what will get the job done. ("Darlin', welcome to Virginia justice," she tells one man. "If you keep still, I won't blow your head off.") The Colonial Virginia world in which Sarah operates needs people like her. It's something of a freeforall, with ineffectual governors coming and going, uncertainty about where to establish the colony's capital (Williamsburg is being considered), and perpetual tensions and threats of fighting. Yet it's also a place where democratic values are coalescing, a development made all the more evident in contrast to London, which Sarah and James visit. There, they encounter poverty and abuse all but directly caused by the old system. They also come across some truly riproaring excitement, complete with duels and romance. McLennan writes astutely about the political anxieties of the era—the novel spans the years 1699 to 1710—and depicts a lively world of pirates and paramours. Some observations are made repetitiously. For instance, American Colonial women are more financially savvy than privileged British women, and aristocrats are profligate. And the good guys are exceedingly good, the bad exceedingly bad; several characters are all but evil villains. Though the novel isn't one of great nuance, it's one of impressive scholarship. It will particularly appeal to readers interested in the early planning of Williamsburg.

An informative rendering of preRevolutionary America, with an inspiring female protagonist.

— KIRKUS REVIEW

The Wealth of Virginia, by Barbara McLennan, is the second book in a planned trilogy by the author.

Intelligently crafted to focus on how England's oldest, largest and richest colony got that way. The first in the series focused on Jamestown, its first colonial structured town, and how it grew and developed.

Author McLennan wisely chose to develop this series into novel format rather than straightforward historical document, since the subject matter itself can be complicated and tedious, and the cast of characters, even in this pared down version is very extensive.

One can easily sum up the reason for Virginia's wealth in the late seventeenth century: tobacco. It was the colony's cash crop, and in those early days, few people lived long enough to die from too much smoking. They usually died from something else, including other people who did not like them.

The huge cast of characters, many held over from the first volume of this trilogy, move the story along at a pleasant reading pace. The author briefly reviews the first book's salient events, to a point where The Wealth of Virginia can stand alone very nicely. Most of her characters are real - or at least based on real people. A few have been fabricated for effect.

The plot, slim and more situational than compelling, centers around the fact that the good people of Williamsburg, Virginia, in the throes of becoming the capital of colonial Virginia, heartily disliked their King-appointed governor, Francis Nicholson. They wanted him recalled. So they sent Reverend James Blair who nobody liked either --and his wife Sarah-- who everybody liked and a small party of servants and aides to go to London and do what they could to a) dump Nicholson and b) suggest a suitable replacement, and, while they were at it, c) do a little shopping for all their friends and neighbors.

That, of course, would only take up a dozen or two pages, so McLennan includes an assault --as soon as the Blairs arrive-- a visit to Newgate prison, an unhappy marchioness who really isn't a marchioness but nobody cares, an abusive, wife-beating, mistress-flaunting marquis --who really wasn't a marquis either, but nobody cared about that either-- a duel--guess who dies!-- assorted other mayhem indicative of that time, a couple of small babies thrown in for warm-and-fuzziness, lots of shopping, a general explanation of what the English "factors" actually did --a fair amount by the way!-- a couple of romances, a marriage, an adulterous affair cum pregnancy, and plenty of situational action to make the book a pleasant and nicely-moving read.

Author McLennan obviously knows a great deal about the early colonial days of Virginia, including its economic history and the movers and shakers of that time. It is no mean task to remain true to the facts of the time and the economy - and fictionalize it sufficiently to keep a solid pace and interest. She succeeds admirably.

This is an interesting and enjoyable read for students and for adults as well - especially for those with curiosity about the seventeenth and early eighteenth century in America.

—FEATHER SCHWARTZ FOSTER,
FOR CHESAPEAKE STYLE, WARSAW, VA

———— THE WEALTH OF JAMESTOWN ————

Loved reading about Jamestown residents, and the intrigue involved in their daily lives. This book brought Jamestown to life. Clothing details, the reality of slavery, women's rights in the colony as compared to England, the accumulation of wealth, politics, romance, this book has it all. Really wanted the story to continue.

Was most surprised about James Blair! He was not the man I thought him to be.

Be sure to read this book!!

—CAROL SCHMIDT, WILLIAMSBURG, VA

"This is a great story about a part of our history that is so familiar, yet still far away. A romance set in colonial times, the story describes strong men and powerful women who face the challenges of a harsh world filled with warfare and piracy. The reader will be a part of a great adventure of colonial Virginia."

—BRIAN A. MOORE, MAYOR
CITY OF PETERSBURG, VIRGINIA

"Everyone loves a great read. And this is a great read! It's got everything a reader craves: intrigue, suspense, power struggles of the mighty and the commoner, and the tantalizing clashes of love and money. It's the inside story not taught in the schools — one of the most tumultuous and exciting periods in history. Louis XIV is on the throne of France, England has just fired a king and hired William and Mary as new monarchs, and Virginia simply wants to sell its tobacco, while pirates threaten commerce on the seas. And the reader is on the inside of the entire theatre of action on both sides of the Atlantic!"

— DR. RICHARD OLIVER, FOUNDER AND CEO OF AMERICAN SENTINEL UNIVERSITY, FORMER BUSINESS EXECUTIVE AND COLLEGE PROFESSOR, AND AUTHOR OF A NUMBER OF BESTSELLING BOOKS.

"It is a privilege for Jamestown Settlement to have been part of the inspiration for Barbara McLennan's latest work. Through her fictional account, a period of Virginia's history is vibrantly retold."

— PHILIP G. EMERSON, EXECUTIVE DIRECTOR, JAMESTOWN-YORKTOWN FOUNDATION

"Great book, enjoyed reading about Jamestown. I did not know much about Jamestown, and was happy to receive this book as part of the first reads books. I loved how the author included historical figures from Jamestown in the novel, and also how she included a genealogy in the back of the book about them. After reading this book I want to learn more about Jamestown, and it's founding members. I shall be recommending this book to my friends and family that love history."

—AIMEE, GOODREADS REVIEW

Author Barbara McLennan has come up with an interesting book, and even more interesting, it covers a little tapped mine of American history: the time around 1685-1700, or, to put it in recognizable terms, the time of George Washington's grandfather. Very few books, fiction or non, are dedicated to that time frame. One jumps from Columbus to the Pilgrims and then to ol' George.

But this block of time, when Virginia was the oldest and wealthiest of Britain's colonies, and becoming wealthier by the year, was a time of hardship, a time of experiment and a time of building. Men were rugged and tough. Challenges and fights to the death were common - over trivial causes. Women were just as tough - but in a different way. They were smart and savvy, and were appreciated for those virtues. In those days of boundless distances, men were away for long periods and it would be the wives who not only ran the home, but the plantation or the business.

Jamestown, circa 1685, had been around for nearly eight decades. Ships from England were arriving regularly with new settlers and manufactured goods in exchange for the commodity of Virginia wealth: tobacco. Tobacco had become such a major gold mine, as it were, that goods were bought sold with tobacco as the unit of currency.

The Wealth of Jamestown is peppered with a very large cast of characters, all real, and a few perhaps "enhanced." But the real people, the Colonial Governors, preachers, and wealthy plantation owners with descendants whose names are well known throughout history, have been immaculately researched, and shed some light on this unilluminated time. Nicholsons, Byrds, Carters, Blairs, Harrisons, Parkes and Custises are names that today are household names in Virginia.

The book discusses not only governors and merchants and planters, but the thriving business in piracy - or, as the pirates considered themselves, merely merchant sailors who a) skirted the French ships that were equally interested in helping themselves to the continent, and b) skirted the laws they believed did not apply to them.

Central to the story is a love affair that had been thwarted by an arranged-for-money marriage. As expected, the marriage was unhappy, so Sarah and William merely "skirted" those laws as well. But the love story is coincidental to what the author is looking to do, and becomes a vehicle for telling the intrinsic tale: how the colony of Virginia operated, how it grew, how the rule of law took hold when Jamestown was the capital of Virginia, and, of course, how it became wealthy.

Author McLennan was wise when she chose to write historic fiction: it gives her far more latitude in stating her point. And, of course, it makes for a much livelier read. Key to good historic fiction, of course, is the "plausibility" issue. Might this have happened? Was it in keeping with the characters? The times? The issues? Might these people have known each other and interacted as portrayed? With the exception of using more modern language, everything in The *Wealth of Jamestown* rings true.

It is a solid good read - not only for history lovers, but even for middle and high school readers who, sadly enough, are usually required to learn history on their own. Barbara McLennan makes it pleasant to learn!

—FEATHER SCHWARTZ FOSTER,
FOR CHESAPEAKE STYLE, WARSAW, VA

'Wealth of Jamestown' draws back curtain of time

Author Barbara N. McLennan draws the curtain of time back in this historical novel, letting us look through the window of the past and see some of Jamestown's most affluent and notable citizens. McLennan focuses on a small circle of friends and family connected to the Rev. James Blair and his wife, Sara Harrison Blair. Theirs is a story of love, power and politics.

The story begins in 1685, right before the Blairs are married, when Sara is only 17. At the opening of the book she is engaged to the sheriff of Yorktown, William Roscoe. Though in love with Roscoe, Sara is pressured by her family to marry Blair.

The story continues as Blair, obsessed with founding a college in Virginia, works to start the College of William and Mary. His pushy, pompous manners and single-minded obsession to start a college and be its first president made a lot of influential colonists angry and unwilling to help him.

Blair also went on a couple of long voyages to England in pursuit of the college, leaving Sara to run the home and plantation, her inheritance, on her own.

McLennan helps us see that the colonies had some very strong women. Rules in the colonies were a bit different than in Europe, and women of substance, education, and birth had a strong influence on the culture and the society that would become America.

"The Wealth of Jamestown" is a book of historical fiction that brings to life the inhabitants of Jamestown and the colonies in the 1600s. An entertaining read, especially for those who love early American history.

For more about the book, including excerpts, go to wealthofjamestown.com.

McLennan's work and education seem to have had a strong influence on her writing. According to her website, she holds doctorate and law degrees and has penned five other books and numerous academic articles.

A former docent at Jamestown Settlement, McLennan currently assists the Jamestown-Yorktown Foundation in preparing for the new American Revolution Museum at Yorktown. She is also on the board of the Chesapeake Bay Writers organization.

Elizabeth Macfarlane of Yorktown loves reading and learning and says she "started writing just as soon as I could put letters together to form words."

—ELIZABETH MACFARLANE, HRBOOKS CONTRIBUTOR, DAILY PRESS, NEWPORT NEWS, VA

The Wealth of Jamestown covers the time between 1685 and 1700 using a romance between the plantation owner's daughter, Sarah, and the young sheriff, William, of Yorktown to illustrate an early history of Virginia. McLennan who serves as a docent at the Jamestown Settlement incorporates many historical characters using her extensive research to enliven a time most are barely aware of.

The first few chapters, with its plethora of characters and actions unfamiliar to modern life, feel dense and confusing at times. However, the reader is then rewarded with a charming love story and a fascinating historical overview. One realizes that with the appalling loss of life through disease, birthing, dueling and skirmishes with Indians encouraged by the French, the survivors, both men and women were strong and resourceful. Many plantations were overseen by the women in the families because of the death or temporary absence of the men. McLennan especially brings to life James Blair, villain, husband of Sarah and clergyman with political connections. The reader will dislike him as much as his contemporaries disliked his rigidity and single-mindedness. Although Jamestown was eventually deserted, many of the characters enmeshed within the story were the antecedents of the founders of the United States. The Wealth of Jamestown painlessly presents an early and difficult time in American history.

—JUDITH HELBURN, STORY CIRCLE BOOKS

The Wealth of Jamestown is tobacco and the streets are paved with gold.

Tobacco was the medium of exchange in the late 1600s. Some planters became so focused on their money crop that they planted tobacco in the dirt streets and roads. With no way to print money and no banks, the colonists used tobacco notes to transact business. So, the streets were literally paved with gold.

McLennan, a docent at Jamestown Settlement, a living history museum located less than one mile from the actual landing site in 1607*, uses historic facts as the basis of her story. Her joy in explaining the origins of our country to thousands of annual visitors, led her to research more details about the major players and events from 1607 to the early 1700s. This book is factual and humorous as McLennan explores human interactions in the growing colony.

By the late 1600s the colony had spread from Jamestown and the capitol moved to Williamsburg and Jamestown remained the shipping center. By this time the colonists considered themselves Virginians. England was where they did business. What happened there had little or no impact on Virginia. Certain natural leaders served in the General Assembly* while becoming wealthy from their golden crop. Benjamin Harrison was one such influential colonist.**

This story revolves around the love triangle between Sarah Harrison, William Roscoe, a business man and sheriff, and the Reverend James Blair, a preacher in the Church of England. Sarah and William were engaged to be married. However, Mr. Harrison determined that her marriage to James would offer the Harrison's more power. Being an obedient daughter, Sarah married the minister. Everyone knew that James did not find women attractive and that Sarah and William were still seeing each other.

Sarah was well-read and an astute business woman who managed the Blair household, properties, and business dealings. James, having no head for business, spent his time as minister of Williamsburg's Church of England, attempting to consolidate his power and build a college. After lengthy negotiations in London, Blair returned to Williamsburg with a charter to build a college. He managed to draw a salary as president of the college that had not yet been built. This alienated his few remaining supporters. Yet, he persisted and eventually the College of William and Mary was constructed.

All of these circumstances lead to unusual situations as Virginia grows and does business with other colonies.

The Wealth of Jamestown is the first of a three-book series that is fun to read and meets Virginia's Standards of Learning. The next two books continue to follow the Blair's and Harrison's as they forge business relationships and meet with unsavory characters.

*That site soon became the primary center of commerce in Virginia. Jamestown had an elected General Assembly in 1619, a full year before the Pilgrims sailed from England. Historic Jamestowne is a national park and the site of major archeology discoveries.

**Two of his descendants became presidents of the United States, Benjamin Harrison VII and William Henry Harrison.

—SHARON DILLON, ENERGYWRITER.ME

Just finished reading "The Wealth of Jamestown".
One word: excellent!
I don't think I've ever read a book of historical fiction before. I really enjoyed it.
Chapter one hooked me, and it was off to the races.
While there were a lot of characters, it was manageable. I never felt I was going under.
The scholarship is evident, but not preachy. The author speeds the plot along. I am a very slow reader, but found this a quick read for me (two days). Decent readers could read it in one day.
I learned a lot about a cast of characters who shaped the town in which I live.
I thought including the Genealogy was great. It seems the author took most liberties with Miss Sarah...who goes from a possible half-wit to heroine. I suppose a woman who could say "no obey" at her wedding shouldn't be underestimated.
And I'll never look at the Indian school again without thinking of the monster, James Blair, possibly taking liberties with the young Indian boys. One certainly doesn't hear this side of the man when taking a tour of the Wren Building.
A fine read... I recommend it wholeheartedly. Well Done!

—J.K. THOMPSON, WILLIAMSBURG, VA
AMAZON REVIEWER

The Wealth of Virginia
by Barbara N. McLennan

© Copyright 2015 Barbara N. McLennan

ISBN   978-1-63393-054-4

Published by

◤ köehlerbooks™

210 60th Street
Virginia Beach, VA 23451
212-574-7939
www.koehlerbooks.com

Cover illustration by Keith Rocco,
provided by the Colonial National Historical Park

THE WEALTH OF VIRGINIA

A NOVEL OF
COLONIAL VIRGINIA

Barbara N. McLennan

To the Beaver family,

[signature] Barbara N. McLennan

Feb. 11, 2017

VIRGINIA BEACH
CAPE CHARLES

AUTHOR'S NOTE AND ACKNOWLEDG-MENTS

This work is the continuation of the story that began in *The Wealth of Jamestown* (Köehler Books, 2013). As with the previous volume, it is the result of several years of research that began when I became a docent in the gallery at Jamestown Settlement, a living history park located near the archeological site of the original Jamestown fort.

Visitors to the Jamestown Settlement are told in very brief texts inscribed on plaques throughout the museum that James Blair was responsible for the removal of three governors. Casual historians who overlook details of that period have perpetuated this story. *The Wealth of Jamestown* is built around the conflict between Blair and virtually everyone else in the colony. *The Wealth of Virginia* takes place a decade later, when the colonists send Mr. and Mrs. Blair to London to secure the removal of Virginia's governor, Francis Nicholson.

While many documents have disappeared over the years, many sources corroborate that James and Sarah Blair visited London during 1704–1705. We know that he made an appeal to the Board of Trade criticizing Nicholson. A painting of Mrs. Blair done by John Hargrave in 1705 in London is now owned by the Muscarelle Museum in Williamsburg. A copy of the painting of Sarah Blair hangs on the wall at the Jamestown Settlement, across the hall from a painting of James Blair.

As with the previous volume, this book is the product not only of my imagination but also of numerous published works, lectures, and comments by people with a knowledge and interest in American colonial history. I would like to thank them for their assistance and interest in this work.

First, I would like to acknowledge the artwork on the cover of this book. The illustration is the property of Colonial National Historical Park; the artist is Keith Rocco. A full-size copy of the painting can be seen in the lobby of the Visitor Center at Historic Jamestown, the site of the historic fort.

My research took me to original documents including letters in the handwriting of James Blair and Francis Nicholson found in the archives of the Earl Gregg Swem Library at the College of William and Mary. Additional original documents also were found at the Rockefeller Library at Colonial Williamsburg. The Library of Virginia, an institution operated by the state of Virginia, provided information relating to legislative and legal matters. Other materials were found in numerous articles published in *Virginia Magazine*, the quarterly journal of the Virginia Historical Society. The *Encyclopedia of Virginia* provided specific information on governing bodies in Virginia, including the Governor's Council and the House of Burgesses, with short biographies of all principal Virginia leaders.

Additional information was obtained from secondary sources. These include Warren Billings's *The Old Dominion in the Seventeenth Century*, a documentary history of Virginia, 1606–1700, and Billings's *A Little Parliament*, which describes Virginia's General Assembly in the seventeenth century. A. J. Mapp Jr.'s *The Virginia Experiment* discusses Virginia's role in the making of America, 1607–1781. W. Kale's *Hark Upon the Gale* provides an illustrated history of the College of William and Mary. Parke Rouse Jr.'s *James Blair of Virginia* provides a detailed biography of James Blair.

Other works consulted include *Spreading the Gospel in Colonial Virginia* by Edward L. Bond, a book that contains the texts of selected sermons including one by James Blair. Another book by Bond, *Damned Souls in a Tobacco Colony*, is an analysis of religion in seventeenth century Virginia. Kathleen M. Brown's *Good Wives, Nasty Wenches and Anxious Patriarchs* is a study of gender, race, and power in colonial Virginia. D. A. Tisdale's *Soldiers of the Virginia Colony* provides an illustrated history of the development of Virginia's militia. David S. Lovejoy's *The Glorious Revolution in America* is an assessment of the upheavals that took place in the colonies between 1676 and 1689 and the origins of political dissent in the colonies.

Daily Life in Johnson's London by Richard B. Schwartz and *1700: Scenes from London Life* by Maureen Waller were used to draw descriptive information about London in the early 1700s.

Finally, on a personal note, I would like to thank my granddaughter Catherine McLennan for suggesting names of fictional characters. I'd also like to thank my other grandchildren, Sean McLennan, Heather Ashley, Cameron Ashley, and Rachel Ashley, for enjoying their reading and letting me know they approve of my writing.

I would also like to thank my critique group, which meets every two weeks under the auspices of the Chesapeake Bay Writers organization. Their comments and statements of praise and support were very helpful during the long slog of putting this story to paper. Last, but certainly not least, I would like to thank my editor, Joe Coccaro, who cleverly turned my meandering musings into a readable novel.

CHAPTER 1

Three women sat in the front drawing room with a young child. Windows were opened and spring light flooded the room along with the aromas of jasmine and honeysuckle. Well furnished, the room had bright purple floral paper covering the walls, Turkish carpets covering the side tables, and a great gilded mirror on the wall.

"Nobody asks me what I think. It's my life," huffed Lucy Burwell. "I'm not a dog or a horse."

Lucy's sister Elizabeth Harrison flashed a grin at sister-in-law Sarah Harrison Blair. Both women giggled at impetuous Lucy, still so sweetly naïve at age sixteen. The year was 1699 and Elizabeth's husband, Attorney General Benjamin Harrison III, was away in Jamestown assisting Governor Nicholson who'd moved the capital city of Virginia from Jamestown to Williamsburg, a small town previously known as Middle Plantation.

Sarah had just finished playing a game with Benjamin Harrison IV and was impressed at how quickly he had learned his letters. The boy was five and had a great head for numbers she thought.

Elizabeth sent for a servant to take her son out of the room. As soon as they were gone Elizabeth asked Lucy in the soft tones of Virginia speech, "Sugar, what exactly did Father say?"

Lucy looked embarrassed. She had lovely dark hair and a bright, infectious smile. She stood from her chair and moved to the window. She was a born dancer and every move she made was as graceful as a bird's. "He said the governor had asked for my hand in marriage and that he was thinking it over. He also said that every family in Virginia would like to count a governor as a member."

Sarah knitted her eyebrows and quietly asked in her deep, melodious voice, "Darling, did he leave it for you to think about it, or did he tell you this was going to happen?"

Elizabeth thought for a moment and knew her younger sister was looking for support more than advice. She said to Lucy, "Darling, you know that Father dotes on you. He'll never do anything that would make you unhappy. Why are you so frightened?"

Lucy seemed to dance in short pirouettes around the bright room, warm with the color of the early spring sun. She finally turned to her sister and Sarah and said, "It frightens me. Governor Nicholson is so much older—he must be over forty. Everyone says he has a dreadful temper. I don't know how Father could even entertain the possibility of a match, but I suppose he has to be polite. Father is a member of the Governor's Council. Mother says nothing at all. If I refuse and Father backs me up, we could have soldiers in the house to carry me away."

This was too much for Elizabeth and Sarah. They both smiled to each other knowingly and laughed out loud.

Lucy continued, "Nicholson is beside himself. He sends me gifts and writes ridiculous poetry. He's serious. This last letter I received, here it is." Lucy pulled out a handwritten letter and read out loud:

Virtuous, pretty, charming Innocent Dove
The only center of my Constant Love.

"Isn't this idiotic? The more I hear from him, the more I can't stand him."

Elizabeth and Sarah couldn't contain themselves. After their laughter died down, Sarah was first to speak.

"You know it used to be normal for brides not even to be consulted on marriage choices. When times were difficult, marriages were strictly business arrangements—meant to transfer lands or rights in business dealings. Even though I was already engaged to another, my father had me married to Commissary Blair as part of a business deal with tobacco factors. I was only seventeen. Times really aren't as bad now. If you're unhappy about the arrangement you should let your mother know. She can talk to your father."

Elizabeth rose and went to her younger sister. She was tall, also dark, but not nearly as pretty as Lucy. Elizabeth was in her late twenties and one of the leading hostesses of Virginia. She embraced Lucy.

"You know we're on your side. I'll talk to Father this weekend. We're having a party for some of the new burgesses. Father and Benjamin would like to get to know the new members better. Virginia is growing so quickly, and we're building a new capital city. People everywhere are flush with excitement."

"I know," Lucy whimpered, almost on the verge of tears, and hugged her older sister.

Elizabeth held her shoulders and whispered, "Don't worry, sugar. The Burwells and the Harrisons take care of our own. After all, who's a governor anyway?"

Lucy looked up in surprise. Sarah said, "The Board of Trade sends over royal governors every so often. Since Governor Berkeley, who was governor for a long time and well before you were born, none have stayed very long. A few were outright thieves and were driven away by the burgesses. The House simply asked that they be recalled. Nicholson isn't a royal personage. He's just a London bureaucrat."

Lucy mumbled, "I don't care how he got here. He's here and he frightens me."

"There's nothing to worry about," said Elizabeth. "Father will hear from all of us this weekend."

Sarah tried to turn the conversation to brighter subjects. "Benjamin IV is very bright isn't he, Lucy?"

Lucy giggled. "Yes, just like you. He always wants to make a deal when he plays, and he drives a hard bargain!"

Elizabeth laughed at that too. "Maybe we should arrange a wife for him? He'd let us know what he thinks soon enough."

Sarah laughed. "Yes, in Europe royalty is married off on the day they are born. Thank goodness we're far away from that!"

Lucy felt a little better and decided she was hungry. "May I go to the kitchen to see if there's something to eat?"

Elizabeth smiled and said, "Yes. And have the servants prepare some tea for us as well."

Lucy bounced out of the room, leaving Sarah and Elizabeth to themselves. Sarah said wistfully, "It brings back bad memories, doesn't it?"

Elizabeth looked at her sister-in-law sympathetically and crossed the room to sit down beside her. "But we've managed. Benjamin is a lovely boy and you can raise him almost as your own. He enjoys when William comes. He loves his rough and tumble father."

They were talking about William Roscoe, Sarah's lover and business partner, and the biological father of Benjamin IV.

Sarah had the child during one of her husband's extended trips to London. Sarah's brother and his wife, Elizabeth, had been childless and happily agreed to raise the baby as their own. In doing so, they protected Sarah from being sullied and provided legitimacy to the boy.

Sarah often visited the child, spending months at a time with him at her brother's home. The boy's father often visited as well. While both Sarah and William were married to others, they also managed to spend much time together at the piers where their two ships were docked.

Sarah was suddenly irritated. She stood and paced the room. "Oh, what a performance all of this is! Perhaps we could get the commissary to go to London again, and I'll have another baby. He despises Nicholson as he does all governors. Maybe someone could convince him to visit the Board of Trade?"

"Benjamin won't want to go again, but we might talk him into suggesting it to the commissary. Does the reverend suspect anything about you and William?" Elizabeth was curious about the opinions of the Reverend James Blair, Sarah's lawful husband. Reverend Blair served as commissary of the Church of England in Virginia, with a seat on the Governor's Council. He was also president of the new College of William and Mary.

"James lives in another world. He's always very polite to William, addressing him as sheriff, as if he were some sort of functionary. William's no bureaucrat. He's been elected to the House of Burgesses by the people he knows, and he's sheriff because his people asked the governor to keep him in that position." Sarah continued, "James is married to his church and the titles he accumulates so long as his appointments come from London with small salaries attached. He lives well so long as I keep our plantation and ships in business. He really doesn't know where the money comes from.

"You know I've had two miscarriages these past two years. Archie, my brother-in-law and a doctor, took care of me and I was fortunate to pull through both times. James thought I had stomach problems, and Archie, though he's James's own brother, never contradicted him. James knows and cares more about London than Virginia. If James suspects anything about William and me he doesn't speak of it."

Elizabeth responded with sincerity, "You know, whatever happens, I'll care for your children. We in Virginia have to stick together, and we need to support Lucy. I think we should mention Nicholson's proposal to Benjamin, as he's also on the Governor's Council. He's so busy. He's even bought some land for a new plantation up the river. He wants to build a great new house and will name it Berkeley after the old governor."

At that moment, two maids brought in the tea and cakes, and Lucy, carrying Benjamin IV, smiled as she sat down beside them.

⋯⋯

When Sarah Blair returned to her plantation, she immediately rode out to see how the tobacco planting was proceeding. She'd engaged an overseer, Mr. Simmons, who had a small plantation of his own. In exchange for his services, Sarah agreed to take Simmons's crops as part of her consignment sold to Cunningham, a great Scottish factor of tobacco. Cunningham paid a higher price for her consignment than Simmons could get by selling tobacco on the open market.

Sarah was dark haired and spirited. She'd always had a head for business, and her father had often involved her in his business decisions. He was Benjamin Harrison II, one of Virginia's great tobacco planters. Sarah was a strong woman of twenty-six, who was used to getting her way through negotiation. She knew how to make a business deal.

She stayed on horseback and shouted to Simmons, "How are we doing? Do you have enough people?"

Simmons was working alongside two indentured servants and four slaves. "We could always use more hands, Mrs. Blair, but all is going according to schedule. If you add more land we'll be in trouble, the seven of us!"

"It's best to do it slowly and carefully. Perhaps if all goes well, we'll add more hands next year. We have the Harrison brand to protect. London loves Virginia tobacco, and we're all living off our reputation."

"Yes, as they're living off their whiskey and tea. What would trade be without tobacco and drinks?"

Sarah laughed. In her mind, she wouldn't mind being out in the field with the men who worked for her, as she cared deeply about the tobacco crop. She was a Harrison, and Harrison tobacco was highly prized because of its quality and sweet taste. Sarah, more than any of her brothers and sisters, knew more about the practical problems of raising and shipping tobacco. She'd ridden out to the fields with her father many times as a young girl.

She looked at the sky, where clouds seemed to be gathering, and said, "Well, good work to all. We'll celebrate when the planting is finished." With that she turned her horse back to the stable.

When Sarah entered the house she found her husband at his writing table. He was preparing a sermon for Sunday. He saw that she'd been out riding, and she'd been away visiting her brother for over a week. He said, "Welcome back, Mrs. Blair. I trust the family is well?"

James was a small man of forty with mousy-brown hair down to his shoulders. He spoke in a high-pitched Scottish accent and wore a white blouse under black ecclesiastical robes. His thoughts were wrapped in his writing. He didn't look at his wife when he spoke to her.

"Yes, James, all is well. Let me get out of my riding clothes, and we must talk. Lucy has raised concerns about the governor, Mr. Nicholson. You know him, do you not?"

Sarah abruptly left James to think about what she'd said. She then went up to her room to change out of her traveling clothes. The Blairs lived in a small wooden farmhouse that had been expanded to include a relatively spacious second floor. Their four indentured servants and six slaves occupied the nearby quarter house. James insisted that he needed at least four slaves for his daily needs.

James considered his current predicament. The Bishop of London had appointed him commissary of the Church of England in Virginia. As commissary, he should have sat on the Governor's Council as the church representative. He'd served in this capacity under the previous governor, Edmund Andros. However, due to recent English law, James had been thrown off the Governor's Council because he was born in Scotland; currently only native-born English or Virginians could serve as council members. The church had no other commissary in Virginia.

James knew Governor Nicholson very well. Soon after James had first come to Virginia, Nicholson was appointed lieutenant governor. Even then, Nicholson was interested in building and supporting the church and education. When James recommended to him that the church should have courts to judge petty offenses, Nicholson at first agreed. However, after consulting with the burgesses, Nicholson withdrew his support. After that James thought of him as an enemy.

James regarded himself as the head of the church in Virginia; Nicholson thought the governor or lieutenant governor was there for the monarch and that the monarch was head of everything in his colony, including the church. That made Nicholson head of the church, with or without a commissary.

Sarah came down and asked the servants to bring some tea. The small parlor included James's writing desk and a few chairs near a fireplace. Sarah sat near the fire, and James stood to cross the room to sit beside her. She turned to look at him.

"Have you missed me, Reverend Blair?"

"Of course! You make the plantation run and my life with it. I would be nothing except for you and your family."

Sarah laughed. "Yes, and now you may be able to pay us back a little."

Sarah thought hard about what she was going to say. Her marriage was a business arrangement. She'd been married to James in exchange for his contacts with Scottish tobacco factors, companies in England that bought and sold Virginia tobacco. James knew people in London because of his position as commissary. She remembered he'd done some work for Nicholson in London years earlier.

"What do you think of Nicholson now?"

James knew that Sarah was going to make a request, but he was a little befuddled as to what it would be. "Well, he wishes to move the government from Jamestown to Middle Plantation since Jamestown's State House burned down just before he arrived. Middle Plantation has always been set aside for the college, and the only large building standing is the Wren Building at the College of William and Mary."

"You think he'll demand the use of the college building? There's no college now. You can do him the favor and ask for something in return."

"The college is mine, Sarah. I'm its president. I raised money here and in England for its building. He should have no right to it. He's not an honest man with which to deal."

Sarah remembered that James had been to London before. She was curious about how James felt now. "Why do you say that, James?"

"When I was in London I did my best to speed the end of Andros, a villain who opposed me at every turn with respect to the college. I succeeded, and at the time I put in good words for Nicholson. He wouldn't have been appointed governor were it not for me. He owes me for my expenses there. He's never paid me."

"That's only wages for services. It's of no great importance. A governor on your side may be worth something. You should politic with him now that he's governor."

"Tell me about Lucy, and say what you'd want me to do."

Sarah then related Lucy's fear of Governor Nicholson.

"Would a father support his daughter against the wishes of a sitting governor?" James said sarcastically.

"James, be sensible. The Burwells are a great plantation family. A governor has little to offer in the grand scheme of things. We all live off the land and what it produces. Colonel Burwell would expect Lucy's marriage to bring more land to the Burwell estates. Nicholson doesn't interest or frighten him. The council and the burgesses expect to run Virginia, as they always have. I'd like you to convince Nicholson to leave Lucy alone."

James didn't understand all of this. He was of the old country where the monarch, supported by the aristocracy, made all decisions. The church in England was part of the aristocracy. The great landed lords of the realm dominated the parliament in England. People of wealth had titles to indicate refined social status.

The assembly in Virginia represented the freeholders who elected burgesses. Nobody had a real title bestowed by a monarch, and these people educated themselves at home. The burgesses in Virginia, to James, were just a bunch of ruffians who opposed building towns and paying taxes.

"I've been invited to see the governor at his offices. I'd invite him down to see the college, but he insists that I see him in his place. I doubt if we'll talk about Lucy, but I'll have some sense of how he wishes to proceed. It probably would be improper for me to say anything about this."

"Be careful when you talk to him, James. He's the governor—King William's representative here. If you play your cards right, you may be able to ask a favor or two from him."

James shook his head knowingly. He wondered what Sarah would want him to request of Nicholson. Sarah, feeling tired, stood from her chair, yawned, and said, "Good night." She then went up to bed.

James, wearing his black ecclesiastical robes, visited Nicholson the next day. He walked briskly, with a determined gait and an air of superiority. He projected this to fend off perceived threats and entreaties from passersby.

James didn't like being out with the yokels who lived and worked in Virginia's capital city. Every person he saw was armed with sword or pistol. There were virtually no streets to walk or ride on, as tobacco had been planted everywhere. He had to be careful not to step on somebody's tax payments. Tobacco was the source of wealth for the colony, and people grew it everywhere because tobacco notes, issued by factors purchasing tobacco for sale, served as the only currency of the colony. If ever a place had streets paved with gold, it was Jamestown, and the weed that grew there was certainly golden. James didn't approve of the stuff or the place it grew in. But it was everywhere, and it was making Virginia very rich.

James entered the governor's offices in a dark and unhappy mood. He waited a short time until two militiamen escorted him into the governor's private offices.

Nicholson, a plump, red-faced man of forty, rose and greeted him. He wore a military uniform, including a sword. His wig was of ordinary quality. He didn't seek to impress with his appearance. "Welcome, Reverend! I'm pleased to see you again in happier circumstances. I hope you are satisfied with the progress of the college. Please sit." Nicholson asked the two soldiers to leave and motioned James to sit in a chair facing him. Nicholson sat down on a high chair behind a high desk.

The room normally served as an office for the commander of the Jamestown militia. It was sparsely furnished, with only the desk and chair for the governor and three wooden chairs for visitors. The interior was all pinewood, lit by one small window. It was a long, narrow room used for the storage of weapons. On the walls hung two long eighteen-foot pikes, a dozen spears, and some muskets.

Nicholson began, "You know I'm planning a new capital city,

and the college will be a major feature of the design." He pointed to some large architectural drawings on his desk.

James replied, "Yes, it would be an improvement to have streets rather than puddles of tobacco to wade through."

"But the puddles have made Virginia rich, and they're paying for our building! Do you know how many people are coming into the colony to seek work here? I think Virginia will double in size in ten years. That's many more Christians for your flock."

James didn't like Nicholson and found the governor's bluster annoying. He responded cautiously, "Yes, I had the good sense to get the building plan from Sir Christopher Wren when I received the charter. We had a ground breaking and part of the building already stands."

Nicholson looked interested, so James continued, "We have a great hall for large meetings and some small classrooms. We have use of three floors of space. The cellars contain a kitchen and storage space. The grammar school is doing well as we have a few instructors. We have some rooms for people to stay, as there are no lodgings currently in Williamsburg. I have an apartment there myself."

"Well, that sounds like a good start. What of the Indian school funded by Boyle's estate?"

"We've barely begun. The governor could help by asking the chiefs to send some boys."

Nicholson made a small note to himself on a piece of parchment next to his drawings. "Yes, we'll do that! I've asked you here because I'm planning to have a May Day celebration on the college grounds and will ask for some of the students to give speeches supporting the college and the capital moving to Williamsburg. I'm sure you favor this. A city surrounding it can only help the college."

"Of course I'll support it. I'll meet with the instructors and choose our student orators. It's only a month away to prepare."

"You realize that I'm moving our whole government to Williamsburg as well. Since the college is the only building stand-ing, the House of Burgesses will occupy your great hall, and my own offices will be moved there as well. I'll be taking one of your apartments for myself."

"The governor is the royal personage in Virginia and, as such, may do as he wishes," James said, trying to restrain him-self. "Do you plan to pay for any of these accommodations, gov-ernor?" James still was angry because Nicholson had never paid the lobbying expenses for the last time James was in London.

"Is it not an honor to have a governor in residence?"

"If you rented a plantation you'd pay the landlord. Am I not also a landlord?" James said.

"But the college belongs to Virginia by royal charter, not to you. You are only an employee. Do you pay yourself rent for your apartment?"

"Of course not!" James said, now clearly agitated. "You have a habit of not paying for services rendered, do you not?"

Nicholson was getting angry with James. "Don't be a dolt! I'm the governor and I'm moving the government to public property, granted by the late Queen Mary and paid for by local taxes. I owe you nothing. King William's board appointed me to this post because I was best qualified and available. If you helped I thank you, but I did not commission you to do anything for me, and I owe you nothing more than I owe any other person living under my royal protection."

James could see that he was close to inciting Nicholson. He'd seen Nicholson's temper before. He stood. "Thank you for advising me of your plans. I will make sure the building will be ready for the use of the burgesses and that your offices and apartments will be made ready. I'll move the grammar school upstairs so the students don't interfere with your work. I'll also see that we're ready for May Day."

"See that it's done soon." Nicholson went back to his plans and James left in as grim a mood as when he arrived.

CHAPTER 2

William Roscoe, sheriff of Gloucester and Yorktown and member of the House of Burgesses, took his ship the *Pretty Polly* to Charles Towne in the spring and fall. The ship usually carried tobacco and trading goods and was armed with ten cannon. By sticking close to the coast and using inland waterways and streams whenever possible, the voyages over the past two years had been uneventful. William was properly licensed by Virginia as a private carrier of goods.

Roscoe was a tall, dark-haired man of thirty-two with very broad shoulders. He wore a small moustache and had clear-blue eyes. An affable, easy-going person, he smiled as the crew got the ship ready for its spring voyage.

Other ship owners were not licensed and were regarded by the colonial government and mother country as pirates. Since the colonies did not maintain large navies, the distinction between privateers and pirates was a moot point. They all operated pretty much in the same manner, transporting goods and sharing the profits with crew members. Pirates got away without paying the license fees, so their crews were a little better off.

On the other hand, if their ships fell into the hands of the Royal Navy they'd face severe penalties. Privateers sometimes seized the goods of other ships if they felt they were armed well enough to get away with it.

William's crew was capable and loyal. He knew them since childhood and most came from Gloucester's coastal fishing villages. The men could handle swords and pistols and knew their way around sailing ships and waterways. William had inherited his father's tobacco plantation, but sailing his two ships gave him the most pleasure and profit. He was careful about arming his ships and took few chances on the open seas.

"We might see some warships, as the war is on in full swing in the Caribbean," William said to George Harris, his captain.

"If we do, let's hope they're ours," the captain said. "I think we can stand up to most pirates, but they're traveling in larger fleets now."

"What do you think of the weather?"

"We'll have a fine breeze going, but we may have to look for shelter inland if storms really pick up. I know a few places in the Outer Banks, but we really don't want to get stuck away from proper winds."

"Let's hope we don't need to look for shelter. Maybe the big boys are down in the Caribbean."

Since he was licensed, William didn't fear reprisals from the Royal Navy. British ships didn't enter Virginia waters very often, as Holland had a treaty with England allowing Dutch ships to trade in Virginia. The Royal Navy tried to avoid direct confrontation with legal ships belonging to foreign powers. For the most part, English ships stayed in the Caribbean, harassing and being harassed by French and Spanish sailors. That's where most trade and pirating took place.

William took his public responsibilities seriously. He never missed a meeting of the burgesses, and as sheriff he was understanding and efficient in seeing to the court's business and conducting elections. He was popular with his people and won his elections by unanimous voice vote.

William shared his business dealings with Sarah Harrison Blair, whose family, the Harrisons, was far wealthier than he ever expected to become. Sarah was part-owner and major-investor in their ships and she'd equipped a crew on their second ship, the *Good Fortune,* to handle transatlantic trade, mainly in tobacco. William also was a business partner of Captain John Crowe of Charles Towne, whose ship, the *Revenge,* conducted business in the Caribbean and across the ocean.

William and Sarah had been lovers for years and spent as much time together as they could. When they were together, they both felt they understood each other, in the manner of people who'd known each other since childhood.

William never missed the opportunity to offer Sarah a compliment. He'd say, "You are lovely today, much as the sea breeze warms a man's heart."

Sarah would usually respond in kind, but she was more business than William. She generally responded with, "Thank you, sir, but a ship needs more than the lovely breeze."

William was an accomplished speaker and had given many speeches to the burgesses. When they were together alone he'd recite a poem or speech from Shakespeare, and Sarah would throw her arms around his neck and whisper, "Don't stop."

William's legal wife and four children stayed in Gloucester and never left his tobacco plantation. His wife didn't care to come to Jamestown, a very rough, uncomfortable place for visitors. Sarah was married to the Reverend Blair, who every so often went to London and stayed there for several years at a time.

Business was booming and trade was increasing daily. People were moving into the colony from everywhere. Charles Towne was growing and building large new buildings, and now Williamsburg had been designated as the seat of a new capital city. As a burgess, William had seen preliminary plans. The new city was to have three great thoroughfares and be designed in a peculiar circular pattern.

William laughed to himself thinking about the plump, new governor with the loud, bombastic voice. Nicholson was going to have three main avenues, with two named for himself: Francis Street and Nicholson Street. The main avenue through the length of the new town was to be Duke of Gloucester Street, named for the ten-year-old son of Princess Anne, next in line to the throne. *Nicholson*, William thought, *thinks he's twice as important as the King here in Virginia.*

Williamsburg was preparing to become a much larger town than Charles Towne. There were plans for a great new assembly building, a governor's palace, an armory, theaters, taverns, shops, and places for visitors to stay. The new governor planned for paved streets with no tobacco growing between the pavements. Some retailers had already opened shops near Bruton Parish Church. They already called their neighborhood Merchant Square.

Now that it was early April, William supervised the loading of goods on board the *Pretty Polly*. His aim was to be back for the governor's May Day celebration, and he had deliveries to make in Charles Towne.

He and Capt. George Harris greeted the crew, ten men all of whom sailed with him the previous year. Harris, who'd captained his first voyage to Charles Towne, stood alongside him, along with Harris's eighteen-year-old nephew, Andrew Morgan.

Harris said to William, "Seems like a nice spring day for sailing. The wind is really up. How much will we carry today?"

"Not as much as in the fall. We have mostly small manufactures—tools, small muskets, some hunting and fishing gear, and some foodstuffs and molasses. We have a few crates of medicines and some books and newspapers. The books and news-papers are the new things. Since Virginia has no printing press, some of the richer planters have started their own libraries by buying books from Europe. We have books and papers in Eng-lish, French, German, and Italian. I thought these items might go down well in Charles Towne where so many people come from different countries and speak different languages."

Andrew overheard. "Did you get some ladies novels? Su-zanne loves to read them in French."

George and William looked at each other and smiled.

"Well, I suppose you could look in the crate and see what you can find. I'll charge you two pennies per book, seeing you'll be working hard for it," William said.

Andrew laughed and quickly went to the stern of the sloop to help with the rigging.

William spoke to George. "What does his mother think of all this?"

"She's a widow, and he's her only boy. But he's eighteen and he's been exchanging letters and gifts with Suzanne through the year. Mrs. Custis Hill has been to the Morgan house a few times, bringing notes from Suzanne's parents."

Mrs. Tabitha Scarborough Smart Brown Custis Hill, a rela-tive of the Dubois family of Charles Towne, was a friend and early political supporter of William. She'd given him a few pack-ages to deliver to the Dubois when he got to Charles Towne. In fact, a number of other people had given him letters and pack-ages to deliver to various friends and acquaintances there. He, George, and Andrew planned to stay with the Dubois while they were in Charles Towne.

"Well, it might still be harmless, do you think?"

"My sister Anne feels as if she's lost him forever this time. Something's made her feel that he might not ever return. Of course she worries terribly, but she worries every time he goes out."

"He's a teenager but strong and responsible. We'll have to keep an eye on what develops there. Maybe he could bring Suzanne back to Williamsburg? Lots of businesses are opening, and Andrew's mother could be a help to them with introductions to people living around."

"He loves the sailing. I think he'd postpone any serious entanglement if he could get on the larger ships."

"I'll talk to Sarah about getting him a spot on the *Good Fortune*. The ship sails for London in June, just after we get back. If Andrew and Suzanne decide something we should know about, they'll have the summer to think it over."

George looked at the sky. "Let's get going. We might as well take advantage of the good weather."

William shouted to the crew to get ready, and soon they cast off, heading for the Chesapeake Bay.

⚓

The weather was warm and stormy, normal for early April. The *Pretty Polly* lurched along the inland bays and then went out to the Atlantic. The sloop went out far enough to avoid the treacherous undercurrents of the Bermuda Triangle. Still, the ocean seemed to boil with turbulence. Waves of twenty feet sometimes slapped the sails, and at one point the sails were taken down to protect them from tearing in the wind.

After two days they passed Ocracoke and the Outer Banks of North Carolina. Three days later they were in Charles Towne. During the journey they'd seen only one navy ship and no other commercial ships. In early April there generally was little traffic as crops weren't yet ready for shipment, and sloops avoided stormy weather when possible along the Carolina coast. The ocean was already a graveyard to hundreds of small, brave ships and their crews.

The *Pretty Polly* cruised into the lively harbor and docked

next to the *Revenge*. The *Revenge* was a much heavier ship
armed with twenty guns and showed the ravages of open warfare
on the ocean with her sides pock-marked by ship-to-ship gunfire.
William waved to sailors aboard the *Revenge*. He, George, and
Andrew alit from the boat, each carrying a few packages. William
stopped to tell the warehouseman where to unload his goods,
and he left five crew members to oversee the unloading.

The three men entered the nearest tavern. They were ready
for some food and drink and thought they might see John Crowe
and some of his crew there. The Carolinas were proprietary
colonies, and some of the proprietors were Virginia planters.
Nobody really knew the geographic boundaries, and popula-
tions were small. Indians moved in and out of the towns according to their ancient traditions, and immigrants arrived
in larger numbers than ever before from many places. Many
came from European countries, escaping religious persecution
and permanent warfare, others from other colonies due to the
growth of Carolina towns and prospects for establishing a peace-
ful life.

William noticed Crowe sitting in a corner talking to two
other ship owners. They were Simon Grey who owned *Sweet
Susan,* a very well-equipped ship with three masts and thirty
guns, and Alonzo Ellis who owned six smaller ships. Grey was
a young man who'd obviously been in many fights. He carried a
small scar to the left side of his cheek. Ellis was a young, blond
man who seemed somehow out of place in the tavern. He looked
like a lawyer or accountant. The conversation seemed serious.
Crowe was a large, grey-bearded man who loved his beer.

William and George ordered crab cakes and beer, enough for
themselves and Andrew. They then drew up chairs to Crowe's
table. Crowe, a swarthy man with an affable expression, shouted, "Welcome to Charles Towne! How was the journey?"

William smiled, sipping his beer. "The weather was more
exciting than anything else. Seas are stormy with quite a lot of

thunder but no damage done. We didn't see much traffic, just one navy ship."

Ellis asked, "Are you fully loaded? I'm surprised you saw no other ships. Merchants will be buying everything now that building has begun on some bigger buildings. Lots of people are putting up residences in the town. Charles Towne is going to be a city."

"We're fairly loaded with building materials, some books, and furniture. No grain this time of year. We dodged every thunderstorm and didn't see anyone else either out to sea or inland. Only one navy ship quite far out, past the triangle."

"We were just talking," Grey said. "Some of the shippers are banding together for voyages. Fifty guns are better than ten or twenty if you meet with hostile people. We expect the next Caribbean trip to be done by fleets of five or more. There are some nasty pirates down there."

Ellis added, "Some are coming up here when sugar isn't in season. We're becoming a serious port, and now that we're really building, the value of shipments here are probably as good as they can find in the islands."

"Yes, and once Williamsburg starts building the traffic will increase even more," Crowe said. "There's nothing of value between the Caribbean and the Carolinas right now. The more we grow, the more attractive we become. Besides, there are few navy ships to protect us here. The Carolinas have very small military garrisons and almost no navy. Government ships are down south harassing each other, while we remain defenseless. We're all adding more guns and fighting men. What do you think, William?"

"I suppose adding guns and men are preferable to begging the Royal Navy to do something. I could raise an issue in the House next time we meet. Maybe the House would pay for some ships to patrol the coast for defense."

Crowe laughed. "Nicholson isn't Andros. He wants to build his town and pave its streets. He cares little for defenses, unless war in Europe erupts again."

Ellis said in somber tone, "It won't be long until that happens. I hope the King's health holds up. Let's drink to that." Everyone raised their glasses and toasted King William, finally at peace and home in London.

"How are things here?" William asked. "Does everyone support the new governor?"

"The governor was appointed by the council who answers to the proprietors," Grey said. "He's a very small fish here. We don't keep governors more than a year or two. More's to be made in business than in being a governor."

"Nicholson will last a while I think, though he's flighty and loses his temper in public," William said. "He gets along with the House and they support the new capital city. The plans are really extravagant, and with times being flush, the planters are happy to oblige him. I'm hoping to be back in time for Nicholson's May Day celebration at the college. Everyone will be there. It will be a big party with drink and fireworks and all the rest."

The three ship owners grinned at that and in chorus raised their glasses and said, "To the governor of Virginia!" William and George didn't join the toast. They were too busy eating. Soon they stood and took their leave.

William said, "We go to the Dubois with some mail and packages to deliver."

"Will I see you again before you return to Jamestown?" Crowe asked.

"It will be a busy week, but we can stop here again, maybe on Friday?" That was three days away, and Roscoe hoped to be reloading the *Pretty Polly* for the trip back by the following week. Crowe smiled and said he'd be there waiting for him.

Ellis said, "I have two sloops to go to Jamestown. Maybe we can send the three together as a little fleet."

William looked at Capt. George Harris and they both shook their heads in agreement. They waved farewell, and the three left the tavern and got into a wagon provided by the warehouse. It was a large rig drawn by two horses carrying various packages to be delivered. The Dubois lived in a town house on the other side of the harbor. There they kept a shop where they made dresses for ladies and coats for men.

As the wagon drew up to the Dubois town house two teenagers, Suzanne and Pierre, ran out to greet them. Suzanne, a pretty, dark-eyed girl of sixteen, and Pierre, a tall, thin boy of nineteen, shouted to them, "Come in, Mother is waiting for you!"

Andrew was first down and first into the house, and Mrs. Dubois, an attractive woman of forty, kissed him four times and embraced him like a long-lost relative. Captain Harris and William took care of the wagon and retrieved some packages before they entered. They soon received the same treatment and quickly presented their hostess with several letters and packages from Williamsburg. Twice a year they came and stayed, transporting shipments in both directions.

Mrs. Dubois offered some tea and fresh baked pastries, and they sat down around a small round table. "I'm pleased you are here safely," said Mrs. Dubois in her deep, French-accented voice. She was a small, blond woman and wore a finely made floral silk dress. "My husband is down at the pier talking to several other shippers and manufacturers. Pirates just outside the harbor have attacked a few small ships. Nobody's been hurt, but pirates are beginning to put together fleets to out-run the navy ships."

"We had no problem, but the weather was a bit rough, and we were spotted by a navy ship. We plan to go back with another two ships. That will be safer, as we'll have more guns."

Andrew asked Suzanne if she wanted to go for a walk. He still had sea legs and had a small package to give her. George said, "You're bored with us already? You know, you'll be on the ship going back, the same as us. This involves your safety too."

"Uncle George, my legs are stiff and wobbly. I need a little walk."

Mrs. Dubois looked at him and Suzanne. "Go down to the dock for a while, but be back in an hour. We'll have an early dinner, and I'll need your help with some measurements."

William and George looked at each other and said in unison, "We'll be the best-dressed sailors in Williamsburg!"

William added, "I have some dress material for you from Williamsburg. I think it's from France by way of Philadelphia. Mrs. Custis Hill wanted you to have it. You know, Williamsburg is a new capital city. It's going to be large and we have a royal governor. Your work would be very much appreciated there."

"We are happy here and happy to be far away from royal governors. Mrs. Custis Hill has urged us the same, and it's true that there probably are more people in Virginia than here. We'll just have to see what happens." She looked out the window when she spoke, with a slight look of sadness. She saw Suzanne and Andrew walking hand-in-hand down the small street.

William said, "They'll have a richer, happier world than we had. They'll be able to live in towns already built for them."

"But there's so much violence, and they are young to be going out on their own. Has Andrew said anything to his mother? We've been corresponding. Does he have plans?"

"My sister knows he wants to be on his own, but he has no estate or property," George said. "His father fished and hunted and left a small house that had a small forge when he passed away. Once Andrew gets his share from the voyage, he can think of what he wants. If he got onto a larger ship he'd have enough to start a small business and build his own house."

"What sort of business would he start? I don't think Suzanne wants the life of a sailor's wife. She's used to towns and has skills herself. She can bake and make clothing."

George said, "Andrew is good with metals. He's particularly good with firearms and has made improvements in the stock pistols the militia carries. I don't know if he's thought about his future, but he has options. I know he wants Suzanne to be part of his future if he could arrange it."

"My husband and I respect him very much, and I can tell that I'd like his mother as well. But Suzanne's my only daughter. We'll be careful before giving them permission to marry."

They sipped their tea and relaxed, and soon Andrew and Suzanne were back. She carried a small book and a broad smile on her face. Pierre looked up from a newspaper he was reading and asked Suzanne, "What sort of book is that?"

"Just a little novel," she said and giggled.

Mrs. Dubois looked at both her children and quietly said, "Time to get ready for some measurements. Andrew first." She spent the next several hours measuring Andrew, George, and William for spring coats. She'd already done a new dress for Andrew's mother, which was wrapped in a cloth package in the corner. She said to William, "What business do you have this time?"

"We'll deliver some manufactures and books and medicines to the retailers and doctors. We'll also pick up some deerskins, rice, or other things. What do you have in mind?"

"I've done some children's clothing, and my neighbor has carved some toys. We also have a new hat maker. We can provide some new spring hats."

William smiled. "I'm sure Virginia will love this. I can pay you in advance this time in tobacco notes?"

"That will be fine."

That week William saw to his deliveries and slowly loaded the *Pretty Polly* for the return voyage to Jamestown. Andrew and Suzanne never said anything about plans for the future that whole week, though they spent a lot of time laughing together, taking walks, and holding hands.

The *Pretty Polly* sat in the harbor surrounded by ships belonging to owners who knew each other well. Two of Alonzo Ellis's sloops, the *Charming Anna* and *Smiling Margaret*, were weighed down with deliveries for the new capital in Williamsburg. They also carried twenty guns each and would be much slower in the water than the *Pretty Polly*. As agreed, all three would sail together, and they devised flag signals to warn each other of approaching dangers. The flags would be hoisted on top of their highest masts and would signal the approach of unidentified armed ships. They also agreed on a signal flag for approaching navy ships.

They decided to use a battle formation, with one ship lined up behind the other in a straight line. That would give them a twenty-five gun, broadside cannon shot from either the port or starboard sides. Because *Pretty Polly* was the lightest and fastest, she led the two others out of the harbor.

The weather was calm as the three ships slowly left Charles Towne. They traveled some distance apart but never out of each other's sight. Andrew spent the early part of the voyage perched high on the topmast with his telescope. He knew how he'd change flags if necessary and situated himself so his right side was closest to the flags.

For the first day, the ships encountered no problems. Calm breezes pushed them along at a steady pace, and the currents, while strong, were manageable. They sailed past the barrier islands of the Outer Banks of the Carolinas. On the second day, Andrew spotted what he thought was a small ship emerging from a narrow inlet between two small islands. It moved slowly in their direction.

"To the stern—a small, low-lying craft of some kind," Andrew shouted.

George gave the order. "Hoist the flag indicating stranger

approaching!"

Andrew moved toward the flag, and as he did so he could see that the strange craft was a galley, rowed by twelve oarsmen. It lay fairly low in the water and making fair progress because of the push of the tide.

William and George alerted the rest of the crew who were busy arming themselves and getting *Pretty Polly*'s ten guns ready for fire. They expected to see their two sister ships soon, and both could be spotted on the horizon. They were fairly close to each other and probably already saw Andrew's danger signal.

The foreign galley was closing on the *Pretty Polly*. George said to William, "She seems intent on getting close to us. Probably she aims to ram us, and her men may be armed and ready to board us. We have no protection from the bow or the stern. If they get close enough to fire muskets, they could do some damage. You're the owner. Should we face *Polly* farther east to take advantage of the wind?"

"How long till our other guns get here? I can see them with my telescope. This strange galley is much closer."

"We don't know if it's alone or with others. I think we should move back to the Ellis ships. We could set up in a proper battle line and face them with half our cannon bearing down on them."

With that the *Pretty Polly* turned back southwest, and the strange galley kept following at a slow pace. Andrew kept his spyglass on her and soon shouted, "There's at least one other coming up behind her. A small, fast sloop."

George thought that his ships were probably better armed than these pursuers, as the three cargo ships had heavy cannon on board. The small ships couldn't be so quick and still carry heavy arms.

He shouted to William, "When we're in position let's wait for these little sloops and see who they are. We'll have no trouble blowing them out of the water."

"But then we risk them trying to board with small weapons.

Even muskets could kill from short range."

"We'll fire a warning shot, and they can send over an unarmed messenger."

"How can we be sure he'll be unarmed?"

"We'll be able to blow their ships out of the water. They wouldn't take a chance by arming one man when a whole ship could go."

"How can we be sure they have any intelligence to know that?"

"We're better knowing about them than not. What if there are whole fleets of them all along the way?"

After several hours the *Charming Anna* and *Smiling Margaret* caught up with the *Pretty Polly*. The three ships signaled to each other and arranged themselves so they were far enough apart so they wouldn't be a danger to each other but could launch a powerful broadside of twenty-five cannon at any attacker.

Four small sloops were now following the small galley. George waited until the galley came into range. He could make out the twelve men on the galley, and a captain stood on the deck of the nearest sloop. The ship flew no flag. It wasn't navy and wasn't a private licensed ship either.

The small sloop overtook the galley and began to turn broadside. George noticed the aggressive maneuver and signaled to his crew to fire three cannon at the leading sloop. Their shots clapped like thunder loud enough to open up the sky. None of the shots hit the sloop, but all fell in the water near it. The splash of the cannon ball caused the small galley to capsize, throwing the twelve oarsmen into the ocean. The crew on the sloop's deck cowered and was drenched by the torrent. The sloop made a sudden turn to get out of range.

With that, William ordered George to follow. When in range again, William shouted through a megaphone, "Halt! Tell us who you are! Send one unarmed man in a life boat to tell us, or we'll blow you away!"

The sloop moved back in the water closer to its three companions. The galley and its oarsmen were brought up onto the lead sloop. Then the *Charming Anna* and *Smiling Margaret* became visible to everyone. The four small sloops, knowing they'd be outgunned, all turned around and moved away.

William felt relieved but knew this was the beginning of very dangerous business. He ordered Andrew to pull down the danger flag and said to George, "Our illustrious governor had better see to defense if he wants his city built. I'm going to raise the issue in the House when we return. I doubt we'll hear much about ships at sea on May Day."

Three days later the three ships arrived safely in Jamestown harbor.

CHAPTER 3

The Burwells held their family conference just two weeks before May Day. The weather was beautiful and dinner was served in early afternoon on large outdoor tables. The smaller children played, the older ones held deep, ardent conversations. Everyone from the youngest to the oldest had something to say.

Lewis Burwell II was a planter, an explorer, and in 1701 the father of thirteen children, nine who were still living. Of all of them, he always thought Lucy was the prettiest. She was born the year after he'd lost his second son to a fever at the age of thirteen. With her gay smiling face, Lucy filled a hole in her father's heart, and he cared for her deeply.

A Burwell family affair was a large gathering. The oldest three Burwell children were married with families of their own. Included were in-laws, cousins, and various other relatives. Altogether, more than sixty people sat at large tables on the Burwell front lawn, a larger group of people than the House of Burgesses.

After dinner and much loud mumbling among the guests, Elizabeth Harrison addressed her father. "Lucy tells me that the governor pays advances, and she doesn't care much for him."

Elizabeth's brother Nathaniel and his wife, Elizabeth Carter, both stood and approached her. All three advanced to where their father sat.

"This isn't England," Nathaniel said. "The King can do what he likes there. His governor—who is he anyway? He shouldn't be allowed to ride rough shod over planters and their families."

Nathaniel's wife was red faced. "Father Burwell, Lucy is too young to be saddled to that fat functionary. My father would never allow it." Elizabeth Carter Burwell was talking about Robert "King" Carter, the largest and wealthiest planter in Virginia.

Lewis, a strong, athletic man of nearly fifty, said, "Everyone calm down. I never said I agreed to anything. Nicholson is a tempestuous person. When I sit with him in the council, I know that everyone is expecting an explosion. But he's energetic and wants to build up the colony. He pays for the grammar school with his own money, isn't that true Reverend Blair?"

James was caught off guard but stood and said in his high-pitched, Scottish brogue, "Yes, he has a temper and can't always be trusted. I've known him for ten years, and I can't say he's done much for the colony yet."

Burwell replied, "But ten years ago he was only lieutenant governor. He supported the college, didn't he? He's paying for the grammar school."

"And he's taken our building for the government." James couldn't cloak his contempt for Nicholson. "He's a middle-level military man who's never had success on the battlefield. He's been aide and assistant to great men but never did anything on his own. I'm afraid if he marries a Virginia girl he'll feel he owns the place. I doubt anyone wants to see that."

Lewis Burwell stood up and paced around the head table. "Nobody said anything about marriage. It's still the bride's father who must give consent. Let's wait and see what he has to say to me on the matter."

Sarah Harrison Blair sat next to her brother Benjamin and kicked him, looking at him carefully. Benjamin coughed quietly and stood. "Colonel Burwell, we are one family here, and we all love and support Lucy. If she doesn't want the governor as a husband, I'm sure many other young women will consent. This is a proper commonwealth that respects customs and the laws. Lucy shouldn't have to marry a man simply because he's the governor."

Burwell took a deep breath. "I expect we'll hear a lot from the governor at his May Day celebration."

The Virginia Assembly had met in a Jamestown house prepared by John Tullitt for which Tullitt received fifty pounds in payment. The council and general court had met nearby in the house of Mrs. Sherwood who also received a small payment for the use of her great entry hall. The ruins of the State House still smoldered from the fire that had destroyed it the previous fall.

Nicholson, who was first and foremost a builder, had begged the assembly to erect a "pile of buildings" that would serve the public use. It was at that assembly in April 1699 that the governor announced a public day of rejoicing on May Day. He invited the burgesses to assemble at the College of William and Mary at Middle Plantation where they could hear and be "witness to the great improvement of our youth in learning and education."

Middle Plantation was located halfway between the York and James Rivers, and several of the wealthier planters had built large brick homes there. The land offered fresh water and a more pleasant climate than Jamestown, which was low-lying and marshy.

The college was only a grammar school. Its students were several dozen boys from age twelve and up who studied Latin and Greek with Mungo Inglis, the grammar school master. For the May Day celebration five of the boys prepared speeches under the guidance of Nicholson and James Blair.

To the celebration all of the boys wore the school uniform of white blouse, navy-blue coat, grey breeches over fine, white stockings, and buckled shoes. Once the crowd assembled in the Wren Building courtyard, the boys marched in lock step behind Inglis and stood in line waiting to speak. On a small, temporary podium all of them proclaimed the advantages of education and begged for support of the college and moving the capital to Middle Plantation.

The first speaker, Jack Armistead, a plump, red-headed boy of fourteen, declared in a thin, high-pitched voice that learning was essential for the public good, for without it how "can laws be made, justice be distributed, differences be composed, or public speeches be begun or concluded." Learning was man's only solace in a world where "all things are perishable except the goods of the mind." James undoubtedly contributed to these remarks, and everyone listening knew it. Young Jack wore a broad smile throughout his oration.

The second speaker, Tom Davidson, a tall, thin boy of sixteen, wore his curly, blond hair down to his shoulders. He deeply intoned the advantages of providing education in Virginia rather than abroad. He argued that English schooling was twice as expensive, voyages to England were dangerous, and Virginia students sometimes couldn't acclimatize to England where travelers often became ill. Many listeners nodded agreement with these facts. Voyages were getting increasingly dangerous, and sicknesses in Europe were well known to those who'd traveled and returned. Many understood also that once a son is sent to England to study there was a strong possibility that he'd decide never to return to the colony.

The third speaker, Orlando Jones, was eighteen and the senior student at the grammar school. He strutted to the podium and argued that the moving of the statehouse to Middle Plantation would be providential. "The colledge will be a great help to the making of a town, and the town towards improving the colledge." He listed Middle Plantation's advantages: a high elevation and fresh water, easy access by land and water, and security from attacks by sea and Indian attack by land. In addition, Middle Plantation offered hills on which windmills could be erected and firm ground on which to erect buildings and houses. He finished by saying that Middle Plantation had already made a start toward being a town: it had a church, several stores, two mills, a smith's shop, a grammar school, and the college. These remarks obviously reflected Nicholson's opinions, and many members of the assembly and council who'd already heard these arguments and seen his building plans recognized them.

The fourth speaker, John Harrington, a dark-haired boy of sixteen, described the origin of the college and the previous support given by many persons in attendance. This was a plea for further support, continued by the fifth speaker, Henry Mason, a small, dark fourteen-year-old, who commented on the great universities of England and asked for support so that the college could grow and take its place among the world's leading institutions of higher learning. Nothing was said about the needs of the church in Virginia, nor of James's desire to produce more ministers of religion. The boys appealed to their listeners' self-interest: the college would promote wisdom and learning, the new capital would be a city of which they could be proud, and the college would provide an intellectual status to the new capital.

Listeners gave the boys an attentive and affectionate reception. The crowd consisted of many of the relatives of the boys who were anxious to show their support. The listeners clearly were impressed by Gov. Francis Nicholson's resolve. If he wanted a new capital, and there was money to pay for it, nobody would be in opposition. The State House in Jamestown had burned twice in the previous thirty years. The colony was growing by leaps and bounds, and a new capital likely would better serve the new businesses that were coming to Virginia.

Lewis Burwell, a member of the Governor's Council and governor of the college—a member of the Board of Visitors—waited for Nicholson to approach him on the subject of Lucy, but Nicholson said nothing. The governor didn't want any arguments before his building plans were approved.

Later in June, when the assembly resumed session at Mr. Tullitt's house, Nicholson recommended formally that the assembly build a State House near the College of William and Mary. He announced that henceforth the House would meet in Williamsburg, in rooms in the college's Wren Building prepared for the members use, and members wishing to stay in the Wren should let the Governor's Council know. Nicholson also sent along a copy of the address given by the third student, outlining the specific advantages of Middle Plantation as a location.

The assembly promptly passed a bill calling for a "Capitol" to be built at Middle Plantation, which should forever be "called and known by the name of the city of Williamsburg, in honor of our gracious and glorious King William."

Members of the assembly had known for months that this was going to happen and were pleased with Nicholson's plans. They had their doubts about the circular plan of the new streets, but Nicholson was the governor, the emissary of the King in Virginia. If he wanted streets named after himself that was his prerogative. They approved of naming the main thoroughfare after the Duke of Gloucester, the ten-year-old son of Princess Anne and her only surviving child after eighteen pregnancies. The Duke of Gloucester was next in line to the throne after Princess Anne, as King William had no children.

When presented with the proposal for the new capital city, the House of Burgesses accepted but was slow to approve of buildings that cost money. Nicholson had his street names but would have to beg for money for a Capitol Building and Gover-

nor's Palace. The House figured that if he wanted these buildings so much, perhaps he or the Board of Trade would pay for
them. The Board of Trade consisted of very wealthy men, and
the governor was very well paid. Nicholson was left with the
Wren Building of the College of William and Mary as his home
and office, great plans, and James Blair as an adversary.

CHAPTER 4

Francis Nicholson was forty-six when he finally became governor of Virginia. He'd spent his career in the military, mainly as adjutant and assistant to higher-ranking officers. He'd been a lieutenant governor of Virginia, governor of New York when New York was part of the Dominion of New England, and governor of Maryland, a very small neighboring colony.

A royalist, he believed in an orderly government and supported the monarchical party in the Parliament. When King James II left England in 1689, Nicholson withheld support for the new monarchs, William and Mary. Nicholson mistrusted and disliked the Whigs who for a brief time dominated the Parliament. The Whigs were responsible for the so-called "glorious revolution" by which Parliament removed the King.

Nicholson believed that all the colonies in North America should be placed under one governor or viceroy supported by a standing army similar to a European country. He'd been governor of New York and lieutenant to Governor Edmund Andros during the time of the creation of the Dominion of New England during the last days of James II. The Dominion of New England had stretched from Massachusetts to the Jerseys. With the King's overthrow and much colonial unrest, the experiment was abandoned. Nicholson still thought it was a good idea and agitated for a similar experiment again. He discussed the idea with his council soon after announcing the move to Williamsburg.

The council met in the great hall of Mrs. Sherwood's house in Jamestown and consisted of eight Virginians, all wealthy planters and long-time leaders of the colony. In July, during hot and humid weather, they held their council even though some members had taken to their beds with the first shivers of malaria. Those in attendance included Lewis Burwell; Benjamin Harrison II (Sarah Blair's father and Elizabeth Burwell Harrison's father-in-law); Philip Ludwell II (Sarah Blair's brother-in-law); Robert "King" Carter (Nathaniel Burwell's father-in-law); William Byrd Sr.; and John Lightfoot.

Nicholson welcomed the gentlemen and asked Reverend Smith to say a prayer of invocation. The reverend stood somberly and said, "Almighty God, please bless this council meeting." He then turned to Nicholson and reported, "I understand that Commissary Blair will soon take his seat on the council."

Nicholson harrumphed vocally and waved his arm at the reverend. "I've written to London on that issue and the Board of Trade will soon determine who can sit for the Church of England in the council." He looked squarely at the reverend who quickly became nervous and asked to be excused from the room.

Nicholson then sat back and asked the assembled council, "What is the proper role of a governor in a commonwealth like Virginia?" The council, thinking he was just being courteous, listened attentively. Nicholson proceeded to answer his own question. "A colony like Virginia is best safeguarded by a militia and a governor who can plan territorially. Planning should take into account all of the King's lands from Massachusetts to the Carolinas."

Benjamin Harrison, perhaps the most senior council member, laughed. "That would be quite a militia. Would the militia be English? That might be a good thing as they would all be over here, and the King would have nobody to fight the French!" The council laughed, but Nicholson didn't. He was serious.

Philip Ludwell asked, "Do you mean to impose martial law everywhere? What about civilian authority? Will there be sheriffs, courts, local magistrates? Will this viceroy do everything?"

Nicholson fired back. "The governor or viceroy would do much more than is done by crown appointees now. It's time for the colony to grow up and that's why I've planned for a real capital city."

Nicholson then announced his plans for Williamsburg and showed the plans for the city streets to the council members. They sat around a long table and the plans were unfurled for them to see. The plans proposed a large city—more than a mile would stretch from the Wren Building of the college to the planned Capitol Building that would be home to the House of Burgesses. A Governor's Palace was to be built on a large grassy mall about halfway between the two large buildings. Facing across the mall from the Governor's Palace would be a large armory to hold the weapons for the governor's militia.

At the time, the town had a church and a few shops; farms and tobacco fields occupied all the rest of the land. The land on which the city was to be built belonged to somebody.

Carter began the questions. "How will you pay for all this? You'll have to begin by purchasing the land if you want buildings in these locations."

Nicholson replied, "We are the government and rule here for the King. I will take the land as the King's prerogative, a simple matter of eminent domain."

William Byrd countered. "But you'll have to pay the owners

the market price for the land. There's not enough in quitrents to cover this property. It's valuable. People are building fine brick homes in the area."

Philip Ludwell added, "Yes, my brother Thomas has a place in Middle Plantation, uh, excuse me, Williamsburg. I believe Mrs. Blair, the commissary's wife, is looking at a plantation nearby. It's valuable land."

Nicholson was getting annoyed. "For years this colony has seen lands grabbed from the King's parcels to enrich individual planters. As the King's own governor I will take the land back. It belongs to the King and nobody else has the right to it."

Benjamin Harrison II stood and in a calm voice said, "My governor, we are your council and love the King as much as you. We wish you to succeed with your plans, but you must understand the wealth of Virginia lies in its tobacco and the ability of planters to get it out of the land. A good part of the King's treasury comes from customs duties collected from Virginia tobacco planters. Tobacco depletes the land quickly, and the more we grow tobacco, the more land is needed."

Nicholson would have none of this argument. "Yes, yes, I've heard this before. But Virginia is the maker of great wealth while its people live like denizens of the deserts and forests. It's time for our richest colony to take its place among the civilized countries of the world. Other colonies have fine cities. Philadelphia and New York have all that townsfolk would require—even Boston and Baltimore are fine small cities. My goodness, even Charles Towne, south of here, is more of a town than any place in Virginia."

King Carter stood at that and went over to the side of the table where Harrison still stood. Both faced the governor. Carter spoke. "Yes, those are fine places I'm sure, but as you say, Virginia has the wealth. The King and his armies didn't found this colony. It was founded by a company that drew the wealth from the land. Only after many of our ancestors died of starvation did the King see fit to name Virginia a crown colony."

William Byrd added, "Yes, and what do we get from the crown? The costs of the King's wars with not much benefit. Hardly a governor has seen to our defenses. Didn't the Dutch send ships up the James to burn five of our tobacco ships? Where was the Royal Navy then? Who protects us from Indian attack? You are the governor. What do you say to defense?"

Nicholson responded, "My first duty is defense, and the building of a capital city with streets and an armory for a militia will add to our defense. Williamsburg is a much more defensible location than Jamestown from attacks by sea. I've made up my mind—the King will take his lands back and will reap the profits from tobacco grown on it."

The council was shocked. Nicholson was talking about their land as well as land being farmed by many members of the House of Burgesses. Nicholson wasn't simply suggesting an increase in taxation; he seemed to be threatening to use the militia to seize property from people already working the land.

"By what right does this Middle Plantation land belong to the King?" Harrison challenged. "We all have proper legal patents granted by the courts. We paid for the land. It's valuable because we made it so. Our people farmed and died on the land and grew our crops, which the King's supporters are happy to buy and resell all over Europe. We pay our quitrents to support the colony, but if we have no plantations there are no profits and no quitrents. We've lived here near a hundred years without cities."

Nicholson was now angry and red in the face. "Yes, and your people forget that they owe allegiance to the King and his governor! Henceforth, I will decide who will get appointments as the King's customs agents and all other colonial offices—sheriffs, judges, and the like. These will be people who'll work for the King, his governor, and his colony! All fees for employment will go to the governor's offices!"

John Lightfoot shouted, "If we are to lose fees paid by those who have appointments and are loyal to us, are we not to be justly compensated? If my nephew makes a few pounds because I got him a position as tobacco inspector and pays me a small amount each month are these fees to stop? Should not my compensation as council member be increased to compensate me for the loss of fees? Where do you expect to find people to occupy these positions anyway?"

"Enough of these complaints!" Nicholson commanded. "I will bring these matters to the Board of Trade and tell you of their decisions."

Nicholson wrote to the board but received no reply. Matters in London were muddled by talk of the King's illnesses, and the board postponed all major decisions.

Chapter 5

O ver the rest of the year, James prepared the Wren Building for the arrival of the House of Burgesses. The great hall was
outfitted with benches that would hold the House with room
for more than fifty members. Small rooms on the upper floors
were furnished with beds and small tables to provide lodging
for members who had no other place to stay. The grammar
school was moved to the highest floor, where James also kept a
small apartment.

By the middle of 1700, it was clear that the House would
be able to move into the new facilities by December. But 1700
was a time of anxiety in England. There was deep sadness in
England and the colony when the Duke of Gloucester died early
that year at the age of eleven. Parliament quickly passed the Act
of Settlement to establish the royal succession. It decreed that
the English monarch should be in communion with the Church
of England—not Roman Catholic—and that heirs to the throne
should follow the line of King James I. Virginia was an Anglican

colony and the idea that the monarch should be required to be of the Anglican persuasion wasn't controversial.

The Act of Settlement was necessary because King James II, who'd been removed from the throne in 1689, had moved with his Catholic family to France and was still alive. He claimed to be the rightful English monarch and had the support of King Louis XIV of France. He'd landed with an army in Ireland in 1689 but was defeated by King William there in 1690.

The London press always carried stories about assassination attempts against King William by people wanting to restore King James II. Political anxiety permeated the English aristocracy and governing classes, including the Board of Trade. Virtually all major decisions were postponed. In 1700, the board restored James Blair to Virginia's Governor's Council but made no other decisions responding to Nicholson's letters.

Anxieties ran deeper in England than in Virginia. News from Europe was intermittent and very late, coming either from notices by the governor, correspondence by individuals with English friends and relatives, or occasional newspapers from London arriving by ship on transatlantic voyages. Virginia still had no printing press of its own and there were no local newspapers. The main form of communication remained personal meetings in homes or taverns; but when news came it was of great interest. The trials and tribulations of European royalty were always a subject for amusement and conversation, though most Virginians felt they were far away from the court and all its internal politics.

Francis Nicholson didn't feel far away from it. He knew that the royal succession would likely affect the makeup of the Board of Trade. He wanted his post as governor of Virginia to be seen as inevitable and permanent, no matter who sat on the board. For this reason, he determined to marry into one of the great planter families. William Berkeley, the last governor to rule for a long period—over thirty years—married Frances Culpeper Stephens, a widow with great land possessions in Virginia and the

Carolinas. Virtually all other governors either had been driven out by an angry House of Burgesses or simply retired because they never intended to stay.

Nicholson wanted to remain in the commonwealth, and a Virginia marriage was one way of cementing his hold on the colony. He waited until the House was in session in Williamsburg before he invited Lewis Burwell and his wife, Martha, along with other members of the Council and their spouses to a gala event in the Wren Building. He had the Blue Room, where the council met, decorated sumptuously and ordered a fine dinner of turkey, crabs, winter vegetables, and fresh baked breads and cakes. He brought out his best wines.

When his guests were seated Nicholson offered a toast to the new capital. All of the guests smiled. Benjamin Harrison III spoke. "Yes, we'll have a fine capital, and with peace we can find the resources to get people of stature to come here. Thank you, governor, for your leadership."

The other council members agreed. William Byrd was especially effusive. "Yes, peace is what we need. It brings plans for a future, growth, and prosperity. It's wonderful to look forward again."

Nicholson addressed Burwell. "Yes, I look to the future also. We need to have a firm grip on our plans and know where we are going next. Colonel Burwell, what does Lucy think of marriage to the governor?"

"That's hardly a matter for public discussion, is it?"

"But we are all nearly one family here, are we not?"

"I'm sorry to tell you but Lucy disdains your proposal, and we, her family, will support her desires. She's very young to marry. My Governor, please look elsewhere."

Nicholson grew red in the face. He stood and pounded his fist on the table. "Am I not good enough? How many children do you have? She is near sixteen or seventeen, is she not? Explain yourself!!"

Burwell, who was a bland, easygoing man, was affronted. He knew Lucy was beautiful and that many young men of Virginia had their eyes on her. He intended to make a good match for her—one that she wanted and would add to his already extensive landholdings. Marriages were still business in Virginia.

"My Governor, I cannot encourage your suit. After all, you have a title of governor but for how long? You're an appointee of a distant government. I'm her father and have to think of her future. Where are your landholdings? What property do you offer? If she wished it, the matter would be different for me, but she doesn't wish it."

Nicholson was enraged. He stood, pounded on the table, and shouted, "If I can't have her, nobody else will. If she marries I'll cut the throat of her bridegroom, the functionary who grants the license, and the clergyman conducting the wedding. I can make life uncomfortable for you in many ways."

The guests were shocked. Burwell's young wife, Martha, the mother of his four youngest children, spoke quietly. "Please, Governor, sit down. This has been a fine occasion, and we thank you for it. Our Lucy will take her time deciding her future. Perhaps you should take some time to think on this too?"

Nicholson calmed down a bit, but he was angry. The council members were all Virginians, all related one way or another to each other and not of his choice. He couldn't easily enter their ranks, but he was willing to harass any suitor Lucy might otherwise meet. He sat and sipped his wine. After Nicholson's temper tantrum, conversation around the table became muted, eventually dealing with such subjects as the weather, the problem of malaria, the value of land in Middle Plantation, and the idea of building a city according to a plan. The conversation, led by Nicholson and James, was difficult for the Virginians in the room to appreciate. The planters and their wives really didn't understand what the governor and the minister were talking about. Most of them had never seen a large town or city.

The matter was made worse by the actual speech of James and Nicholson. James spoke in a high-pitched, Scottish brogue. He spoke much more quickly than Virginians who generally used a calm, lilting, almost musical tone of speech. Nicholson seemed to speak in clipped tones. To the Virginia ear, he sounded like a dog barking.

Nicholson, the governor and emissary of the King, believed in decrees from above. He thought it was right and just for a royal monarch and his governor to decide if and where towns were to be built. Nicholson loved to build, and he thought of towns and buildings as jewels in the monarch's crown. Nicholson also believed in education and supported the church out of personal conviction. He spent his own money supporting schools and churches in every colony in which he'd lived. He thought of himself as a sort of royal personage and acted as though he were a minor royal monarch.

James also saw the world as a hierarchy presided over by a monarch who was one with the church. But James wasn't interested in building something because the monarch might like it. He thought of the world as a class structure made up of a ladder to prestige and income for the clever man to climb, and James aimed to climb as far as he could go. If he had to tear something or someone down in the process, he was willing. If he had to use the church to get where he wanted, he'd do that. If he had to use church and political connections to tear down a governor, he was able and happy to do that as well. James, as much as Nicholson, wanted towns and cities built, preferably with churches as center pieces.

Benjamin Harrison III, the attorney general, addressed Nicholson. "My Lord Governor, how can a city just be brought to a place because you have a plan? Who will live here? Why would they come?"

"They'll come because we are a capital city. We have the seat of government, the assembly, the courts, and a college. People doing business here will need places to stay. They'll be well off and will support shops. People who have crafts and things to sell will come because of the wealth of the place."

Robert Carter couldn't follow the logic. "But our wealth has nothing to do with education or government. We earn our profits by mixing our labor with what comes out of the ground. All government does is tax it. Most Virginians of wealth try hard to stay away from government."

A round of laughter broke out all around the table. Only James Blair didn't think it was funny. "My governor is wise in wishing to build towns. Towns are the center of civilization, where people of education and means can meet and share opinions."

William Byrd agreed with Carter. "Yes, we have no problems expressing ourselves to each other at public and private meetings. How would elaborate buildings add to what we already have, my Governor? Inns, taverns, theaters, shops are for visitors, are they not? We have no great difficulty buying what we need now. So long as we raise the tobacco, we can keep buying."

Nicholson couldn't follow Byrd's logic. "But don't you think Virginia should have a fine State House? This is a rich colony, but to the rest of the world it appears poor, for lack of civilized attainments."

"What makes a city or town civilized?" Byrd retorted. "Don't you have to tear down the trees, befoul the water, and push people around to do the building? For what purpose and whose benefit? People from distant places may like what they see, but what do the people here get from such building?"

Nicholson thought the discussion idiotic, and so did James. Both had seen London and lived there. Nicholson had already erected other towns and buildings. James had lived in London twice and enjoyed the cultural life there immensely. Both liked the idea of a town where people could flaunt their power and wealth, view and be seen by others, and outwit and outclass competitors. They thought a town was the best place for civilized people to move up the social ladder—to get closer to those at the top and to treat contemptuously those beneath them.

James continued, "When I was last in London I told Dr. Locke of our lack of cities. I was embarrassed to say that Virginia was simply built the wrong way. In Massachusetts people weren't permitted to live far away from each other. They built towns at the beginning of the colony."

Byrd couldn't contain himself. "Yes, and what is Massachusetts compared to Virginia now? People who couldn't abide the Puritan religion have been exiled and hanged. Many left for other places. Connecticut and Rhode Island are colonies founded by people leaving Massachusetts. I was born in London myself, and I can tell you, it's a place many people don't care to live in. If we build a town, I hope you will make it suitable for people—not for the rats and vermin that populate London."

"Please, sir, we're here to eat and enjoy," Nicholson admonished. "If we set out the streets they will be to our liking. I assure you the new Duke of Gloucester Street will be a wide thoroughfare."

Everyone calmed down, but the rest of the dinner remained tense.

Though Francis Nicholson felt no love for James Blair, the Board of Trade directed that James should be returned to the Governor's Council in 1700. The board felt it necessary that the Church of England be represented on the council, and James was the logical choice. He'd married a daughter of one of the Virginia plantation families, and he'd lived in Virginia for fifteen years.

Virginia had no high-ranking clergy—no bishops, no archbishops, nor anyone related to these high functionaries. Indeed, it was very difficult for the church to recruit ministers to go to the new world. Virginia was the richest colony but one where living was rough and violent. In 1700, the church had thirty-six ministers for sixty-five parishes and no ecclesiastical school in the colony that might produce more ministers. The college remained a grammar school.

Anglican ministers in Virginia were at the mercy of local vestries who decided what each minister would be paid and how long he would be employed. Every year one or two Virginia ministers returned to England because they found riding circuit among the parishes too difficult or they were on the verge of starvation or they feared the violence of their parishioners. Or they simply couldn't stand James, who made matters worse by keeping all money provided by the English church to Virginia as if it belonged to him personally.

If ministers were going to be better paid, the House of Burgesses or the governor would need to find the money for them. In 1699, the House rejected a plan put forward by James, and the Board of Trade supported the House decision. Blair proposed that the clergy be given lifetime tenure, moving costs, a house, a library, and four or five Negro slaves. Clergy widows and orphans would be aided. All this would put the clergy in a situation far wealthier than many members of the House of Burgesses. The burgesses never really bothered to vote on the proposal, just issued a resounding "no" in a voice vote.

When Nicholson became governor, the Anglican ministers of Virginia already distrusted James. The English reverends despised him as a Scottish hireling. Almost all of them knew he was greedy and self-centered. The vestries, controlled by the planters, were frugal but wanted to control their individual parishes. When Nicholson threatened the planters with a proposal to take over all colonial offices, leading vestrymen began to support James.

All this played out in letters to and from the Board of Trade by James, Nicholson, various Anglican ministers in Virginia, and some planters over the next two years. The board remained uninterested in making major decisions. Politics was again in the forefront.

⌁

King James II died in France in 1701, leaving a Catholic son, James Francis Edward, recognized as King of England by Louis XIV, at James II's death. The Board of Trade felt relief, as the Sun King wasn't very interested in backing a military restoration in England. The young pretender was French with few supporters in England. King Louis was much more interested in placing his grandson on the throne of Spain and became engaged against Austria in the War of the Spanish Succession.

Matters became more complex when King William died in 1702 and was succeeded by Queen Anne. The Queen was immediately drawn into the great European conflict, which pitted France, supported by Spain, Portugal, Savoy, and Bavaria, against Austria. Austria had the support of Holland and Prussia. In 1702, very soon after taking the throne, Queen Anne lent her support to Austria. This entailed the raising of a new army. War again would afflict trade on the high seas and affect the livelihoods of Virginians.

Under the Act of Settlement, because Anne had no living children, next in line was Princess Sophie of Hanover, a granddaughter of King James I. Princess Sophie would be followed on the English throne by her Protestant descendants.

In 1702, Williamsburg, the new capital of Virginia, was named after a dead king and its main street for a dead heir apparent even before the city's streets were fully laid out. Nicholson's preferred street plan had the streets arranged in a cypher of the two letters *W* and *M* superimposed on each other, standing for the monarchs William and Mary. The streets would meander along the shapes of *W* and *M* regardless of the lie of the land. The only living person whose name appeared on street names was the governor, Francis Nicholson, who took great pains to plan the town. He was so obsessed with his building projects that he didn't care if he made powerful enemies, and he'd already made many. He was king in Virginia, atop the government and atop the church. His main problem was how to keep it that way.

<center>~~~~~</center>

The members of the Governor's Council in Virginia, though far from the politics of Europe, knew they were again to become its victims. By 1702, King William's War was replaced by Queen Anne's War. War with the Spanish and French in Europe was waged by large armies, decimating hundreds of thousands of people living in their way, mostly in central Europe and Germany. In North America, it took the form of raids on outer settlements by Indians supported by the Spanish and French and attacks on port cities and shipping.

In June 1702, Benjamin Harrison II invited some members of the council and a few friends and relatives to his home for a small birthday celebration for Benjamin Harrison IV, now seven years old. He planned some festivities for the children and an afternoon of quiet discussion among the members of the council, without the presence of the governor.

Lewis Burwell, William Byrd, John Lightfoot, Philip Ludwell, and Robert Carter attended along with spouses and some family members. Benjamin Harrison III attended since he was attorney general of Virginia, as did James who sat on the council as representative of the Church of England. Altogether, about thirty people occupied the Harrison house, and all were in some way related to each other.

The tobacco was planted and the weather fine, but the men were concerned about the safety of the seas in getting their crop to Europe. The elder Harrison began the discussion. "Well, we have a new monarch and a new war. When will this end do you suppose?"

Byrd responded, "When kings and queens stop coveting each other's lands. Are we that different?"

Carter laughed along with the rest and finally said, "We have smaller fish to fry. We need to feed our children and servants and see that our children are well situated after us. We don't need wars to do that. We need good weather and enough rain and simple hard work."

Lightfoot laughed also but said, "My dear Carter, the land is here for us to take or purchase. How many thousands of acres can each of us have or hope to get? Some of us will own more land than some European kings. But we can't prosper without trade and earning some hard currency."

Byrd responded again, "Yes, my son William II writes from London that the Queen is well loved, but going to war is a happy frenzy for the English. The treasury will be emptied buying armaments and supplies for the troops. Our own Daniel Parke thought he'd become an aide to a general. Now he is aide to a duke. Churchill's been given the title of Duke of Marlborough and leads a large army on the continent."

Harrison spoke sadly. "Yes, poor souls of Europe. So many Germans and Swiss are coming here to escape the bloodshed. Well, our Daniel will bring us pride. There's nobody who can stand up to him in battle."

That brought uproarious laughter. Each of them recounted the tales of arrogant Daniel Parke, fighting duels and threatening friends and enemies alike. Sarah Blair, sitting in the rear with Elizabeth Harrison, commented. "Jane will be very pleased. Daniel's success will be good for the prospects of his two daughters, Frances and Lucy. Every young man of Virginia will court a hero's daughter."

Byrd and Carter agreed. Byrd said, "Yes, they seem like fine girls. What do you think, Philip?"

Philip Ludwell, brother to Jane Ludwell Parke and uncle to the two girls in question, was also a member of the Governor's Council and married to Hannah Harrison, Sarah Blair's younger sister. Everyone in the room was a sibling or cousin, naturally or by marriage, to everyone else.

Philip said, "Jane is delighted. As you know, we never expected Daniel to survive his debtors here in Virginia. He sends no support back to the family, but Jane is taking care of the plantation and doing quite well. She's grateful not to have to pay his debts, which I'm sure have grown along with his pride. When tobacco is doing well, so do the Parkes! The estate he left here is quite large."

Benjamin senior interrupted, "That brings us to the main issue before us, the behavior of our current governor." Everyone had a complaint:

"He will bankrupt everyone with taxes for his building plans!"

"He'll do nothing to protect the ships at sea!"

"He's a threat to the orderly government with his threats of taking over appointments!"

"He's angry and bad tempered and doesn't know how to deal with complicated issues!"

Harrison calmed the group. "Yes, yes. We all know that. We are his council and bear some responsibility. If we leave it to the burgesses, we could have riots and the new Wren Building could burn, and not accidentally."

When it became obvious that the men generally agreed about the governor, James Blair stood and moved to the center of the small parlor to make his suggestions. "The current Board of Trade still has some Whig members, though Doctor Locke is ailing and off the board now. I believe that if the council drafts a letter to the board complaining about Nicholson's behavior, the current board will take the accusations seriously. Nicholson has no strong supporters on the board."

The council members murmured to each other. "A letter from the council by itself could hardly be taken seriously," said Lightfoot.

James replied, "I could go to London and represent our interests to the board before they get the letter. That would give us an idea of our chances and who would listen to us."

Benjamin III intervened. "A letter from us has to include the entire council and be argued in fine legal terms. The board would want a respectable presentation."

"Yes," said James. "We should talk about our letter in detail before it's sent, but I do think I should go." He looked at Sarah. "I'd like Mrs. Blair to accompany me. It's about time that someone in Virginia saw a real town, and she could finally meet the people she's been trading with these last few years."

Sarah was surprised at James's announcement and wondered why he might need her in London. He probably had some social engagements that would require the presence of a spouse. She shuddered to think about the priests and bishops she'd have to meet. But she began to seriously consider a voyage to Europe and the opportunity to shop there.

Benjamin Harrison II, Sarah's father, said, "Well that's a good idea. We'll work on a letter and you can get ready to go by this time next year. That should give us plenty of time to draft our complaints. You know, James, we in Virginia are very good at drafting complaints to authorities."

That brought howls of laughter from the group. Everyone remembered Bacon's Rebellion of thirty years earlier and Nathaniel Bacon's long declaration of grievances against authority. This council, however, wasn't planning a rebellion. The members simply wanted to replace the governor, and they had to get the Board of Trade to consider their wishes. The meeting soon broke up to play cards or billiards or take walks in the late spring air.

CHAPTER 6

Sarah Blair knew a great deal about tobacco and visited the plantation fields every day. Good tobacco came from carefully cultivated and dried leaves of the plant. The crop sprouted from very small seeds that had to be transplanted to small hillocks. Spring plants needed rain, and once the crop began to grow plants had to be weeded, worms had to be removed, lower leaves removed, and suckers cut off. Removing the flowers from the tobacco plant was a painstaking and delicate job.

Sometimes Sarah worked alongside her field workers in the mornings. She particularly enjoyed removing the tobacco flowers and was quite skilled at it. She always felt that the job was better suited to women than men as women had more patience with delicate tasks.

Sarah knew that tobacco allowed the Harrisons to thrive and prosper. She knew that plantations had to grow to survive and that profits from tobacco had to be invested in other businesses. While her brother also owned a plantation his wife ran that. Benjamin Harrison III was more interested in public service. He was a lawyer and enjoyed the roles of attorney general and member of the Governor's Council. Younger than Sarah by three years, Benjamin III spent most of his time in Jamestown seeing to legal matters affecting the colony. Sarah Blair and Elizabeth Harrison grew close and understood each other well.

Sarah was determined that her illegitimate son, Benjamin IV, would favor business over public service. She wanted him to know where his livelihood came from. She often brought him out to the fields with her, and she made sure he knew his numbers. Sarah knew how to make a deal, engage a factor, and keep accounting books. She intended that Benjamin IV would carry this knowledge forward.

Although reluctant at first to leave the Blair plantation and her son, Sarah became increasingly excited about going to London with her husband. The visit would enable her to shop directly from retailers and manufacturers instead of placing orders from afar. She began to make lists of items to buy, from household goods to clothing to weapons. She planned to visit Virginia friends, relatives, and neighbors over the next several months to see what everyone else might want directly from London. She could offer a better price than they could get from their English factors.

The two ships Sarah co-owned with William Roscoe, the *Pretty Polly* and the *Good Fortune*, were docked at a pier on the York River. Many growers along the James River had begun to build piers and keep ships alongside their plantations.

Sarah and William kept a cottage near the York pier and saw to the loading and unloading and other maintenance tasks. They loved working together on the ships and taking meals on them and sometimes sleeping on them and making love, but Sarah had never sailed on one of them.

Sarah left her husband preparing one of his letters. "I'm going to the York to see about the ships. I may stay a few days, if some work is to be done."

James replied, "That's well. I'd like you to hear this letter when you come back. We should also see about writing to people in London, advising them of our visit next year."

"Yes, we'll have to think about that. I'll also have to inform Cunningham, our factor in London."

"Cunningham is a good Scottish company. I'll write to my brother William to tell him to see about anything we could do in advance."

"Well, I'm off." With that she went down to the stable and had a horse attached to a small wagon. She took two strong-armed servants, one to drive the wagon and the other for simple protection. She never went anywhere without armed protection. She could handle a pistol herself, and she'd taken out small animals menacing the crops since she was a small child.

She took the wooded path to the York and arrived about four hours later. When she got there the two servants tied up the wagon and immediately went out to the ships. Sarah entered the small cottage. Inside she found William, his captain George Harris, and Andrew Morgan, George's young nephew. They were sitting around a small, round table talking about the last voyage of the *Pretty Polly*.

William said, a little amused, "We were fortunate to have a fleet with us. I doubt we'd be alive if we took the voyage alone. We'll have to look for trading partners every voyage now."

"From a high mast it would be useful to have a real weapon, a gun that could shoot straight for more than a hundred yards," Andrew added. "I swear I saw the first small ship's captain, but there was nothing that could be done except call in the cannon."

George countered. "Yes, it would be wonderful to shoot, but there's more safety in numbers."

Sarah took off her outer cape, a heavy, red wool garment. The June weather was warming up, and she felt freer in her simple muslin dress. She embraced William who stood and embraced her. "Nothing to worry about," he reassured her. "We're all fine, and *Polly* never received a shot."

Sarah looked up at him, and he quickly related the adventure of the voyage back from Charles Towne. Sarah said, "This has got to stop. The people of Charles Towne will be worried now that there's a new war with the French and Spanish."

William related the last of the news he'd heard. "The town is building a wall, a sort of fortification on the land side. Armed ships will patrol the harbor, and the people of Charles Towne will need weapons. They have only a small militia and worry about attacks from the land."

"Oh, I wish I could get the Dubois to come to Williamsburg!" Andrew said. "I fear for them terribly when I'm away."

George smiled and said, "He worries for Suzanne but hasn't yet asked for her hand."

"I haven't the money to ask for it. Her parents will want to know I have a way of supporting her."

William added, "And then there's religion. They are Huguenots and devout."

"They've already told me that they would allow any protestant religion. It's the Catholics they're against," Andrew said. "I'd do whatever Suzanne asks. Religion won't keep us apart. Mother will understand."

Sarah took a few steps towards Andrew. "Would you like to accompany me on a voyage to London? I'll be going this time next year, and you'd be paid for work on the ship, and you could be a help to me once I'm there. Perhaps we could look over new weapons. There should be quite an array now they're at war again."

Andrew smiled. "I thank you, Mrs. Blair, but I hoped to go sooner than next year."

"You give your mother too much to worry about," George said. "You can start your forge with what you got for this voyage. Maybe you can improve your musket or try to make a new rifle that would shoot straight. Fewer ships will be going now that there's war. We'll have to worry more about French and Spanish warships than the clumsy little pirates. Some of the warships will have sixty cannon."

Sarah said, "I plan to take the *Good Fortune* loaded with good cured tobacco. The reverend has official business in London, so I suspect we'll go in a small fleet including a warship."

George and Andrew stood up to leave. George said, "We'll be taking our leave now. There's fishing and crabbing to tend to."

Andrew looked at Sarah as he stepped through the door. "You're very kind, Mrs. Blair. Perhaps it would be a good idea if I accompanied you to London!"

William walked to the door with them and smiled. "There's time. We'll talk further, and we'll be back in Charles Towne in the fall."

⚜

William returned to the cottage later in the day, alone. Sarah was waiting. He took her into his arms. They hadn't been together for more than a month.

"Are you pleased to be going?" he asked. "Sailing a ship isn't for everyone, you know."

"I know, but likely I'll never go again. This time we have money to spend and I could act as factor for friends and family. I'll shop for them and make a little profit besides."

"If you were my wife I wouldn't permit it. The ocean is dangerous, as is London. You'll need guards the whole time you are there, and you'll have to be careful about what you eat."

"I know, but James has made a public issue of it. He's not going for himself but for the council. They're all anxious to get rid of Nicholson. Since I'm the Harrison in the family and deal directly with our trade, he felt it important that I be there to accompany him."

"Do you expect to go to official meetings? I doubt that women are allowed into their pristine aristocratic chambers."

"I know, but James probably needs advice on what he says to the Board of Trade. He really doesn't know much about trade himself."

"Promise me you'll practice with your pistol. It will be reliable and accurate compared to the usual pistols carried by the militia. Go out and shoot some varmints in the field."

"Oh, William, I'll take Andrew and a few other servants. I'll have protection."

"Don't be foolish. You should be armed and ready at all times."

"Yes, darling, I'll do as you say."

Sarah raised her arms to put them on his shoulders. The size of him always astounded her. He could easily have lifted her with one arm; his shoulders were enormous. He looked the part of a town sheriff, with his great power and straight back.

"I missed you, darling," she said. "We should take advantage of our time together. Who knows how long I'll be in London?" He smiled, took her hand, and they both went out to the *Pretty Polly*.

⸺⁂⸺

Sarah Blair was used to making purchases through her tobacco factors. They bought her crop a year in advance. Against the price she'd receive for the tobacco, she ordered all sorts of goods for her personal and household use. Virtually all tools, furniture, cutlery, and chinaware came from England, though Sarah had a few Dutch dishes and rugs imported from the orient. Fabrics for clothing also came from England, though Sarah had seen some silks from France.

Sarah visited her sister-in-law Elizabeth almost every week, mainly to keep an eye on little Benjamin. The first time she had the chance she asked Elizabeth, "What would you really like to have from London? James tells me it's the center for everything we'd want to buy."

Elizabeth laughed. "I would love a light-blue silk gown and new furniture for the new plantation house. Are you going to fill up the *Good Fortune* with the wishes of the ladies of Jamestown?"

"Of course, why do you think I'm going?"

"Have you thought the whole voyage through? Why does the commissary want you along?"

"Not because he gets lonely, I assure you. He knows his way around London society, and they know he's married. Somehow I fit into his plans, though he hasn't explained it to me."

"I'd take my pistol if I were you. People who've been to London hate to talk about it. You should especially talk to Mrs. Custis, who is now Mrs. Hill. She's buried four husbands now. I know she has a full correspondence with London and French relatives. She might be able to give you some letters of introduction. She certainly knows what to buy and which shops to patronize. What does William think about you going?"

"He's worried. I know we'll miss each other, but we can't change facts. We can only take advantage of the opportunity. I'll likely take young Andrew Morgan as protection and probably one or two servants. I'll certainly take my maid, and James will take a few servants as well. I imagine we'll have a full plate of invitations once James and the council finish with the letters they're writing."

"Young William Byrd is there, as is Daniel Parke. Have you spoken to Jane Parke yet?"

"No, but I feel close to her and will try to make whatever amends I can with Daniel. I think he's very caught up in English society and English life. I don't want to add to her troubles."

"Do you think he's got more debts? He's got a high position next to a duke."

"With him, the more he makes, the more he owes. If he has anything left at all, after the gambling and women, it would surprise me. I doubt he'll ever come back to Virginia."

"Jane will be relieved to know that, but what of Lucy and Frances? They're already marriageable. Does he care nothing for his legitimate children?"

"If I see him, I'll mention them to him."

Elizabeth took out some writing paper and began to make a more detailed list of clothing, furnishings, tools, and whatever popped into her head. As she showed the list to Sarah, Sarah suggested more items. When they were done Sarah asked, "Does King Carter want anything for his new house?"

Elizabeth burst out laughing. "What do you think? You could bring back half of London and that wouldn't be enough for him." She looked at Sarah and said quietly, "I mean it when I say you should protect yourself."

"I don't worry about physical danger, but it's supposed to be an awful dirty place, full of illness and vermin."

"Yes, be careful what you eat and where you go. Keep servants and guns at hand. Has the commissary told you what he'd like you to do?"

"Only that I'm to be gracious and look the part at the various places to which we're invited. Cunningham, my factor, will likely arrange meetings and parties as well. I'll need to get proper clothing and the like when I get there. Also, James mentioned that he'd engage a portrait painter for us. That's apparently what's expected in English society."

"Well, you'll both be hanging, whenever you get back. You'll need to build a house big enough for the paintings!"

Sarah didn't say so but she didn't want a big plantation house. Whatever she earned from this voyage she was going to use to buy more land, as would her father. She resolved to do some target practice with a pistol before she embarked. She also wished to see Mrs. Scarborough Smart Brown Custis Hill and Jane Parke before she left.

CHAPTER 7

In early September, Sarah and William met at the York pier to load the *Pretty Polly*. The main cargo was cured tobacco, and that year had seen an especially fine crop. William helped the crew and servants roll on the hogshead barrels, while George Harris helped with the arrangement of the barrels below deck. Sarah kept an account of everything placed on board. Loading the small ship took two days.

Sarah asked, "William, have you seen to the cannon?"

Andrew, George's young nephew, heard the question and quickly answered, "They're all clean and ready to fire. We have new equipment, and I've made a few improvements in the loading mechanisms. Would you like to see what I've done?"

Sarah was delighted with the invitation. She had an interest in firearms and knew how to use them, but cannon were a new proposition to her. "Of course, show me the way!"

Andrew took her arm and led her onto the ship and then into the hold. There were five gun ports on each side of the cargo deck. A cannon stood at each gun port, each with piles of shot and powder kegs. They were neatly arranged, and Andrew was very proud of his improvements.

"Here, Mrs. Blair, I've only worked on two of them. You can see that I've rifled the interior of these two muzzles. That will make the shot spin when it's fired and should make for better accuracy. Without the rifling, the shot simply goes up and down into the water. We don't even expect it to hit anything, just make lots of noise."

Sarah laughed and saw William in the corner, also smiling. William said, "We're well armed this time. Andrew will be up top all the way, armed with his new rifled musket!"

Andrew proudly said, "Oh yes! I'm sure I could hit something at two hundred yards, though I'll have trouble reloading up there."

Sarah smiled at the young man. "Well, let's hope you don't have to use the weapons. Be sure to keep safe as can be. You know I'll want you for London?"

Andrew looked embarrassed. "I'm sure I'll want to go, ma'am. We'll talk again on our return?"

"We'll make a list of things to buy to build a proper forge. You can tell that to your intended in-laws."

Andrew blushed. He knew everyone saw how he felt about Suzanne, but until he could be on his own, he felt it was his business and his secret. "I'm grateful for the opportunity. I promise I won't delay in letting you know."

William lifted Sarah up to the deck and then disembarked with her. They strolled slowly to the cottage, and once inside both sat quickly, as loading a ship was hard work. They were both weary but satisfied at the prospects.

"We should do well with this load. Crowe expects to transship the tobacco to the Caribbean, under what flag I don't know," Sarah said.

"He doesn't care. With the war it takes ingenuity to get the tobacco to market. If the French will give the highest price, that's what we'll get."

"How kind of the French to enrich Virginia's English. What sort of war is this?"

"We should be happy. It only drives prices up. I'll try to get something in hard currency, not just tobacco notes. That will be useful to you in London."

"Amazing that they take gold currency, wherever it comes from? This voyage may be dangerous. Be careful, William." With that they embraced and said their goodbyes.

The next morning the *Pretty Polly* joined six sailing ships at the mouth of the Chesapeake Bay. All carried cargo and heavy armaments. The seven ships held over a hundred cannon and all crews were armed with pistols and muskets. They set out in fine, bright fall weather, helped along by a brisk breeze. They sailed in a diamond shaped formation and kept close contact with each other through the use of flags and bullhorns. After a few days at sea they found no pirates off the coasts of the Outer Banks of North Carolina. Pirates evidently were now in the Caribbean, where the pickings were better for unmarked vessels; possibly pirates with the war at sea were happier seizing rice ships from the Carolinas than tobacco ships from Virginia.

The small merchant fleet sailed into Charles Towne harbor and peacefully docked and unloaded the cargo. The town, in just a few months, seemed larger and busier, and the docks held many heavily armed ships. William, George, and Andrew saw to the unloading of the tobacco and left four crew members as guards until the tobacco auction two days later. They then hired a small wagon and horseman and loaded some personal packages for the Dubois.

When they arrived, they entered the small dress shop and found Madame Dubois alone at her sewing table. She immediately stood and crossed the room to greet them. After the normal ritual exchange of hugs and kisses they delivered the packages—some woolens and linens shipped out of New York and Philadelphia, some personal letters, and a few newspapers in French. Andrew soon asked, "Where is everyone? How is it you are alone?"

"The men are at the battlements. Everyone in the town is helping to fix the western wall."

William was curious. "Do you expect an attack?"

Mrs. Dubois looked up with a worried look on her face. "We hear only rumors, but the Cherokee come and go and have good intelligence. They warn us that the French and Spanish are paying northern Indians to stage raids in the west. Nobody really knows, but we hope the wall will help. We're moving some cannon to that side as well."

"A hard decision for a small port. You'll need to protect the harbor as well."

"Yes. We have some fully loaded ships at the mouth of the harbor, but you know we can hardly defend against armed warships. The English fleet is in the Caribbean. If any warship came here, we'd been on our own."

Andrew couldn't contain himself. "Where is Suzanne? Do you plan to stay if war appears closer?"

Mrs. Dubois looked at Andrew. "If war comes here, it will come everywhere. This is where we've built our home. Suzanne is helping out at the wall. Many of the women are working alongside the men or are keeping the campfires and preparing food for them. She should be back quite late tonight."

William stood and thought about the situation. "We would be happy to take you and your family back to Williamsburg with us. It's a new city, not even built yet, and quite far inland. We're also at peace with our Indians. Perhaps you'd like to think about it."

"We have much to talk about, don't we? Andrew and Suzanne, I think, are not really ready for a new life together?" She looked up at George, Andrew's uncle, when she said this.

George shook his head knowingly. "I've had long talks with my sister. He's still young, only eighteen, and needs to set himself up in some business."

Andrew was flustered and immediately interrupted. "Uncle George and Mrs. Dubois, Suzanne and I have talked but I haven't yet asked for her hand. I want to have a forge and business before I do that."

"Ah, but that takes time and effort," Mrs. Dubois said.

"My father's small forge is in good condition. I can reopen that. But I'd like to outfit it with new equipment before I set up a business. Mrs. Blair has offered to take me to London with her next year. I can get what I need then and have some money to spare from my earnings on the long voyage."

"But you wouldn't be back for more than a year, and the oceans are very dangerous," said Mrs. Dubois.

"I know. I'd like to talk to Suzanne about our future together. It wouldn't be fair for me to ask her to simply wait that long."

"Well, we understand each other. Nothing will take place this year in any event. Suzanne is only seventeen, and another year's waiting will not be a bad idea. We'll all be busy with war preparation. Even a dress and coat shop has to produce coats for the generals and soldiers."

"Thank you for your hospitality, but this trip we'll be staying with Crowe and visiting the governor," William said. "It's all to do with military preparation along the coastline."

Andrew was surprised to hear that. "Shall I go with you or down to the tavern?"

"Don't be silly," Mrs. Dubois said. "You'll all stay for dinner tonight and Andrew will stay with us until you have to leave. You'd want to see our new wall, won't you Andrew?"

William and George looked at each other and agreed to the arrangement. They stayed the night, and Mrs. Dubois measured each of them for a new coat for the winter, using some of the wool fabric they'd brought with them.

The following week, *Pretty Polly* left Charleston loaded with cannon and a cargo of manufactured goods and rice. Everyone on board held thoughts of war; especially Andrew who feared this was going to be the last year of his life.

The *Pretty Polly* sailed back to Jamestown accompanied by only two other ships, the *Harriet Dee* and *Merry Marjorie*. Among the three, *Pretty Polly* was the most heavily armed. They decided to stay quite close to each other, and George took the position of captain and leader of the group. *Pretty Polly*'s main mast was the highest of the three, and Andrew atop the mast would be the first to know if they were to meet with any trouble.

The first day at sea was uneventful, giving William, George, and Andrew some time to talk to each other. Andrew had not told them anything about his conversations with Suzanne and the Dubois.

George could hardly contain himself. As Andrew traded places atop the mast with Henry Cooper, another young crew member, George finally said, "Well, do you have news for me and your mother?"

William quietly walked to the other side of the boat and became partially hidden by the mast and rigging. Andrew soon said to his uncle, "There's nothing to tell. I love her dearly but can't give her a home now. With the war coming to Charles Towne she doesn't want to leave her family, and neither would I. The place is new with not that many people to defend her. I left them my two new pistols. She, her brother Pierre, and I had some target practice shooting seagulls. She knows I'll be going to London. I hope she'll wait for me."

George felt relieved and very proud of the young man. "We'll leave it all in God's hands. Perhaps the war will be kind to us, though usually it isn't. If you gave away your pistols what do you have for firing a shot from up on the mast?"

"Don't worry, Uncle. I have two loaded long muskets that I've rifled. I also have one pistol. I've found a place to store them up high, though they will only give three shots. It should give us time to set the cannon, if need be."

The second day at sea was windy, though not stormy. The small sailing ships made great speed and soon were off the islands of the Outer Banks. George felt the possibility of a great storm coming on and asked William's thoughts.

"We could try to get closer in, maybe near a cove for shelter," George suggested.

"If there are any bandits we'd be sitting ducks for them."

"I know, but we have danger from the storm, and this time of year heavy cargo ships aren't the most seaworthy in high winds."

William paced the deck nervously. After a moment he said, "Let's see if we can find a cove off one of the islands that we can defend. We have ten cannon ourselves, and the other two probably are able to fire off theirs. Get Andrew to tell them to get the cannon ready."

George motioned to Andrew, who immediately waved his danger flag. Then the three ships turned west and followed the Outer Banks, a meandering coastline dotted by numerous coastal islands.

After making a slight turn, Andrew shouted below, "I see a sloop, much larger than we are, off to the port side hiding behind bulrushes." He raised his danger flag again and the three small ships proceeded cautiously.

The large sloop remained partially hidden, but soon a small dinghy with a small sail and carrying about five men emerged from the tall grass. They apparently came from the larger ship and headed directly toward the *Pretty Polly*. They were outside normal cannon range. A man in the prow of the dinghy held a bullhorn and shouted, "Stop. This is private water for Captain Fielding. He wants to know who you are."

George responded, "We are the *Pretty Polly*, and we are here with two sister ships bound for Jamestown. These are English waters, not belonging to anyone other than the crown. Who is Captain Fielding?"

"A proper Englishman from North Carolina with a proper

armed ship!" As he said this the dinghy came closer, aiming for the bow of the *Pretty Polly*.

Andrew shouted, "Get the cannon ready. These men are armed!" With that he took one of his muskets and aimed at the man standing in the dinghy. He shouted, "Turn around, or I'll fire!"

The *Pretty Polly* crew scurried about the deck and below. Soon all of *Pretty Polly*'s cannon were ready to fire. William and George took out their pistols, fearing the five armed men would try to board before their preparations were ready. George fired his pistol at the dinghy, but the shot fell well short and landed in the water.

Andrew, seeing his uncle had fired a shot, fired off his newly improved musket. He caught the man in the dinghy square in the chest. The man lost his breath, clutched his throat, lost his footing, and toppled over into the water. Andrew then took up his other musket and fired again, this time hitting the head of a second man. The dinghy, now with only three men, quickly turned back toward its mother ship.

"What now?" George asked William.

"We must move the ship into a broadside position so we can fire a clear broadside shot. The wind favors us now. When all three of us are lined up we likely can give Mr. Fielding a proper battle."

Andrew had come down from the mast and heard his uncle's conversation with William. Andrew spoke up. "Move us so the two new cannon face forward. We'll get a much better range with them and maybe we can scare them off."

George and William shook their heads in agreement. Their small fleet—the *Pretty Polly*, *Harriet Dee*, and *Merry Marjorie*—formed a battle line. All three had pulled down some of their sails to weather the storm. *Pretty Polly*'s portside cannon faced toward the large sloop that now emerged from behind tall grass. Two of these cannon were Andrew's newly rifled guns.

The wind picked up and was near hurricane force, driving rain at them. The sky was very dark, and every so often they could hear loud claps of thunder.

Andrew reloaded his two muskets, and he knew he'd likely killed the two men. The men in the dinghy had done nothing for the man who fell overboard. The man who'd been hit in the head was slumped over covered in blood. Andrew was near tears.

"Terrible things happen, Andrew," George said to his nephew, seeing Andrew's remorse. "We can't control everything. You and the new guns likely saved yourself and us. At home, you'd be a hero. Now go see to your new cannon. We'll likely be using them soon." George patted Andrew on the back and took a few steps with him as two men in the prow shouted, "The sloop is moving! Her sails are up!"

George beckoned to Henry Cooper to mount the tallest mast, so he could spot what was happening. He climbed up in heavy wind, carrying only a bullhorn. Once up, he had to lash himself to the mast to keep from being blown off.

The sloop followed a smaller ship and came directly at the battle line and without warning fired four cannon shots.

"Two large sloops coming our way!" Henry shouted. "The forward one is firing!"

The three cargo ships were being tossed around by the heavy weather and had little control over the direction they faced. They were merchant ships loaded with cargo, heavy in the water and not very maneuverable.

Andrew saw to the cannon and went back up on deck. He saw the large sloop and shouted, "I think we can do her some harm now, Uncle!"

George smiled. "Well, go do your worst. He's already fired at us."

Andrew went below and directed the firing of the two rifled cannon and three others he hadn't worked on. The two rifled cannon were centered along the *Pretty Polly*'s portside, with another to the left and two others to the right.

As he prepared to fire, the sloop kept its progress and was now only about a hundred yards away. Andrew aimed the first cannon low and the second one high. The three other cannon aimed at the deck level. He gave the order, and the five cannon, one after another, fired in a cloud of thunder.

When the smoke cleared, the large mast of the tall sloop was hanging over at a rakish angle and its sails were beating about the crew on deck. She also had a hole in her lower side and was listing out of control. Andrew's two cannon had done the damage; the balls from the other three had made a large noise and much smoke but had fallen short into the water.

William could see the crew from the large sloop abandoning their ship. Some were swimming; others escaped in small boats and were hastily heading toward the second ship. William shouted to Andrew, "Better reload!"

Andrew ran down below and hastily readied the five cannon again. He waited a while and then went back on deck. "What's happening?" he asked.

Henry shouted down from the mast, "They've turned around and run away!"

"And now we have a prize to show for our efforts," William said. "We'll have a look at the sloop once the storm's finished."

They maneuvered their way to the edge of the nearest barrier island, which provided some shelter from the brunt of the storm and was covered in grass and infested with mosquitoes. The three ships dropped anchor and stayed there for nearly two days, waiting for the storm to pass through.

Nobody came to retrieve the damaged sloop once the storm lifted, so they sent a few crewmen aboard to see if she could be moved. With a few repairs they were able to lift a few sails, and the new sloop, with the name *Dangerous* painted on her stern, followed them into the docks at Jamestown.

The *Pretty Polly* arrived in Jamestown in early October 1702. Small ships hugging the coast had seen the prize and raced to Jamestown to tell everyone the news of its capture. Capturing a large pirate ship was a cause for celebration and fireworks. Governor Nicholson and half of his council lined up on the pier to inspect the sailors and the new ship. The crew members were a bedraggled mess, having been at sea for close to two weeks, but they smiled when they received three huzzahs.

William, looking very tired, spotted Benjamin Harrison III, attorney general of Virginia. "Can you prepare the papers?" William asked Harrison. "This would be a good ship for Sarah and the reverend to take to London. It can be equipped with quite heavy armaments."

"Of course. Will you dock her here or on the York?"

"Probably on the York. We have better facilities for working on her there."

"You look tired. Why don't you come home with me? Sarah's there and you can have a few words with Ben IV."

William laughed and quickly said, "How can I refuse an invitation like that? Of course I'll come." The attorney general waved for his cart and William took a seat next to him behind the driver.

"I haven't been feeling that well these last few days. I hope you don't mind if I just get some sleep."

"Of course! Elizabeth can have dinner waiting. I'll ask Archie Blair to come over to look at you. Maybe he'll have some medicines to make you feel better."

When they got to the plantation house, young Ben ran out to the cart. "I heard about the prize! Was it very exciting? Did you blow your cannon?"

William lifted his son to his shoulders and carried him into the house. "Of course, yes to all of the above. What should we name her? She's ours now, and we have to give her a proper name."

"I'll think about it," young Ben replied. "I bet Aunt Sarah has some ideas!"

Elizabeth and Sarah greeted and embraced William, and then Sarah walked upstairs with him to a room that had already been prepared. When they got to the room she said, "You're not looking well. What's the matter?"

"Just a general feeling of sickness. I've lost my appetite and vomited a little and have a headache and some back pain. I think a little sleep will do me a lot of good."

"Well, darling, you're a hero and deserve to sleep a bit. What about George and Andrew are they also not feeling well?"

"Well, we were stuck in a small cove for a couple days and the mosquitoes were just terrible. All of us felt a little the worse for wear because of them."

"Archie's coming over with some medicines. Let him look you over."

William embraced Sarah. "Oh, how I missed you, but I must sleep now." With that he lay down and closed his eyes.

A few hours later Archie and James arrived. William had just awakened and Archie went up to see him. He took one look at him and quickly closed the door. Archie asked, "How long have you been ill?"

"Probably a week or so. Do you know what this is?"

"Well, your skin is developing a yellow pallor. I'd say this is a case of yellow jack. Have you been near mosquitoes?"

"They ate us all alive for near three days. Why? What's the prognosis?"

Archie bent over William and examined him. He looked in his mouth and his eyes and felt for his temperature.

"William, we all love and admire you and you have a fine family. If this is what I think it is, I'm afraid we have no cure. We'll have to pray for you. You are a strong, healthy man but you should think about getting your affairs in order."

"Oh my! I survive the guns and cannon but fall to this?"

"You may not fall. There are cases of people surviving, but there is nothing I can do to help you. I'll send Sarah and Benjamin in to talk to you. If you feel clear in the head, you should say what you wish for your estate now."

Sarah and Benjamin III entered the room a few minutes later. Sarah was near tears but managed to control herself. Benjamin, in most lawyerly fashion, said, "I'll draw up a document which you'll sign outlining your wishes for your estate. The widow gets a third of everything with the rest for the children, but you might want to mention specific bequests to your children."

"They're so young. James is ten, Mary eight, William six, and Wilson four. My wife is with child now. What do they know of estates?"

"They'll not always be this young, and you're the owner of a prize ship. Unscrupulous lawyers will come to see your widow. They'll try to break the contracts without a clear statement of your wishes."

"I want all three ships to go to Sarah Harrison Blair who'll use them for proper business."

"Do you wish to include that as a condition?"

"No. How do I give the ships to Sarah?"

"You can sell them. She's your partner and can buy out your shares."

"What of my family? Will they get anything from the ships?"

Sarah thought and then said, "Can we agree that the widow should get one third of one third of the profits, for five years—when James becomes 15? After that, he'll be on his own."

"Why one third of one third?"

"She's entitled to one third, and you own only one third of the first two ships. What should we do about the prize?"

William quickly answered, "I want you to have it free and clear, to do with as you like."

Sarah was weeping now. "Oh, William, how are we all to get on without you?"

Benjamin looked at his sister. "I'll draw up the papers and bring them up for signature straight away." He stood up to leave the room.

Sarah, with heart heaving and a face wet with tears, said, "No. Wait."

She collected her thoughts and then said, "I know the law has its rules, but we should make sensible choices while we can. William, I want your family to have the *Pretty Polly*. It's a fine merchant ship and you've given your life to protect her. I'll see to her being refitted, and if your family wants her renamed we can do that. That will give the widow one third, isn't that right Benjamin?"

Ben shook his head in agreement. Sarah went on. "What of George's family and the crew? They must be depending on the profits?"

William was becoming weaker but answered, "George has a wife but no children of his own. She had about five but all died very young. The crew, well, you know them. They're young and mostly fishermen. But yes, they wanted the profits from the ship. They needed the pay for the things a family wants."

"I'll take care of them," Sarah said. "You can put this in William's will. I'll give ten pounds to every widow for the next five years, and I will see that any family member who wishes to work on a ship can be taken as a crew member. Is that sufficient?"

"Ten pounds is much more than any of them would have gotten, even George."

"We can afford it, but is it your will that they get less?"

William looked up at Sarah. "No, you have the head for figures."

Benjamin interrupted, "Five pounds would be normal for pensions. Do you want to go higher than that?"

Sarah responded quickly, "If they die it's because they took the prize which enriches me. I want their estates to share that, not just have the legal rule. Let's give them seven, will that be acceptable?"

William smiled weakly and looked at Benjamin who put on his legal face and said, "Then it's settled. The *Pretty Polly* to the estate of William Roscoe, and seven pounds[1] pension for five years to the estates of the crew." With that, Benjamin left the room.

William said to Sarah weakly, "You know you're the love of my life. We've had much joy together, and we can proud of little Benjamin. I've never seen a child as clever as he."

"Yes, that's true. And he loves life—all due to you. My father will take over his education soon I'm afraid."

William laughed weakly. "Make sure Ben marries well. He's got a great head for business and will do well with a good dowry."

"Don't worry your head about that. He'll be well cared for."

"I'm curious. Have you ever been in a marital bed with the reverend, your legal husband?"

"That's a silly question. He likes only young boys, and I fear for the children of servants in our house. I fear for the boys who'll be coming to the Indian school he's building. I've never lain with him, and he's never asked me. You're my one true love and always have been."

"Yes, Nicholson has promised some students." William was drifting. He clearly had chills and a high temperature. His skin was becoming a decidedly yellow pallor. He said, "Promise me something, Sarah."

"Whatever you wish, my love."

"When the time is right, don't be afraid to give yourself to another man. You deserve more than wealth. Virginia will give you that. Think of yourself. If you can, have another baby. You're a fine mother."

---

1   Seven pounds in 1702 would be equal to about $1,600,000 in 2009 money.

"What a request! How can you think of that now?"

"But now's the time to say what we really mean to each other. I know you'll see to my family and friends. I want you to try
to be happy, my love."

They looked at each other quietly, and soon the door opened.
Benjamin presented the document. "Before you sleep again, sign
this." He brought a quill and ink to William's bedside, and William scrawled his name in the proper place.

⁕

The following week William Roscoe lay dead, along with
George Harris and half the crew of the *Pretty Polly*. Andrew
Morgan suffered a milder version of the illness and survived.

William's body was transported to his plantation and received by his grieving widow, Mary. He was interred in the
churchyard at Denbigh Parish. At the funeral James gave the
eulogy. The funeral was well attended, including many members
of the House of Burgesses. Sarah Blair didn't come. She stayed
at home and wept by herself.

Over the next several months the *Pretty Polly* and *Dangerous* were outfitted and renamed. Mary Roscoe asked that her
ship be renamed *Sweet William*. Sarah named her new sloop the
Brave William.

CHAPTER 8

Sarah Blair always looked forward. Death and disease were part of life, and she'd seen much of both. She'd been to funerals for her mother, aunts, uncles, cousins, babies, servants, and slaves. But she felt the loss of William deeply. He was more than a lover to her; he'd been her partner in every sense. They'd planned their future together.

Sarah knew she had responsibilities, and she took them seriously. She ran the plantation, saw to the business of operating trading ships, and approved of the hiring of the captains and the crews. And she was going to London with her husband.

In this moment of crisis, she turned to her family. Soon after William's funeral, Sarah visited her father, Benjamin Harrison II, and stayed for a few days. Her father lived in the old plantation house with his three youngest children. His wife, Hannah, Sarah's mother, had died four years earlier of malaria.

Benjamin II was a man in his late fifties and quite fit for his age. He was near six feet tall, as all the Harrisons were quite tall.

He had a ruddy complexion because he still rode out to see his tobacco crop several times a week. He occupied himself more and more with the colony and his children and grandchildren. Though many men of his wealth would have sought a young wife, he wanted peace and to see to the education of all the Harrisons to follow.

When she arrived, Sarah still mourned for William and choked every time she tried to speak. She tried to overcome the feeling that the joys of life were over, but she could barely look up at family members who offered solace and gathered around her.

Her father tried to be sympathetic. He said, as they sat in the front parlor of the old farmhouse, "William was a fine man and a wonderful business partner for you. We all miss him, and you've done right by his crew and family. We're proud of you. The whole colony will look up to the Harrisons knowing you have something to do with our business."

Sarah said very little but was grateful for kind words and the company of people she loved. Her sisters Anne and Elizabeth sat on either side of her. Her teenage brother Henry sat across from them. Her sisters were both attractive girls in their late teens and not yet married. Elizabeth, the younger one, asked, "Have you thought of what you're taking to London? It's only a few months away when you'll be on the ship. You'll need clothes when you get there."

This talk didn't really interest Sarah, but she said, "I don't know. William brought some nice things from Charles Towne last spring. I'll take them. Probably I'll have to have things made when I get there."

Her father suggested, "You should talk to Jane Parke and Mrs. Custis Hill. They can tell you what to get and where to get it. The factors will see to payments."

"I'm not worried about that. I hardly think about London now."

Benjamin, a bit annoyed, said, "You should. You go there for us, in fact for all Virginia. James knows his politics, but he doesn't understand the council or our meaning in sending him. The board reflects the new Queen and her Tories. James won't have as many Whig friends to help him this time. You'll have to let the people know the seriousness of this visit. Not everything is decided in formal meetings, you know. You'll meet the members of the board informally and their families likely. You should let them know you support the Queen and you should think about what you'll be saying to them."

Sarah looked up at her father with admiration. He'd built a plantation that in Europe would be a small empire, and he spent virtually nothing on himself. He still lived in the same wood farmhouse in which she and her three brothers and three sisters were born. He only thought of the colony and settling more land. He'd been hesitant about owning his own ships for trade, but he approved of Sarah's move in that direction. He encouraged Benjamin III to do the same, and he adored Benjamin IV.

"I'll do as you say, Father, but I hardly know what to expect. I've never been in a town, much less a big city. You know I can say my mind. I'll be well prepared to do so if I have the opportunity."

"You must make your opportunity. You'll be a wealthy woman in a place that worships wealth above all things. James knows the politics and backstabbing that goes on. You have to make your place there, a difficult matter for a woman."

"Well, I'll talk to Jane and Mrs. Custis Hill. They may have some ideas about the politics," Sarah said.

"Lady Berkeley, Jane's late mother, was married to three royal governors. Her family, the Culpepers, will be worth knowing. They may not be on the board but they'll know all the members well. Jane can write some letters of introduction for you. Also, Daniel Parke, Jane's husband, is an aide to the Duke of Marlborough. The duke's wife is well acquainted with the Queen. You should see how high you can go. It's a strange society, people always climbing all over each other to get to their top."

Sarah broke a small smile at this advice. She stood up from the small couch where she was sitting and went over to her father and embraced him. "Oh, Father, I think Virginia will survive my being in London for her. Just keep the tobacco and ships moving."

With that she went upstairs to her bed. She was very tired thinking about everything all by herself. She missed William badly, but she had to talk to someone. The next day she left for the plantation of her childhood friend, Jane Parke.

When Sarah arrived Jane and her two teenage daughters, Frances and Lucy, greeted her warmly. Jane and Sarah had been friends since childhood, and Sarah had always fussed about Jane's two daughters. This time they fussed over her, as her sorrow was palpable. They took her quickly into the front parlor where tea was waiting for them.

Jane Ludwell Parke, a woman in her thirties, had a stately bearing. She wasn't beautiful but radiated patience, wisdom, and intelligence. She had light-blue eyes and light-brown, curly hair, was small boned but was robust and energetic.

Jane lived in a large, well-furnished plantation house that showed signs of European taste. Descended from colonial governors and English aristocrats, Jane embellished the house with portraits of former governors, their wives, coats of arms, gold candlesticks, maces, weapons, and numerous other indicators of power.

The house, Green Spring, had been the home of several sitting governors who'd rented the place while Jane lived on another plantation some miles away. Jane rented Green Spring when she needed money. Her husband, a gambler and philanderer, always ran up his debts and she regularly heard about these from his business agent in London, Perry and Lane. Jane tried to keep the plantation afloat, but keeping up with Daniel Parke's debts was a challenge.

Jane took Sarah's hand and said, "We grieve with you for William. I know how you depended on him."

Sarah looked at Jane and said, "Thank you, but life has to go on. The girls are so pretty. You must be thinking of husbands for them?"

"They're still young, Frances seventeen and Lucy sixteen. They have their share of would-be young suitors, but I think I'll wait a bit. Daniel is quite a success serving the duke, which might help their prospects. But he keeps adding to our bills."

Sarah shrugged and smiled at that and said, "Well, I'm here. Tell me everything I should know about London."

Frances and Lucy perked up their ears, as they loved to hear their mother talk frankly about their father, but Jane would have none of it. "This is between Mrs. Blair and myself and will be of no interest to you." She looked at the girls crossly, and they both soon left the room.

"What an example Daniel sets for these girls! They will both be handfuls for any husband. I'm afraid I've really spoiled them."

"Don't be silly. They're just young and independent. It's good that they have minds of their own. Surely they want to marry?"

"I'm sure they do, but there aren't any gallant knights hanging around the Virginia woods. Well, we have time for that. You'll need to know who to meet, how to meet them, and what to say when you get to the great city."

"Only for starters I suppose, don't you think? Do you want me to try to see Daniel?"

"Wait a bit before you contact him. You should be settled somewhere to your liking first. Then you can have some suppers and invite people. I'll write some letters of introduction. Who is getting your town house for you? You should take your own servants who you trust. London is a wild place, really quite dangerous if you don't know your way about."

"Our factor, Cunningham, will rent the place, and James's brother William will come down from Scotland to inspect the place before anything is rented. Do you have other ideas?"

"My cousin Marjorie will be a good person for you to know. She's a Culpeper and married to a young earl who has a place in London. I write to her three times a year. Do you remember her? She was here, when she was about ten. My parents had Culpepers out from England every once in a while. They stayed here for about two years, and Marjorie and I became great friends."

Sarah thought but couldn't remember. She was wondering if Jane was going to say anything more about Daniel.

"Marjorie and the earl visit the court and know the people there, but she tries to stay away from it," Jane said. "She's our age and has three young boys. She'll know the right parts of town and the right places to stay."

"Perhaps we should write to William Blair to consult with Marjorie in advance."

"Either way—if you like what Cunningham provides you can stay. If not, after a few weeks if you don't like the place you can move. You won't find the place that expensive, unless you start gambling the way Daniel does."

"What would you like me to say to Daniel? We certainly expect to see him, along with Byrd. He's been a burgess and member of the Governor's Council."

"Well, he thinks he's much superior to all of Virginia now. But not so superior that he doesn't take our money. You might remind him that he has two marriageable daughters who adore him. I wonder if he ever thinks of them."

"Surely he does. I'll write you whenever we get there and every chance I get. I promise I won't be timid talking to Daniel."

Jane spent the next few days writing letters of introduction for Sarah to take with her. She also invited Mrs. Custis Hill to come to tea.

The next day, when Mrs. Custis Hill arrived, Sarah felt some-what better. Mrs. Custis Hill had known William very well and was warm and sympathetic. She was a bright, energetic woman of sixty who'd once been a great beauty. Born in Virginia, her father had once been Speaker of the House of Burgesses.

"It's hard to be a strong woman, but what would the men do without us?" Mrs. Custis Hill said.

She immediately had Jane and Sarah laughing. "I've been here longer than most everyone, so I have stories to tell. But don't let me bore you."

Nobody was bored, and she went on to relate stories about the various burials of her numerous husbands. She finished and looked Sarah in the eye and said jovially, "I'll write some letters of invitation to my English relations. Be careful about them, all very clever people. They know their way around the place. One of them came here to sue me for my widow's share—said she was related to a son of my dear Mr. Brown. William had the House of Burgesses dismiss the claim. London lawyers! What a lot!"

Sarah remembered. "Yes, you paid William with the *Pretty Polly*. I helped him outfit the ship and it started our business. His family has renamed her *Sweet William*."

Mrs. Custis Hill sighed. "Well, that's fitting. You did well by them. Now I have advice for you. Find a proper business agent other than your factor. You might want to buy more than clothes and jewelry, and be sensible about what you consider. Also, get a smart Jewish banker to keep some cash on hand for you. Don't worry about the interest they charge you, use them to look for investments. They are heavy into the Caribbean trade, and they'll keep you up to date on business here and on the conti-nent. Remember you're going to England for us and you're rich. You aren't a success if you merely remove the governor. Your duty is to come back richer than you ever were before."

James Blair believed he couldn't get along in Virginia with fewer than four servants. He needed them to help him dress, prepare his food, see to his horse, and keep his home comfortable. Sarah Blair had two personal maidservants, but she tried to be out as much as possible and tended to her horses herself. She normally took two manservants, Henry and George, on journeys of any distance and danger. Both were always armed and handled a pistol and musket comfortably.

The Blairs were living on a rented plantation. They decided that since they were to be in London for probably more than a year they would take all of their household help with them. Sarah planned to give up the lease to Philip Ludwell, her brother-in-law and landlord. She would rent the property again on their return.

In addition to the eight servants, Sarah also took Andrew Morgan and his close friend David Simmons. Both young men would sail and be paid as part of the crew, but Sarah promised Andrew's mother that she would keep a special eye on him once they arrived in London. She also told Andrew that he and David would be staying with the Blairs once in London and would be expected to provide security whenever they needed it.

The Blairs sailed on the *Good Fortune*, Sarah's own ship, fully equipped with twenty cannon. The ship was part of a flotilla of six ships that included a British warship, *The Endeavour*. The five merchant ships carried cured tobacco, and Virginia's planters, large and small, depended on their safe arrival with the factors in London.

Once on board, the Blairs kept a comfortable stateroom. James had the use of a writing desk and carried with him a petition to the Queen asking for the removal of Nicholson. Sarah carried some forty letters of introduction to Virginia friends and relatives. Several were for members of the Board of Trade.

Sarah had never traveled by ship, though she knew how the ships were built and had personally seen to their equipment and maintenance. She'd never experienced the swell and fall of the ocean waves or the terror of a thunderstorm at sea. At first she had no difficulty.

June 1703 was a sunny, calm month, and she ambled around the *Good Fortune* trying to get as much fresh air as possible. James stayed in his cabin preparing letters and remarks for when they arrived.

After a week at sea the weather changed somewhat, and Sarah could see white caps and the deeper swell of the waves. She began to feel some seasickness and cut back her eating. Soon she retired to her cabin. She lay in bed with a wet cloth over her head. James smiled amusedly at the sight of his powerful wife reduced to being queasy. He'd made the crossing in each direction three times before and was quite used to the rolling sea.

James tried to take her mind off her discomfort. "Can Anne bring you something? The servants will be happy to fuss a little over you."

"I know, but what can make the nausea go away? I'm not used to this."

"You should make sure you eat and drink nevertheless. It can't go away if you starve yourself."

"Maybe some clear soup? I'll try a little."

James called to Anne, Sarah's elderly maidservant who'd been with her since she was a child. Anne was black, of Jamaican descent, and married for many years to Henry, Sarah's manservant, who was also from the Caribbean. Both were now in their fifties but very fit.

Anne came into the stateroom and immediately took the

cloth from Sarah's head, moistened it again, and put it back on her head.

"She's willing to try some clear soup," James said. "What do you think?"

Anne shook her head. "Not a good idea if she feels like lying down. I'll get some prepared for later, but now she needs something cool and clear to drink. Could you swallow some apple cider, Miss Sarah?"

Sarah could only groan but shook her head yes. Anne went out and returned in five minutes with a cold tankard of apple cider, which she held to Sarah's mouth while Sarah tried to drink. The first few swallows were difficult, but soon she felt a bit better. "Now you should chew on some hard biscuits. There's a reason sailors always have them handy," Anne said.

Sarah smiled but remained quite pale. "How is everyone else doing? Am I the only invalid?"

Anne laughed. "Andrew's fine, but David is son of a tobacco farmer, and now he wishes he was back on the farm. Andrew is taking care of him. He's been feeding David apple cider and hard biscuits for at least two days."

"Oh dear, I hope we won't have six weeks of this."

"You mustn't think of that," James said. "Get into a routine and stick to it. Anne has brought some sewing and mending projects. The men are working on leather liveries for horses. You need to prepare for what we'll see when we get to London."

Sarah began to move a little and soon was out of bed. She took out her leather bag carrying the letters, but the moment she held one she began to feel sick again. She then took another hard biscuit and said, "I need some fresh air. I think I'll go out on deck and see how our crew is doing."

Anne held her arm as she made her way to the short stairway that went up to the deck and captain's station. Sarah managed up by herself and spotted Andrew standing near the main mast looking up. She asked him, "How are we doing? Where's David?"

Andrew pointed up to the top of the main sail, where his friend was hanging on for dear life. "David wasn't feeling well, so I thought it a good idea for him to see the ocean from on high. He's not feeling sick now, just a little frightened."

Sarah laughed. "Very clever. I'm not feeling well myself. How do you propose to frighten me?"

Andrew chuckled. "You won't be sick long, Mrs. Blair. The weather will soon calm down."

"I hope you're right. Are the cannon well prepared, and have you brought some pistols?"

"Oh yes, and I've worked on one that I think you should have for yourself." Andrew reached for a leather bag he'd tied to his side. Out of it he pulled a pistol. The gun was made of black gunmetal and had a simple, smooth-oak handle. He handed it to Sarah. "This one is light and shoots straight for more than a hundred yards."

She smiled gratefully. "Is there a place I can try it?"

Andrew chuckled. "Just don't kill the captain or the Royal Navy commander. That would make people angry."

Captain Edward Spenser listened to this conversation and finally interrupted, "Mrs. Blair, I'm pleased you're feeling a little better. If you want a little target practice, I'm sure you can find some birds to aim at once the sea calms down a little. But please, don't shoot an albatross. Seamen think that's bad luck. Give the birds a sporting chance." With that he laughed, took Sarah's arm, and led her to a place on the port side of the ship facing away from the other ships in the flotilla.

"You'll have plenty of room here, and it's out of the way."

"Thank you, Captain Spenser." With that she sat down on a small barrel and inhaled the sharp ocean air. She looked at the new pistol and felt its weight. Her strength began to come back. She raised the weapon and aimed it. "Have we some shot and powder? I'd like to try it."

Andrew was delighted and quickly provided powder and

shot. He demonstrated the loading and aiming of the weapon and stood quietly while Sarah took aim at a black spot in the sky some two hundred yards away.

"If that's an albatross and I got him, nobody will ever know."

For the next eight weeks, James Blair prepared his papers while Sarah Blair practiced her marksmanship. Both felt ready for London when they arrived in September.

CHAPTER 9

Good Fortune's eight week crossing had been largely uneventful. The crew had spotted a few other vessels but none were
threatening. Except for a few thunderstorms the passage had
been calm.

London was just a few days away and the weather was glorious with a slight breeze, deep-blue, purple skies, and a gentle
swell of the waves. Sarah and James came out each morning to
see if they could spot land. Sarah shot a few seagulls but finally
put the pistol away. She just didn't feel it was sporting to kill
birds in flight, especially since they were an omen of impending
land. Soon they entered the mouth of the Thames, and birds and
ships of every size began to appear.

As the ship proceeded, the sky seemed to take on a haze.
The weather warmed a bit, but the air turned from light brown
to almost black, not the usual humid, yellow haze that naturally
enveloped Virginia in the summer. Soon, the haze seemed to
engulf them entirely, and it carried a strong, unpleasant odor.

James said to Sarah, "That's London you smell. More people in one place than you can imagine."

"Is that the people I smell? It's worse than our pigs and goats."

"You haven't even gotten there yet. People of high station wear facemasks to protect themselves from inhaling the soot. The buildings are quite black. It comes from the burning of wood and coal for cooking and everything else." James shrugged when he said this, as if he remembered something unpleasant that he didn't want to think about.

"What do they use for clothing?" Sarah asked. "You would hardly wear your best to be covered in black soot whenever you go out."

"You'll find life different here. People will wear heavy cloaks to cover their clothing, but they don't attempt to stay outside very much. It's not Virginia, Mrs. Blair. Conversation and action take place indoors in drawing rooms, courtrooms, and any other kind of room. There are buildings and rooms for every occasion."

Sarah didn't react quickly to the idea of living entirely indoors. The idea was simply hard to imagine, but she was game now and looking forward. Though the air was getting grayer by the minute, she could make out docks and wharfs. She was ready, but she resolved to herself that she would get out and keep her pistol handy for protection against varmints, animal or human.

She saw large and small ships and barges and, as they proceeded, more and more of them. Several tried to signal the captain indicating that they would transport goods to shore for them. These cargo ships immediately backed off when they spotted the warship *Endeavour*. Smugglers apparently ran a good business helping foreign ships avoid customs officers. As the *Good Fortune* approached the docks between Windsor and Gravesend, the river teemed with boats, and the captain did a fine job avoiding being rammed. Two pilot boats captained by local fishermen came alongside and helped along the way.

Finally, after eight weeks at sea, the *Good Fortune* docked in London. The Blairs and their household disembarked first, followed by their personal and household baggage. The unloading of the tobacco was left to Captain Spenser and his crew. An agent from Cunningham, the factor, waved to them and would see to the warehousing of the cargo.

Sarah was delighted to walk down the gangplank to solid ground, but she was appalled at the filth of the place. Not only were the mixed odors of animal excrement and discarded offal from nearby slaughterhouses almost overpowering but the street itself was covered with at least four inches of oozing black slime. She could see rodents roaming all over the place, and if she weren't so concerned with the nuts and bolts of disembarkation, she'd have shot a few.

Tied up at the pier, waiting for them, was a great black coach drawn by six black horses. The coach was large enough for all of them, as Andrew and David chose to ride up front with the driver. Henry decided to ride on the back along with the footman. The driver bowed to James and introduced himself as George Pickering, engaged by Cunningham to take the Blair household to a town house near Whitehall where the Board of Trade held its meetings. Blair's brother William would meet them at the house when they arrived.

Cunningham's agent, David McAllen, stood next to Pickering and introduced himself. "Welcome to London, Reverend and Mrs. Blair. I trust you are well and I'm sure you want to get to your lodgings as soon as you can. You must be very tired."

"Yes, thank you for your services," James said. "I'm sure we'll want to talk with you about details of living here. Is our lodging fully furnished and serviced?"

"Yes, fully furnished, though of course you may add to what we have there. The house belongs to a lordship who is off at the war. You have a housekeeper and valet waiting for you, and you should have a prepared meal for tonight. I'll be over tomorrow to discuss details and provide you with payments on the cargo. Tobacco is getting a good price now, as we've had fewer shipments and demand is high."

Sarah thanked McAllen. Then she and James and the maidservants climbed up into the coach. There they found some beer and cold sliced roast beef. Sarah decided to sit near the half door, which had an open window above it. She munched on the beef and now looked forward to seeing the sights. The men loaded the luggage on the top and rear of the coach and soon they were off across London.

James was delighted with how smoothly everything was going. He said to Sarah, "We'll be comfortable. You'll be content. Our street is home to some high lordships and is quite clean and safe. London is more than the waterfront."

Sarah simply shook her head and looked out the half window as the coach lumbered through paved streets with buildings erected on both sides. She'd never seen a town before and London was more than just a town. Over half a million people lived there, ten times the number in all of Virginia.

The coach lumbered through small streets and wide thoroughfares. Some small squares housed mainly grocers, butchers, bakers, and taverns. There the aroma of baking bread and other foods were a wonderful respite from the generally offensive London air. They rode through areas that seemed to be engaged mainly in the dress trade, where both ladies' gowns and men's coats were on display on racks near the entrances of shops. People were everywhere, some very well dressed in elaborate cloaks and masks. Others looked decidedly downtrodden, dirty with soot and dressed in little more than rags.

They passed large bank buildings, jewelers and silversmiths, hat and peruke makers, and printers. London was full of posters stuck on the sides of buildings, announcing meetings and special sales of particular merchandise. They also passed theaters and parks. On some streets peddlers hawked various items they seemed to carry with them. These included light garments, kitchen implements, and toys. Many foods seemed to be sold that way, particularly puddings, pies, and fresh bread. Sarah enjoyed the sights and smells, until they came to a corner near a large, green grocer.

As the coach was making a turn, a small, thin man leaped up on the left side of the coach and grabbed the half door near Sarah's seat. He shouted something she didn't understand and reached in towards her with one arm while keeping his balance with the other.

She leaned backwards and glared at him. He was covered in soot and gray grime and his face carried a fierce expression. She said in her broad Virginia drawl, "I don't understand you, sir, and it's dangerous for you to hang on to a coach protected by so many powerful men."

The man waved his hand around and shouted something again. James was cowering in the corner, but Anne would have nothing of this person. She said to Sarah, "Mrs. Blair, push him off or ask Henry to do it. He's up to no good. He probably thought he could find a purse to snatch."

Sarah took out her pistol and with her left hand she grabbed the man's dark, greasy hair. He kept shouting and she firmly shoved the barrel of her gun into his mouth. She said, "Darlin', welcome to Virginia justice. If you keep still, I won't blow your head off."

James sat up and looked at his wife knowingly. "Please, we can leave him off at one of the prisons. Don't shoot him. It will make a terrible mess of the coach." With that he told the coachman to stop at Newgate prison. George Pickering looked at his new passenger with the pistol in his mouth and smiled. "Yes. That's the right place for thieves and pickpockets."

After lumbering through more cobblestone-paved streets for another half hour the coach arrived at the great prison, at the corner of Newgate Street and Old Bailey. The prison occupied an old fortress situated in an ancient city gate just outside the old city.

Pickering shouted to two guards, "Take our pickpocket please. Mrs. Blair is here from Virginia and would like her pistol back."

The two guards moved quickly and detached the dirty man from the coach and returned Sarah's gun to her. They laughed hilariously and shouted, "He's a poor example of London hospitality. We'll try him by next week, but he'll need some payment for us to keep him."

Sarah looked at James, not comprehending. "The poor fellow has no money, and to be fed in the prison he'll need something to pay the jailer," James said. "Look at him. He has nothing and now he'll have to contend with murderers and highwaymen, and the jailers aren't much better."

The dirty man was weeping, and James shouted, "Let us know when the trial will be. You can reach us through the factor, Cunningham!"

Sarah fished into her pocket and pulled out a few shilling coins. She shouted to the weeping man who still was being restrained by the two guards. "Please come here, my dirty sir!"

The guards brought the man closer to the coach, and the man was still weeping. Sarah said, "I suppose you wanted more than this from me, but I believe in helping those in need. Make these do until your trial."

With that she pressed two shilling coins into his hand, looking at James while she did it. James nodded that he thought that was enough.

The coach moved on as the dirty man was taken inside the

ancient prison. In another hour they came to Whitehall and stopped in front of an elegant, four-story brick house that was to be their home.

⟨ ⟩

The small street that held the Blairs' rented large brick house was home to eight other similar town houses. The houses stood back from the main cobbled street by about twenty feet, but all of the neighbors could see the great coach and the new arrivals. Maids in white aprons and liveried servants stared.

Andrew and David were first off the front with George Pickering. They helped the Blairs and the others out of the coach and then turned to unpacking the baggage. Sarah and James walked up to the front door knowing they were on display. Sarah smiled to herself, for she knew that the neighbors likely never saw such an assemblage before.

Andrew, now nineteen, was taller than most Englishmen at six foot three. His hair was light blond but his sunburned skin showed his regular outdoor living. He was tall and thin with very light-blue eyes. David, about twenty, was fully six foot eight. His father was a man of normal height, not even six feet tall, but his mother was a full-blooded Pamunkey and related to the chiefs of the Powhatans. David had light, chocolate-brown skin and straight, raven-colored hair down to his shoulders. Both boys spoke with a light Virginia drawl and laughed as they handled the heavy trunks as if they were children's toys.

Small children holding their nursemaids hands stared and laughed at the two boys. Some older children, aged eight to twelve, managed to come to the front of their houses and heard every word the boys said. Obviously many adults watched from some distance.

Once inside the house, the housekeeper, Mrs. Goodman, and the valet, John Pierce, greeted Sarah and James. Mrs.

Goodman, a small, plump woman of about forty, was dressed in the customary white apron and wore a small, white cap. John Pierce was about thirty, about the same height as Sarah, and stood very erect. He was dressed in a dark coat and white breeches.

The new arrivals were shown to their rooms, Sarah and James being on the second floor, the servants on the third and fourth. The second floor held some guest bedrooms. The lower level held an office with room for a library, a large dining room, a large parlor, and quarters for Mrs. Goodman. The kitchen facilities were in a separate building to the rear of the main house and could be reached by a covered red brick paved walkway. The rear of the house also held a stable, a well and laundry area, a few other small buildings for storage, and a small garden.

Mrs. Goodman helped to situate the servants upstairs, and Anne and Henry decided not to say anything until they could speak directly to Sarah. Anne knew Sarah from the day she was born and had led Sarah's household staff all Sarah's married life. There were few secrets between them.

Sarah and James went to their room, which held some massive wardrobe closets and a large four-poster bed. They changed out of their traveling cloaks and into more comfortable, lighter clothing. "Is this our house?" Sarah asked James.

"It's rented, but it's ours to do with as we see fit."

"Do the servants belong to the house?"

"We don't need to keep them, but we need some people who know the town and how houses run here."

"How do we know they won't be thieves?"

"Well, Cunningham has vouched for them. We know that much."

"Well, this is my household then, and Anne and Henry will supervise the staff and report to me. I trust them and will have no others."

James knew the determination of his wife and was tired.

"We don't have to decide that right now, do we? Let's wait a few hours. My brother William should be here soon. We'll introduce everyone and talk about details tomorrow with McAllen."

They both went downstairs to the front parlor where Mrs. Goodman met them. "Welcome to London. I hope you find the rooms comfortable?"

Sarah was curious and feeling the grime of the long voyage and the filthy tour of London. "Where does one wash or take a bath?"

Mrs. Goodman smiled. "His lordship had no use for baths but one can be purchased and put upstairs in your suite. There's ample room near the bed. We'd have to carry water up for it of course. The servants can get fresh water from the well out back and wash there as they see fit."

"Is there a place with clean water for swimming?"

"I'm not sure what you mean," Mrs. Goodman said. "There are several relatively clean ponds not far from here but people don't swim in them."

"Our David swims every day. His people are very strict on personal cleanliness. How far to the river and how dirty is it near here?"

Mrs. Goodman was about to reply, but they all heard a sharp rap at the door. John, the valet, opened the door and received the visitors, Mr. McAllen of Cunningham and William Blair, James's older brother. At the sight of James and Sarah, William broke into a broad smile and rushed over to embrace them.

"Oh, my dears, how wonderful to really see you! God has been good to us this day." William couldn't believe his eyes in seeing James for the first time in eight years and Sarah, his sister-in-law, for the very first time. He pulled her to him and kissed her four times, twice on each cheek.

William, like James, stood about five feet six inches. Sarah was taller than both of them. William spoke with a Scottish brogue, but a very deep, sonorous voice. Like James he was an

Anglican minister, and he spoke in soft, mellow tones and obviously could give a proper sermon.

"I'm sure you're weary and have many questions, but it's time to give thanks that you are here safely. We have a fine church around the corner and I know the minister well. I've asked him to lead his congregation in thanksgiving. Bring everyone, please. It's not far. We can walk, and I'm sure many of your neighbors will attend. You can meet them after the service."

James was delighted that his brother had organized this first day. "We have quite a crowd," he said and motioned to the servants to come down. When all of them assembled Andrew and David joined them, and William looked at them in astonishment.

"Well, this will be quite an occasion. I think the press will report on the new arrivals." He couldn't believe the height of Andrew and David and, for that matter, of Sarah. He immediately acknowledged Anne and Henry. "I hope you are comfortable and will come."

Used to speaking her mind, Anne said, "I've already said my prayers. It takes more than one person to prepare meals. Henry and I will stay and help Mrs. Goodman prepare the food for our evening meal." She looked at Mrs. Goodman as she spoke.

Sarah looked at Anne and responded, "The meal can wait. I'm sure Mrs. Goodman is well prepared. You and Henry will come with us. You're part of our household and I want the neighbors to know that." She and Anne looked at each other, and Anne knew when Sarah was determined to have her way. The full group went down to the church together.

CHAPTER 10

W ell, how do you like the neighbors?" asked James as he and Sarah walked back to their new home. She was tired but had enjoyed the exchange of greetings at the church. The reverend was a plump, jolly man who refused to leave Sarah's side while she greeted his parishioners. She was used to large family gatherings, but she never had to learn the names of over a hundred people at one time.

Several of the neighbor ladies had already invited her to tea, and James received a generally warm welcome from many of the men. He wasn't certain if all the kind wishes were from neighbors, but he'd been invited to hunt, to play cards, and to visit the theater. He realized that he and Sarah would need a stationer to print proper calling cards so they could invite and reciprocate to invitations. He just hoped that Sarah would seem more positive about the house so he could go ahead with the printing.

"Let's see where we are tomorrow," Sarah said. "I'd like a

short ride around the neighborhood, and I want to know how we'll be getting provisions. We can't just go out and shoot a turkey as we do at home."

They returned to the house, and Mrs. Goodman had a warm roast beef dinner prepared. She'd set the table in the downstairs dining room for the Blairs, William Blair, McAllen, Andrew, and David. The other servants were served in a small building located next to the kitchen in the back garden. The main house served wine and the back garden served beer.

After they'd eaten, the Blairs and their guests went into the parlor to rest. McAllen had a small drink and noticed the Blairs' weariness. "You've had quite a day. I returned here today because there was a message at my office from Newgate prison. Is there something I should know about this?"

James explained the events of the coach ride and the man dropped off at the prison. "My goodness, on our first day here! Mrs. Blair wished nobody any harm, but the man attacked her. We let the prison guards know they could contact us through you as there'll likely be a trial and we'd be witnesses."

"If his people would like to talk to you, shall I tell them where they can find you?"

"You really don't know what the man wanted, do you?" William Blair interrupted. "Do you think he was a thief?"

Sarah laughed. "If he was, he's not good at it. I'm not sure I know what he said. I couldn't understand him, but he looked desperate. I think you can let them know where we are. What are the prospects for someone like him?"

McAllen became very serious. "Once he's been accused of a crime, he'll likely be sentenced. Very few get off free. If he's in debt, they'll keep him until he pays the debts off, and if he's as poor as you say he looks, he's likely to die in prison. Only the rich and adventurous survive our prisons, though some of them live very well there. Why don't you wait and see if anyone turns up for him?"

William Blair said, "Yes, London is harsh with its poor. Many have little to eat without some thievery and the churches hardly can help that much. Maybe you should consider a little kindness if that's possible?"

McAllen added, "If they don't look dangerous, I'll send anyone who asks to see you here. They'll have to be quick if they want to avoid the trial. You can withdraw the charge if you so decide and I can let Newgate know of your decision."

"So much for one day," James said. "Let's leave more for tomorrow. Will we see you, Mr. McAllen?"

"Why don't you take a few days? See if the house and street suit you. If you ride around a bit, you may find neighborhoods more to your liking. There's no reason to stay if you don't like it. You're paying a goodly rent on the place." With that he stood up. John brought him his outer cloak and he said goodbye. William Blair expected to stay several days, and John showed him to a room on the second floor. James and Sarah went up to bed while Anne and Henry helped Mrs. Goodman clear away the dinner dishes.

⁍

The next morning, David asked Sarah where he could wash. She could think of nothing better than a barrel of water next to the well. He looked glum, and she knew she'd have to find a better alternative. "We'll go out later and see how far we are from provisions and the ponds and the river. We have a lot to learn about this place. We need to get everyone some proper clothes also, especially you David. I don't think there are many breeches and coats in London that will fit you."

David was amenable to a short wash but looked unhappy. Andrew slapped him on the back and shouted, "Race you to the barrel!" The two of them tore through the downstairs and found the outside well. The servants were busy doing the laundry left from the eight-week voyage when the boys arrived. Andrew found a hogshead-size barrel and began splashing water from the well buckets. David and Andrew laughed, and their laughter could be heard across the street.

Sarah and Anne took the time to look over the kitchen and asked Mrs. Goodman how she bought the food for the house and how she paid for it. They worked out a list for the next few days and prepared to visit the food shops. James began to unpack his books and papers, while John helped to sort out his clothes. Sarah left her clothes for her maid Martha to organize.

By the middle of the day both Blairs were ready to go out. They decided that they'd take some refreshment in the town and were ready to leave when there was a loud rap at the door. John opened the door to look down on a very dirty young girl carrying a baby.

"How may I help you?" he said.

The girl looked frightened and very quietly said, "Mr. McAllen of Cunningham sent me to talk to Reverend and Mrs. Blair. May I speak to them?"

Anne saw the young girl who seemed to be covered in soot and grime. The baby's wrappings weren't much better. Anne said, "The Blairs will talk to you, but only if you clean yourself a little. You can't enter the house like that. Who knows what you'll bring in with you?"

The young girl, flustered and frightened, looked at Anne and began to weep. "What can I do? I have no place to wash or clean clothes to wear."

Anne took the baby from the girl and ordered John to show the girl to the back garden and the well, still being used by the boys. "Tell those boys they're finished for today. They can show her how to get a decent wash. I'll tell Mrs. Blair we have a visitor." Looking at the baby she said, "This little fellow could use some clean wrapping as well."

Anne was a mother of four boys who were all married with families of their own. The Harrisons had found places for the boys with various Virginia families, and Anne already was a grandmother of eight. She knew all about babies, and she'd never seen one in such shabby wrappings. She took the child up to her own room and pulled out some pieces of muslin she'd brought with her. Placing the baby on the bed she undid the rags and saw she was a girl. Anne wiped her bottom and rewrapped her in the clean muslin. Anne hummed and sang through the whole process, and the baby relaxed and smiled. She was only four or five months old.

When Anne finished, she went down to Martha's room and told her about the visiting girl in the back garden. Martha looked through her own things and pulled out a lightweight, floral dress and some stockings. She took some towels and the clothes downstairs.

Anne then went in to see Sarah. "We have some visitors."

"Who's this?" Sarah said laughing. She immediately took the child and played with her fingers a bit.

"There's a young girl here sent by Cunningham. I sent her out back for a wash, and Martha is giving her something to wear. She looks very poorly. I didn't want to let her in the house with all the vermin."

"Maybe she'll need something to eat. Is she nursing the baby?"

"Probably, but she's scared to death. I don't know what the sight of David will do to her."

"Are the boys giving her a bath?"

Anne laughed. "John was supposed to order them out, and Martha's down there now." Martha was Sarah's personal maid. She was about thirty and had been with Sarah a long time. Sarah knew that Martha could handle the boys.

"Well, we've already done some good," Sarah said. "Let's hear the story of the dirty man. I'll get James."

With that, Sarah went down to the office where James was still unpacking and organizing his papers. "We have a visitor sent over by McAllen. I'd like to bring her in here for our interview. She's already had quite a fright, and this room is less intimidating than the other rooms on this floor."

"Well, let's bring in some chairs and I'll move some of the papers to one pile in the corner. Will Anne and Henry be here for this?"

"Yes, I'll get John to call them both when she's ready."

James didn't understand why his visitor wasn't ready, but he never questioned his wife when she was being decisive.

After a half hour, James heard a light tapping at his office door. He rose and opened it and saw a very young girl holding a small baby. "Please come in and sit," he said and she entered the room followed by Anne, Henry, and Sarah. They took seats around a fireplace facing each other in a small semicircle.

"First, would you like some refreshment?"

"Thank you, sir, but I've already had a piece of bread and some cheese."

"Tell us your name. How old are you?"

"I'm Mrs. Percy Clarke. My first name is Susanna. It was Percy you dropped off at Newgate yesterday."

Anne took the baby. "Is she yours?"

"Yes, mine and Percy's. We call her Amy, for Amelia. Percy and I've been married a year. I'm nearly fifteen. Percy's seventeen."

Susanna began to relax and tell her story. "Percy's no thief or bandit, but he can't speak clearly. Also, he has trouble expressing himself. We've been in terrible poverty since our lordship ordered us from his house. We both worked for him very diligent-like, but when he found out his lady trusted us he wouldn't have us in the house."

Sarah couldn't understand what Susanna was saying. "Who's the lordship?"

"He's the Marquis of Northampton."

"I don't understand why you were ordered from his house."

"Well, the marquis and his lady don't get along. She's much younger than he is, and he develops terrible tempers, jealous like. He gave her a good black eye more than once. Well, he's jealous, but he also has his other lady friends. He doesn't give his lady much to spend, though she brought him a fine dowry. He treats her as his property and everything she once owned belongs to him. Now, she brought Percy and me from her home in Essex and she's always trusted us. His lordship hates to see her comfortable in any way, so he threw us out. We didn't know London, and I have the baby and can't work. Also, Percy was a house servant and had trouble finding another place. His lordship gave us no time to look for places, and my ladyship wasn't able to ask on our behalf."

"What do you suppose Percy was saying when he jumped up on the coach?"

"He likely was asking if you had some work. He's no thief, milady, and I'm sure wished you no harm. He'll die in that awful prison unless you can help him."

"James, doesn't their lordships have to know about this? Aren't they responsible?"

"This is England, Sarah. A marquis is a high peer, just below a duke. What Susanna says is true. He owns all and can do what he likes with it."

"That includes people? What does the church say to that?"

"The church can't order a marquis about. He is a very high peer and probably welcome at the Queen's court."

Sarah couldn't swallow the whole situation. "I'd want to send a message to them before we do anything permanent. Send a few pounds to Newgate so Percy can be put in more comfortable surroundings and let him know that we won't press charges. Then

I'll send the bill for Percy to the marquis."

James was beside himself. "You can't do that—tell a marquis what his responsibilities are and how much it will cost him! That isn't done in England."

"That's nonsense. Servants are part of a family. Without them a family couldn't live. A man should have no right to dismiss his lady's servants and not give her resource to hire others. What sort of marriage vows do people take here?"

"Calm down," James said. "I'll send a message to Cunningham to pay for Percy for two more days at Newgate in their best accommodation. I'll also say that we won't press charges and that Susanna will stay with us until they find suitable work and a decent place to live. Is that sufficient?"

Anne and Henry nodded in agreement, and Susanna smiled happily and said, "Oh, wonderful." The baby was beginning to fuss and needed to be fed. Anne took Susanna's hand and led her out of the room. Henry then followed.

"I'll write my message to Cunningham now."

"Write another one to the marquis. Andrew and David will deliver it and let her ladyship know what's happened to her servants. If I were her, I'd want to know."

"Sarah, these are people unlike any you've ever met. I don't know what a message would accomplish in that domestic situation."

"I don't care. Write it out. It's not the few pounds, it's their lack of concern and responsibility that bothers me."

"Just remember, this is England. We have a queen and dukes and marquises and earls and barons, all in a row. Everyone knows his place here."

"Places should be earned, and people who hurt their own can't really be tolerated anywhere."

The next morning Sarah called for Andrew and David and told them to deliver a handwritten letter to the Marquis of Northampton. "Where can we find him?" asked Andrew who was looking forward to a long ride around the town. Susanna stood behind Sarah, holding the baby, but didn't leap to give directions.

"We know how to ask, all we need is a general direction or a name of the house." David looked at Susanna when he said this, but she looked down at her feet.

Susanna said, "Mrs. Blair, I fear for these boys. They've never seen the likes of his lordship, and they can't know the proper ways of talking to people like that."

Sarah wouldn't listen to this kind of talk. "Andrew and David have killed more than their share of varmints. I'm sure they can see to their own safety. I want this letter delivered today, as Percy will likely be here by late tomorrow. Now tell them how to find his lordship's house."

Susanna spoke quietly. "Be very vigilant if you see him. He'll think of you as servants or less, and he always carries some kind of whip. His house is served by over a hundred, and you'll have to go through a long line of people before you see him. If her ladyship is nearby, she'll be kind to you if you tell her it's about me and Percy."

David couldn't stand this. "But how do we find him? Where's his house?"

"The house is called Ravensport. It's very large, past the large park, and overlooks the river. It's situated quite high and has very clean air. It once belonged to a royal mistress, I think his lordship's mother. Just go right along the main thoroughfares and head towards the river. You'll be there in less than an hour."

Sarah looked at the two boys. "Now remember, you're not there for yourselves but for the Reverend Blair and myself. The letter is by Reverend Blair's own hand. You may stay for a reply,

if his lordship receives you himself. Be polite, but this is business. Make sure he understands why you're there—to deliver
this message from us."

"Yes, ma'am," said David. "Do you mind if we take our time
a bit to explore?"

"Just be back before dark. We're receiving visitors today and
won't need to go out. You can use both horses or take the cart.
The cart should be more comfortable for exploring, but be kind
to the horses. I don't know how well they'll do with you two at
the reins. Would Henry also like to go with you? If he does I'll
give you a few shillings. You may want to eat or buy something."

"I'll ask him before we leave," said Andrew, and he and David ran to the back stable to get the cart and horses ready. Henry
decided not to go with them, but Sarah gave them a few shillings
anyway.

The boys decided to deliver the letter and then see about
some fun later. They followed the main road nearest the river
and asked several people who were walking along the road if
they were on the right path to Ravensport. Every time they asked
passersby they got a look that said, "You shouldn't be going to
that place." One man driving a small cart full of farm produce
pulled up his shoulder and said, "His lordship is in a poor mood
today! Be careful around him."

In less than an hour they found Ravensport, fronted by a
massive, black wrought iron gate that protected a long road up
to the most massive building they'd yet seen, except for Newgate
prison. The dark, brick house seemed to spread wings and was
five stories in some places. Some corners had parapets.

An elderly man, slightly stooped, stood guard at the gate.
"What do you gentlemen want?"

David stood, alighted from the small cart, and bowed deeply
to the guard who was barely five feet tall. "Sir, we're here to deliver a letter to his lordship from the Reverend James Blair and
Mrs. Blair who have just arrived from Virginia."

The guard opened the gate. "Well spoken, young man. Go straight up and give a firm rap at the door."

The cart rattled, but the two horses seemed very game and were enjoying the day out. The boys tied the cart to a short post near the front entrance of the house and climbed a few steps to a rather large front porch. They then rapped on a tall door that David could step through without bending. They could hear muffled shouting inside. After a few minutes the door opened slightly and a nursemaid holding a very young baby admitted them.

David bowed to her. "We're here to deliver a letter to his lordship from the reverend and Mrs. Blair." He took the letter from inside his coat, but the young woman said, "Oh wait, sir, his lordship is in a snit upstairs. Perhaps her ladyship can take it?"

Andrew answered, "Of course. I think the letter is probably to her ladyship as well."

As he finished speaking a very pretty, young woman of about seventeen came toward them. She was dressed in a gown of light-blue silk that showed off her light-blond hair. She wore gold and diamond jewelry that sparkled in the sunlight of the fresh autumn day. "How can I help you? I'm the Marchioness of Northampton. His lordship is having words just now with his butler and valet and some other people but will be down shortly."

She stared up unbelievingly at David, and he handed her the letter, which she opened and read immediately. "Oh dear, Percy's in Newgate? How awful. It's my fault—I should have given them some money to tide them over. Is baby Amy well?"

"She's fine, ma'am, and has about six women to fuss over her just now," Andrew said. "The reverend will allow them to stay with us until they find a proper place."

Andrew looked at the marchioness who was young and pretty, but her cosmetics and jewelry couldn't completely hide two black eyes. Suddenly, all of them heard some shouting, a few shrill shrieks, and something crashing. A door slammed and soon his lordship, stepping heavily, came down the broad spiral stairway.

They all stood in the front hallway. A large metal chandelier and great high windows lighted the room. The ceiling, more than two stories high, was painted with frescoes. Portraits of great people they didn't recognize and some armor and weapons decorated the walls. The ceiling was so high that David felt comfortable, and he smiled at the marchioness.

The Marquis of Northampton, red faced and smelling of drink and lack of bathing, looked at the two young men. "Who are you, and who let you in here?"

The marquis was plump, about five foot six, and about thirty years of age. His wig was askew, and he seemed to bark rather than talk. He wore riding boots and carried a riding crop in one hand. He looked at his young wife holding a letter. "Give me that. I'm sure it's for me."

The marchioness handed him the letter. "It's from the Reverend Blair, and it's about Percy and Susanna. Read it. Your cruelty is known all over the city, now stretching all the way to Virginia."

"Don't be so insolent! What are you doing here anyway? Go to your room and take the baby with you. I'll deal with these people." He then looked at the two boys. "Well, I have the letter. What do you want now?"

"We await a reply," Andrew said. "If you want to send a written one, we'll wait for you. The reverend and Mrs. Blair want to know that you accept responsibility for your servants."

"Who are they to tell me my responsibilities? This is nonsense."

The marchioness was beside herself. "You needn't be so cruel and unfeeling. You threw them out with a small baby and gave them no money and no place to go. It's a wonder they've survived these three weeks."

"What do I care about it? I have a hundred other servants

and now they know what can happen to them, and you, madam, are still here. I ordered you to leave." He then raised his riding crop and moved toward his wife.

David, revolted by the smell of his lordship, stepped in between the two. He was more than a foot taller than the marquis and much more agile. "Your lord and ladyship, we did not wish to cause a family argument. We only wish a reply to the letter."

The marquis looked at David and screamed. "You unwashed heathen! Who let you in here?" With that he raised the riding crop and would have brought it down on his wife, except David stopped the whip with one hand and lifted his lordship up off the floor with his other arm.

"Sir, I wash every day, which is something that might improve the aroma of you. I'm not a heathen but a Christian as are my parents, and I've delivered a message to you from an officer of the church. You should show some respect or you might land on your head."

The marquis began to scream expletives with both arms flailing as David held him high up over his head. Andrew asked the marchioness, "Would you like to come with us, ma'am? It doesn't seem safe for you here, and you can give the Blairs your response in person. We have a small cart but we can seat four. We have two horses."

The marchioness was shivering and weeping. "I'll need to get some things, and I want the nurse and baby to come also." With that she ran up the main stairway and disappeared into a room upstairs.

The marquis was still flailing. "I think I'm going to be sick. Put me down at once."

David waited a minute and calmly said, "We'll wait for the lady. When she's out the door, I'll see to your safety."

Soon she was down and Andrew took from her a small sack of things that she'd just thrown together on one of her bed sheets. Andrew gave her his arm and moved toward the door, which caused the marquis to shriek. David finally lowered the marquis but still restrained the arm that held the riding crop.

The marquis looked straight at Andrew. "What is your name, and who are you to give my wife your arm?"

"My name is Andrew Morgan, and I'm staying with Reverend Blair. This lady will be safe with us, I assure you." He motioned to the nurse holding the baby to come with him and she followed them through the front door and down the stairs.

David let the marquis down. "I can't say I've been pleased to meet you, sir. My name is David Simmons, if you want to know."

The marquis was infuriated. "You'll all be hearing from me, make no mistake!" With that he grabbed his own stomach and threw up all over himself. David hurried out the door and to the cart where everyone waited for him. They quickly drove off, back to the house in Whitehall.

⁕

David took the reins and drove the horses back to Whitehall. In the front sat the nurse who held the baby. In the back seat sat Andrew and the marchioness, who shivered and wept all the way, mumbling, "He wants to kill me. He wants to kill me." Andrew put his arm around her, but she couldn't be comforted.

When they arrived they noticed a variety of carts and coaches in the front of the house and could hear the loud shouts of children from the back garden. They halted behind a large coach and disembarked slowly and carefully. David lifted the nurse holding the baby out of the front seat; Andrew did the same for the marchioness. David went up the doorsteps, but before he could rap on the door John, the valet, opened it to admit them. David led the marchioness and Andrew, followed by everyone else, inside. Lady Northampton was still weeping.

"My goodness, my lady, have these boys been terrible to you?" John asked. "What brings you here?"

Anne was close by and placed a shawl over the marchioness' shoulders. She gave the group a curious look but then said to the marchioness, "Come into the back room and stand by the fire a bit. Would you like some refreshment? Something to drink?" The marchioness shook her head, but it was unclear if she meant yes or no.

As Anne spoke, she wiped the marchioness' face with a soft piece of muslin. Anne motioned to Henry who took the young woman's hand and led her to the back room where various foods and refreshments were on tables ready to be served. Mrs. Goodman was busy decorating trays to be served, and two maids were already carrying some out the door.

Mrs. Goodman gasped when she saw the young woman. She saw Henry holding her hand and spoke quietly. "Your ladyship! We're honored to have you. Please rest here a bit." Mrs. Goodman drew a chair near the fire and Henry eased the marchioness into it.

In the meantime, the Blairs and assembled guests sat in the parlor waiting for refreshments. These included several neighbors and Baron Cooper, the Earl of Exeter, and his wife, Marjorie. Marjorie was the cousin mentioned by Jane Parke to Sarah before she left Virginia. Two of the neighbor wives were well acquainted with Marjorie, and the group had divided in two—men smoking by the fireplace, women conversing in a circle of chairs.

Anne entered the parlor and whispered to Sarah, who immediately stood and made excuses. She followed Anne to the hallway and saw Andrew, David, and the baby marquis' nurse. Martha and Susanna had also appeared. Martha was holding baby Amy and Susanna was carrying the baby marquis. "John, bring more chairs into the drawing room," Sarah said. "Andrew and David, what's happened?"

Both began to speak at once, but when Sarah heard that the marchioness was in the rear with the food she immediately went into the back room. Lady Northampton had stopped crying but still had trouble speaking. Both Anne and Henry stood behind her and Henry was trying to hold a mug of beer to the marchioness' lips.

Sarah pulled another chair next to the lady, still dressed in fine, blue satin and wearing diamond jewelry. She said to her quietly, "Welcome to our home, my lady. I'm Mrs. Blair. I hope Andrew and David didn't upset you too much and that they behaved properly?"

"Oh, Mrs. Blair, they've saved my life and behaved wonderfully. Don't be displeased with them. I hope I'm not imposing too much on you. I understand that you're new to London."

"This is our second day. I'm afraid that fortune has brought us together in unexpected ways. Let me take you upstairs. You may want to wash your face and refresh yourself. Perhaps you wish to stay with us for a time? We hope to get Percy out of Newgate by tomorrow."

"Yes. I'd like that. I must think about what to do next, and I value your advice."

With that, Sarah, the marchioness, and Anne went upstairs. Anne brought up the knotted bed sheet containing Lady Northampton's belongings, which Andrew had left by the front door. The nurse, Susanna, and the two babies went outside to a small cottage that contained Susanna's guest quarters, while David and Andrew went out to the garden where about eight children of various ages were playing. They immediately joined in the games and began by tossing a few small boys up in the air and catching them.

⌐⚜⌐

Upstairs the marchioness, visibly shaken after a terrible morning, gathered her strength and looked carefully at Sarah. Sarah, while no beauty by English standards, stood straight and tall; she was obviously physically strong and intelligent, features very unusual for English ladies. She emanated a decisive presence, and the marchioness was impressed with the evident happiness and normality of the Blair household.

"I'll be putting your household to a lot of trouble if I stay, will I not?"

"Absolutely not! We'll find room for you and your nurse and baby. You'll have a bed of your own and all our hospitality. Think of this place as yours, for as long as you need it. We'd be no different in Virginia."

"But I must pay you. These boys risked a lot, and I'm sure they saved my life today. I and the baby would be dead now, if it weren't for them!"

"There'll be no talk of payments. We owe each other respect and comfort in time of need. The reverend wouldn't have it any other way."

"You're very kind, but if I stay here, this matter won't be over. The marquis will surely want some revenge. Oh, I fear for your two beautiful boys!"

"Don't worry yourself about it. Would you like to come down to the parlor and meet my guests? I'm sure they'd be delighted to meet you. If you're not feeling well, you can stay here a while. Anne will stay with you, if you like."

"Oh, of course, I'm interfering with your plans for today. If you like, I'll come, or I could spend some time with Susanna."

"Oh, please come. I'm sure our guests will want to meet you and they'll make you comfortable. They're only neighbors, family, and friends of friends. While you're here, you're family also."

The women went down to the parlor, where a room full of people awaited. When the marchioness entered the room, the men bowed and the ladies curtsied. Mrs. Goodman had told them who she was, and she far outranked them all. James went to her, introduced himself, and led her to a chair nearest the fireplace. The guests behaved with great formality until Marjorie, who couldn't contain herself, blurted, "Florence, what's happened? Is the baby well?"

Lady Northampton, otherwise known as Florence Roberts, was delighted to see Marjorie and stood to embrace her. "Oh dear, I'm afraid I'll be the talk of the city again. But I'm rescued by Andrew and David and the little cart and horses."

She then made a brief curtsy to all assembled guests. "Please sit. I hope we needn't be too formal here. I'd like it if you'd all address me as Florence. Have the boys told you about this morning's events?"

James brought her back to the chair where she was sitting, and two maids brought in trays with cakes and tea and left them on the table. James said, "No, I'm afraid they're outside making sport with the other children and didn't bother to tell us anything."

"Well, I suppose you're all dying to hear this." Florence then related the events of the whole morning, how the marquis was drunk very early and had arguments with two of his mistresses, while the third barricaded herself in her room. All three mistresses were residents at Ravensport, a great house that had four courtyards. She related how she'd decided to vacate her room before the marquis could see her and that she took the baby downstairs with her, just as Andrew and David arrived with the letter. She then described the altercation and ended with the remark, "He'll want some revenge. He might even challenge them to a duel, even if they have no rank. He loves to murder, and I'm sure I wouldn't have survived today if it weren't for the boys."

Marjorie was first to speak. "The boys have no business in a duel—they know nothing of sword play in a dueling arrangement. They can just refuse."

Florence had heard this before. "He'll demand my return with apologies and some kind of compensation from them. He can make it quite legal as he knows many judges."

Tom Adams, who lived directly across the street, cleared his throat. "Forgive me, my lady, but there are many lawyers and judges in London. The Reverend Blair and I know many of them, and duels technically are no longer allowed under the law, no matter who the judges are. I can assure you that I'm an experienced attorney, and I'll take a personal interest in this."

Adams's wife, Emily, spoke next. "Yes, we're all aware of the marquis' reputation. He took to mistress a lady just two streets from here. That was a year ago. Her husband was a military man and he challenged him, and now she's a widow. I don't know the details, but evidently there was some injustice on the dueling field."

The men mumbled among themselves, and then Jack Elliott, who lived three houses away, said, "Not to worry. The boys may refuse or accept and choose the weapons. Being from Virginia, they probably can handle pistols well?" Jack was a captain in the horse guards who served the Queen. His wife, Betsy, was a close friend of Marjorie.

"Perhaps we should call them," Sarah said. "I know Andrew is very practiced with a rifled musket of his own making. He's used pistols, mainly for shooting varmints around the garden. Both are good huntsmen. David is magnificent with bow and arrow."

Jack smiled. "Well now, we haven't anything to worry about. The marquis will be a fool to challenge either one."

The whole party laughed at that, and Florence said, "Would anyone mind if I went outside a bit. I'd like to see the baby. He's named Charles, and I call him Charley, and this is the first day he's out of his room, not that he's noticed. He loved the cart ride."

All of the women stood and in a group followed.

⟨·⟩

Jack Elliott knew the Marquis of Northampton. He'd been witness or assisted as a second on four duels, all won by the marquis over the last two years. Though he encouraged the Blairs not to worry for Andrew and David, he knew the marquis to be devious and blood thirsty.

The marquis presented a difficult problem for militia and courts. A marquis held too high a rank to be dragged before an ordinary court, and only the monarch could order his arrest. The marquis had killed nearly a dozen men over the last several years. The horse guardsmen, who were the Queen's own cavalry, couldn't do anything to stop him. Known over London as the "Blues," Jack Elliott's regiment was fed up with the marquis.

Jack put on his blue horse guards uniform and mounted his great white horse early the next day and ambled over to the Blairs. He rapped at the door and John eventually answered; everyone in the house was still asleep.

"What can I do for you, Colonel Elliott?"

"Can you wake Andrew and David and bring them out here?"

"Of course. It may take a few minutes. They're of the age of very sound sleep. Will they need horses to come with you?"

Jack smiled. "Yes. Have two horses saddled and tell them not to be anxious but to bring whatever pistol or weapon with which they feel comfortable."

Henry came out to the front door. "What shall we tell the Blairs?"

"Tell them not to worry but that I've taken the boys down to the horse guards' barracks. There I'll instruct them as to what may happen if they accept a challenge. They can practice shooting down there, and they'll learn something of the etiquette. Tell Reverend Blair if a challenge should be delivered he is only to accept conditionally. He should tell the messenger that Andrew and David will consider a response, but none will be made today. There's no hurry in this matter. Tomorrow is Sunday, a day for prayers and not for killing."

"Will you bring them back today?"

"They're safer with me, as a challenge needs to be in person. This way they can't be challenged by surprise. Also, I'll send

some guards out here this morning to protect the house and her
ladyship. You never know what the marquis will try to do. He
has some thirty armed guards working for him, but he won't
challenge Her Majesty's horse guards. You're best to stay at
home today. My wife will be over in a few hours, and the neighbors can help out. Whatever you do, don't show or use weapons
should the marquis' guards come to call. That could complicate
matters."

After about twenty minutes Andrew and David emerged, still
sleepy, but armed with pistols, muskets, and a bow and quiver of
arrows. The colonel smiled to himself at the sight of them, and
knew the boys hardly needed practice in the use of this equipment. They rode off, leaving the rest of the house in peace on a
warm sunny Saturday.

Babies started crying, and the Blair house soon began to
stir. Mrs. Goodman and Anne prepared a large breakfast for
twelve people, including the baron and Marjorie and their three
young sons, who were staying for a few days. Also included were
Lady Northampton and William Blair. Without Andrew and
David there was a great deal of breakfast, and Anne saw to it
that Susanna and the nurse and the rest of the servants ate well
that morning.

After breakfast, Susanna said to Henry and Martha, "If we're
all to stay at home, how are we to fetch Percy from Newgate?"
She couldn't conceal her concern for Percy and soon began to
weep. Martha tried to comfort her, but they all felt as if they
were under siege. The Virginians couldn't accept the idea, and
Henry went to talk to the Blairs.

Henry found James in his study. "Perhaps I'll go to Newgate
for Mr. Percy?" asked Henry.

"Let's wait a bit," James said. "Perhaps the horse guardsmen will let someone out for that or send one of their own. It's a wonderful day, Henry. Try to enjoy it."

Sarah couldn't abide the idea that killers were planning to come to her house. She said nothing to anyone, but she loaded her pistol and tucked it away in a deep pocket. If someone threatened her or one of her own, she'd get a shot off before anyone knew it. She didn't care about the advice Jack Elliott had left; if she was threatened, she'd defend herself.

After breakfast, Sarah and Marjorie relaxed and soon Florence joined them in the garden. James decided to work on a sermon, as he'd been invited to speak at the local church the following day. The women sat watching the nurse, Susanna, and the two babies.

"Why did you come?" Florence asked Sarah. "What do you expect to do here?"

"Why, James needs to advise the Board of Trade as to the deficiencies of our Governor Nicholson. Nicholson's quite arrogant and has lost the support of most of his council. I'm here to help James, as he's not as familiar with our business as I am."

Florence was surprised. "You handle the business? How unusual. Women here lose everything when they marry and are little better than property after that. If I need anything I must beg the marquis for it."

"Yes, that's the law. But many women try to handle their own property by pawning jewelry and silver plate with the goldsmiths and silversmiths," Marjorie said. "I know quite a few women who buy their clothes for what they get for their jewels. Sarah doesn't need to worry about that."

"Yes, I handle our accounts and will be dealing with the major purchases. I've been advised to get a banker, and I have a few recommendations as to who to contact. Of course Cunningham, our factor, has been helpful."

"You'll need some clothes for formal evenings, if you're to meet and talk to members of the Board of Trade," Florence said.

"They're all lordships and most have investments in the colonies. You should try to meet them in as cordial a setting as possible, if the reverend has to make a presentation to them later. I can help you. I know the dressmakers and the hairdressers. You'll really enjoy meeting them."

Marjorie smiled at Sarah. "Now you'll really get to know London, especially with Florence to help!"

"Yes, I suppose so. What do you think I should do first? Buy the clothes, or engage a banker?"

Both Florence and Marjorie laughed. "Nobody I know engages a banker before buying what's needed," Florence said. "Mrs. Blair, I'm sure you have excellent credit. As soon as we can get out, I'll take you to the town. You'll love it!"

A rap at the door announced the arrival of two horse guardsmen sent by Colonel Elliott. They informed John that they were to do sentry duty and that nobody could enter or leave the home without announcing themselves to the guards first. If the marquis sent a challenge, it would be left with them and the guards would relay it to the Blairs.

For the next two hours the two guardsmen moved their horses slowly up and down the street. After midday a coach carrying four armed men dressed in elaborate green and gold livery approached the Blair house and stopped at the front entrance. The two horse guardsmen signaled the passengers to stay in the coach, and through the window the senior guard received a letter and a glove on a silver tray. He exchanged a few words with the driver and ordered the coach to leave.

The guardsman immediately brought the tray containing the note and glove to the front door where John took it inside to Reverend Blair. James looked at John. "So, it's actually come? I can't believe this. What's happened to this country?"

John shrugged. James put the tray on his writing table but decided not to open the letter as it was addressed to Andrew and David. These first few days in London made James Blair very anxious. All this talk of jails, guns, and duels were more like Virginia than anything he'd remembered of London. He decided that everyone should calm down and wait for the return of the two boys and Jack Elliott before any letter would be opened.

⚬⚬⚬

Once they received the challenge, James asked one of the horse guardsmen about retrieving Percy from Newgate. "Can we send a servant to get him, or can I go myself?"

The guard thought about the request. "Reverend, stay inside and bide your time till tomorrow. We have reason to fear that the marquis will try to cause some mayhem today, and we can better protect you if you remain in your own home. When Colonel Elliott returns, we can see about retrieving someone from Newgate."

The conversation with the guard made everyone feel even more vulnerable. The marquis, a known killer with his own army, had only one day to create more turmoil, as even he wouldn't do anything on a Sunday. But it was already afternoon and the marquis' men still had to report back to him that the Blairs were being guarded by horse guardsmen. The afternoon dragged after that, though the neighbors visited with quite a few children. Two more guardsmen arrived and two stayed inside while two patrolled the street.

For the children the Blair house became a joyous picnic. Jack and the two boys returned near evening. They seemed happy and confident, though David, who'd never aimed a weapon at a human being, appeared a little anxious. The three entered the house and went back to the Blair office where James worked on his sermon for the next day.

"We are back," Jack announced. "I understand there's a challenge."

"Yes, here it is." James handed the silver tray, the glove, and the letter to Andrew. "It's addressed to you and David, but since you're mentioned first, I suppose you should read it."

"Is Mrs. Blair about? I'd like her to hear this," Andrew said.

"Let's go into the front parlor," James said. "Her ladyship and some of our other guests should probably hear it also."

They moved to the front room, and James motioned to John to inform Sarah and the guests of the boys' return. Soon the full household of adults listened.

Andrew said, "Please, Mrs. Blair, read this so we can all understand what it says." He could read only a bit and David couldn't read at all.

Sarah took the letter, opened it, and saw the elaborate cursive writing. She immediately gave it to James, saying, "The reverend should read it. He heads the household, and this involves all of us."

James read out loud:

To defend my honor, I send this challenge to Andrew Morgan, who forcibly removed my wife from my home, and David Simmons, who assaulted me at the same time. I challenge them both, one at a time, to meet on the field at St. James Park. I propose Wednesday next, at daybreak. The challenge will be to the death unless proper apologies are made and compensation given and milady returned unharmed. Signed by the Marquis of Northampton.

James looked up at Jack. "Can we avoid this?"

Jack thought a bit. "Reverend and Mrs. Blair, I know the marquis well and have seen his duels more than once. He's devious and bloodthirsty and likely won't accept a simple apology. He's been humiliated in his own home and his wife ran away from him."

Florence shook her head. "Yes, I fear to return now. It might

be a death sentence for me. He's killed other people of rank before and has no special respect for me. He'll want the baby returned more than anything else."

"Is this a challenge to restore his honor?" Sarah asked. "How
can murdering two new visitors to the country who came to deliver a message uphold his honor? He's a predator who hurts
everyone who comes in contact with him. Can no judge or court
or militia deal with this?"

Jack shook his head as if he expected to get a question like
this. "Yes, he sees it as his honor, and he gets away with it because he holds high rank. His family was granted the title many
years ago, and they are high aristocracy. There are those who'll
say he isn't above the law, but in fact he is. The truth, Mrs. Blair,
is that if Andrew and David could accept and defeat him on the
dueling field, they would be doing a great service to England."

"You advise them to accept the challenge?" Sarah said.

James was shocked at this thought. "This is abominable.
Two boys in our charge on a killing field? It's unthinkable. We
should pay him what he wants."

Sarah looked at Andrew. "I promised your mother that you
would grow up here and come back a strong man ready for the
world. I would go back on my word to her if you died in a silly
duel the first week we arrive here."

"Please, Mrs. Blair. Apologizing won't settle anything," Andrew said. "I have no argument with the marquis and neither
does David. We did him no harm, just protected his wife and
baby from endangerment by him when he was drunk. Also, I
think I can handle him in a fair fight."

"We should send a note back, however you decide. Wait a
few days," Jack said. "Maybe he'll change his mind. In the meantime, these two know what a duel is, where it can be fought,
and what conditions to demand. I'll be happy to deliver your response to the marquis and to act as your second if there should
be a duel."

James was very troubled. "Does the church not preach against dueling? How can a member of a minister's household properly accept a duel?"

"This is England, James. Apparently, they have a different concept of honor here than we do," Sarah said. "In Virginia, fighting someone you don't know isn't considered honorable. We distinguish between those who fight for their honor and those who enjoy fighting for the sport of it."

"Well, our laws and customs are the same. It's the practice that's different. I've made some recommendations to the boys if they should decide to accept, and again, don't do anything too quickly," Jack said. "I'll ask a member of the Queen's Privy Council to warn the marquis against this fight. The boys have no rank or history here and it should be beneath a marquis to fight them. Even if he won, he'd gain only embarrassment for doing it."

Florence became flustered. "All of this is my fault, isn't it?"

"Don't be silly," Marjorie said. "It's not your fault if the marquis drinks too much and takes too many liberties with other people."

"But if he hadn't become annoyed at Percy and Susanna, none of this would have happened. By the way, when can we get Percy back from Newgate?"

"Don't worry," Jack said. "I'll send one of the guards for him. Is he properly paid for?"

Sarah said, "I left him a few shillings. We thought it would be enough."

"They won't argue with a horse guard. Don't worry. We'll get him back by this evening. He'll have much to give thanks for tomorrow. I hope the reverend remembers him in his sermon."

Jack smiled on his way out. "Remember to tell me what you decide."

Percy returned by nightfall and was greeted warmly by Susanna. She said, "Why you've made quite an entrance here, transported by the Blues themselves!" He was quickly ushered into the front parlor where the whole household and guests looked at him.

He announced for everyone to hear, "I'm in your debt forever, Mrs. Blair. The coins you left me were enough for the first decent meals I've eaten in weeks. And you've protected my wife and baby all the while. God smiled on me when I mounted your coach to ask for work."

"Well, you're quite welcome I'm sure. Have the guards left?"

Sarah opened the front door and saw two men in blue uniform on horseback ambling up the street. The guards stayed through the night.

CHAPTER 11

James felt the pressures as head of a household under duress. He disapproved of open violence but knew he likely couldn't avoid confrontation with the marquis, a powerful landed aristocrat. James decided to ignore the present dangers where possible. His sermon the next day lasted more than two hours, glowed with references to the gospel and nature's bounty, and finished with a request for prayers of thanksgiving.

He mentioned the kindnesses of his neighbors and the warmth of feeling towards new acquaintances. He didn't mention Newgate Prison or guardsmen at his house but pointed out his houseguests, Lady Northampton, her baby, and all of her staff including Susanna, Percy, and their baby. The parishioners seemed relaxed and considerate and very impressed with Lady Northampton, who sat in front in the parson's family pew with Sarah and Marjorie. David and Andrew sat in the rear with Jack Elliott and his family.

The day opened gloomily with a soft rain, which grew heavier as the day progressed. After the church service all returned to the house by coach and carriage. Sarah, James, Andrew, and David rode back together and reflected on their situation.

"Have you thought about the challenge, Andrew?" asked James.

"Yes, sir, I have. I believe I should accept, and I know how I would frame my answer. He's not the only person who thinks of his honor. He insults me if he calls me a coward to my face."

"He hasn't done that. He's only asked for the return of his wife."

"But she's not a prisoner or a slave. The world here knows that I don't own her or keep her. She can return if she wishes."

"That's not the way aristocratic society here will interpret it. Whether you like it or not, you boys behaved like rescuing knights for a lady in distress. According to custom, if you rescue her, you own her. I know this doesn't speak of reality, only social custom. He has to demand some redress or be seen as a cuckold."

"But you heard her ladyship. He keeps three mistresses in his house and mistreats all of them."

James responded, "Yes, the rules are different for lords and ladies."

"If you accept, you must win. There can be no truce once that's done," Sarah said. "You must kill him. He mentioned the duel to the death in his challenge. He's very confident. How do you feel about that?"

"I think he's no different than a rat in the street or a varmint in the field. His life is a disease in itself," David said. "The world will be better without him. It won't be difficult or an honor to kill him, and the rules won't matter much once he's dead. Colonel Elliott explained that to us."

"But this is a formal contest. You'll have to specify your choice of weapons and rules of engagement to follow."

Andrew shot back. "Yes, but the moment he violates any of

the rules he'll get both of us at once. No swordsman can handle both a sword fight while defending against an arrow in his chest."

Sarah looked up and giggled and James said, "You should not accept unless absolutely necessary. Maybe he's thought of that and will reconsider. We want to bring both of you back to Virginia uninjured and in one piece."

"Reverend and Mrs. Blair, you brought us with you to help protect the household," Andrew said. "We know that any insult to us is also an insult to you. It would not be honorable of us to allow insult or injury to come to this house without a proper fight."

The boys knew that the written challenge response would have to be written by the Reverend Blair in his most elegant cursive handwriting, embellished with circular patterns and whatever other decorations formal writings required. They soon arrived at the house and quietly the boys helped the Blairs disembark from the coach.

<hr/>

Within the hour, the house was very full again with neighbors, houseguests, children, and babies all bumping into each other and talking all at once. Mrs. Goodman and Anne kept the food and drink going and cleared some of the upstairs rooms for the children to play, as it was too wet outside.

Andrew and David were excited about the prospect for a fight and decided to go out to the garden to practice. Though it rained steadily, David didn't mind taking out his bow and arrows. He erected a target of green garlands that hung from a tree about a hundred yards away or so and sunk every arrow through the wispy, green stuff. Andrew cleaned his pistol but didn't fire it. He'd always been told not to discharge shots on a Sunday. He took turns with David with the bow until the green target was gone and the arrows had to be retrieved.

After about an hour the rain seemed to lighten, and the boys went to the back of the garden to take down the target. Near the rear they noticed a clearing in the brush that created a space of about a foot high through which someone could enter from the outside.

"That looks freshly made," David said. "What do you make of it?"

"Maybe we can expect some visitors from this direction? The marquis would want to retrieve the baby, and he knows the garden's the best place to do that."

"Let's find some sharp brambles to greet them with. We can keep an eye out for them if they come, and I'll keep the bow handy."

"Yes, I'll load the pistol too. Let's tell Colonel Elliott what we've found."

David broke branches off some rose bushes and filled the space. The boys then went to the Elliott house to tell Jack what they'd done. He returned with them and went directly to the garden without going through the house. He inspected the space and said, "That should put a sting into them if they try and slip through. Good work, boys."

The three went inside and spent a relatively restful Sunday. After supper the neighbors departed. Lady Northampton asked to be excused early, as she was quite tired and anxious. She'd barely said a word all day. Andrew and David also were weary from the past week's events and went to sleep early.

⸙

The babies cried early the next morning as the sun came out brightly, promising a beautiful new day. Andrew and David slept through half the morning, and when they arose it was to the sound of horses and guards shouting.

They quickly dressed and went downstairs and out the back where everyone sat in the garden and the babies rolled over on blankets in the warm sun. Anne took the boys to the back kitchen and gave them breakfast there. They gulped down their food, remembering the find of the day before.

David jumped up and ran into the back of the house where he'd placed his bow and arrows. Andrew never went anywhere without his pistol, which he kept in his belt. While David retrieved his bow, Andrew went to the rear of the garden to inspect the space filled with rose brambles. He noticed that it seemed untouched and he relaxed a bit. He then went back to the nurse who was now lifting baby Charley. Andrew lay down on the baby blanket and immediately received baby Amy to hold. Susanna laughed at the sight of him.

"She's had her eye on you from the beginning! I think a lot of other young ladies will also."

Percy now came over to Andrew and bowed. "Thank you for what you've done for her ladyship. It had to be done by someone and soon. I'm pleased it's done by someone as honorable as you, sir."

"I did nothing, and I'm pleased we didn't harm you too much. How did you fare at Newgate?"

"Well, the few shillings went a long way, getting me out of the rat pen. My room was passable and the food edible, though I was done with the shillings by the time the guard came. I don't know what would have happened to me if he hadn't come when he did. But what a sight he was too. A great black horse! I rode back here astride the horse holding on to the guard all the way. I've never seen anything from such a height!"

Susanna smiled. "I think he loved his two nights at Newgate, especially waving goodbye from the back of a guardsman's horse."

Andrew smiled. "Well, you're fortunate Mrs. Blair didn't blow your head off. She didn't plan on killing a complete stranger on the first day she arrived here."

The nurse was walking baby Charley around the rear of the garden, and Andrew heard a strange rustling noise. Then he saw a movement near where he'd placed the brambles. He stood and took out his pistol, which he'd loaded before coming down for breakfast.

David, on the other side of the garden, fully a hundred yards away from the edge of the yard, raised his bow, loaded an arrow, and pulled back the drawstring. He waited along with Andrew and after a minute they both saw the movement of two men dressed in green and gold. The intruders stood, drew their swords, and ran fiercely towards the nurse and baby Charlie.

Andrew fired his pistol in the air and David let his arrow fly at the green-clad man closest to the baby. The man, only five feet away from the child, was red-faced with eyes bulging. As he lunged forward, David's arrow struck him square in the chest and drove him backwards into his partner. Andrew ran towards them holding his short hunter's knife.

As the second man rose, David shot a second arrow. This caught the intruder in the shoulder causing him to fall back and lose his sword. The two men gasped and tried to cover their wounds and soon two guardsmen appeared.

The lead guardsman, sword drawn, said to the two wounded men, "Who are you, and why are you here?"

The lead intruder, bleeding profusely from the arrow in his chest, couldn't speak. His lieutenant responded, "Sir, we're sent by the Marquis of Northampton to retrieve his son."

"Did you think of knocking on the door and asking?" said Andrew.

The green uniformed intruder looked at Andrew. "We also came for a response to his lordship's challenge."

The guardsman replied, "Sir, you've broken and entered into a home with desire to harm the occupants. You've come with drawn swords. You may not return to your place of residence without answering to the Queen's justice for this. Are there just two of you?"

"We have a coach and driver waiting for us in the rear."

"Well, you will go to Newgate to await trial. Your driver may tell your master where he can send lawyers for your defense." The guard signaled to his subordinate to chain the two men together so they could be dropped off as criminal prisoners.

"Please, sir, may I retrieve my arrows?" David asked.

The guardsmen looked at the two prisoners and realized now what had happened. The senior guard asked, "Can they be reused?"

"Oh yes, sir, they are very fine and true. I'd like to keep them."

"Well, if you can get them out, I suppose they're your property."

David leaped over the baby blankets to the two men and went down on one knee beside them. Chained together they sat, back-to-back, on the ground bleeding. With all his strength David removed his arrows. The shoulder arrow was more difficult than the chest as it had gone all the way through. The chest wound bled more, though both men seemed as though they were going to live. When David finished, the guardsmen dragged the two men away.

Andrew and David knew now that they had to accept the challenge. They went inside to ask the reverend to write the formal letter for them.

All of the houseguests witnessed the events of the back garden. Lady Northampton clutched Charley, while Susanna held baby Amy. Both young women were pale with fright and anxiety, and the babies cried. Servants surrounded the Blairs and their visitors. Sarah and Marjorie tried to be composed, but Marjorie's three boys thought the events were very entertaining. They shouted, "What fun to be from Virginia! Can we have bows and arrows? Can we have a pistol? Huzzah for the guardsmen! Huzzah for David!"

James knew he'd have to compose a response for the boys. He was head of the household and neither of them could compose and write a proper formal letter of response. He said to them, "Can you remember everything Colonel Elliott told you?"

Both replied at once, "Of course."

Andrew continued, "He said he'd be our second and would deliver the message himself. He said he would support us with the translation of the rules and would handle our weapons until we needed them."

The three went inside to the Blair study and James took out the challenge. He read it over and following the normal form he wrote: *The undersigned accept the challenge issued by the Marquis of Northampton. He has committed criminal acts against our household for which he should apologize. We will face him consecutively at a place and according to rules to be determined by seconds and in the presence of witnesses. If he should violate any of the rules, he will face us together and no rules will apply. Andrew Morgan will use his pistol as first choice, and his second weapon will be a hunting knife. David Simmons first will use a long knife and second a short knife. The marquis may choose any weapon he wishes. The challenge will be to the death.*

James said, "Take this to Jack Elliott. He'll be at the barracks now. Tell him to make any changes and bring the document back to me for signature."

The boys took two horses down to the horse guards' barracks and asked to see Jack. He immediately saw them and took the document. "I'm happy to help. You know you're providing a great service to the Queen and our sense of justice here. I hope you aren't injured in the process. You aren't really required to accept this, as you have no rank. You're not even from this country. There'll be no embarrassment if you just return the lady and the baby to the marquis."

"She fears for her life," Andrew said. "We'd have to force her to return. We couldn't do that." David shook his head in agreement.

"Well, then it's settled. Ask the reverend to shorten this. Leave out the language about the rules, weapons, and to the death. I expect the marquis to violate the rules. He thinks his title and celebrity put him above the laws and rules that apply to everyone else, but he hasn't ever handled two opponents at once. I doubt he's even thought about it. I'll arrange everything. Just be certain that you have all your weapons with you and that they're ready to be used. Each of you should have a loaded pistol and a sword. David should bring his hunting bow and quiver. If there are no rules, any weapon will be allowed."

Colonel Elliott then took the document over to his writing desk and made some marks and corrections on the paper. He gave it back to Andrew.

"Thank you, Colonel. We'll do as you say, but we don't use swords. We're okay with slashing knives. David likely would use his short knife first. He'll simply throw it."

"That gives you not much to defend yourself if you should miss."

David said quietly, "We don't miss, sir. If you're in the woods in Virginia you don't get many second chances."

The boys returned to James with the document. He changed it so it simply read: *The undersigned accept the challenge proffered by the Marquis of Northampton. Rules will be determined by the seconds in front of witnesses.* James signed the document in his most elaborate handwriting for both boys, who then returned it to Elliott. The back and forth took almost the whole day.

Finally, with the final acceptance in his hand, Elliott looked carefully at the two young men. "Have either of you killed a man before or seen a man killed?"

Andrew replied, "Everyone in Virginia has seen a killing or two. I've shot two pirates myself. I blew one's head off with my musket."

David spoke more thoughtfully. "We come from a place with fewer people and danger everywhere. I haven't killed a man, but I've taken many deer and two great brown bears. I've killed four large wolves. I'm not afraid to aim my weapons at the marquis. I'm sure I could take him."

"Well, be prepared. I'll arrange a place in a park, an open field, probably near some trees. The duel will be at daybreak and will pit Andrew first since he uses a pistol. The rules will specify the first round to be pistols, and unless the marquis raises an objection, you can use yours. If he violates the rules, David can let an arrow fly or throw a knife. Without rules the marquis will face both of you at the same time with all weapons allowed. Be very attentive and quick to respond."

It took two more days to complete the arrangements. On a Friday, just one week after they'd arrived in London, Colonel Jack Elliott came just before daybreak to the Blair residence and asked for Andrew and David. Four guardsmen accompanied him on horseback. A coach was waiting and into it climbed Sarah Blair, Lady Northampton, Andrew, and David with all of their weapons. They drove off without delay.

Reverend Blair, his brother, and the Earl of Exeter, his wife Marjorie, and their children remained at the house in Whitehall. They prepared to immediately go to church where the Blair brothers planned to lead the congregation in prayer.

The coach and horse guardsmen lumbered along for about an hour, picking up some interested bystanders who followed the party on foot. Soon they came to a large green space, one of the Queen's parks. They continued into the center of the park, where they found a large green field surrounded by copses of oak and mulberry trees.

Waiting on the field stood the marquis and eight men in green and gold. The marquis wore a magnificent coat in royal-blue silk and white breeches and stockings. His second was a doctor, dressed in the traditional black coat. The doctor held a carved, wooden box that contained the marquis' pistol.

The horse guardsmen and Colonel Elliott arrived at the center of the field and exchanged some words with the marquis and his second. Andrew and David, both wearing leather Virginia hunting attire, climbed out of the coach carrying their weapons. Colonel Elliott signaled them both to come to the center of the field where the marquis and his second waited.

"It is customary to ask if this fight may be avoided," Elliot said. "Your lordship, will you take back your challenge? These young men hold no rank in England and have committed no crime here. As you know, duels have been outlawed by the Queen's justice."

The marquis looked at Elliott and never looked at the boys. He said, "State the rules please."

Elliott continued, "The rules establish pistols for the first round. You will meet, show each other courtesy, then turn and take ten paces. At the signal, you will turn and fire. It's agreed that I will give the signal, which will be the word, *Fire*. Any turn or use of weapon before the signal will be a violation of the rules. After the pistol shot, if both are still standing, you may use your second weapon of choice. There will be no further signals. I see you have a sword, my lord. Mr. Morgan will use a long knife as his second weapon."

The marquis and his second bowed their heads in agreement. "And after I've killed this one?" asked the marquis.

"Mr. David Simmons has chosen his short knife as his first weapon, to be followed by a long knife. For your second challenge, you have chosen to keep your sword. Is that correct?"

The marquis and his second indicated agreement. They looked at each other and the marquis opened the wood box so he could see the pistol. It was a glowing piece of jewelry, with gold metal and pearl inlays. While the marquis admired the pistol, David looked around and spotted a slender oak tree about fifty yards away. He wore his bow and carried a leather bag holding his quiver of arrows and his knives. Nobody except Andrew saw him run behind the tree from which he could easily see the field and hear Elliott clearly.

The four horse guardsmen stayed on their horses fully armed. The marquis' men stood on foot behind the marquis, also heavily armed. Jack spoke clearly and said, "All except the marquis and Mr. Morgan will leave this field." All armed men and interested witnesses backed away from the field, far from the contestants and from David, who had a clear line of sight.

The marquis' doctor joined the marquis' eight armed men who stood holding various pikes and swords. The four horse guardsmen followed them. David, out of sight from everyone, loaded an arrow and waited. Sarah and Lady Northampton remained in the coach about a hundred yards away. They could see fairly well.

Florence said to Sarah, "You see, he didn't even ask if I was here and would return to him. He just wants to kill the boys. That's his idea of sport!"

"I don't understand how a place this full of people can allow this kind of behavior. It's as if he loves to be seen and doesn't care about consequences," Sarah said. "Does he never think of anything other than himself and how he looks?"

"No, he's a marquis and he always acts the marquis. I don't suppose the boys understand any of this?"

"No, they think he's a varmint on two feet. His clothes won't impress them."

At that moment they heard Elliott shout, "Turn around and

raise your weapons! At the first count you may take a pace. Begin. *One....*"

When he shouted "*Eight!*" the marquis turned ready to fire. At that moment David released the bowstring. The arrow arced high above the field and its whistling sound distracted everyone. The marquis, who intended to shoot Andrew in the back, looked up momentarily. Before he could get off a shot, David's arrow pierced his neck just above the collarbone. The marquis dropped his gun and grabbed at his throat, but his face went from red to blue to white in a matter of seconds. Not able to breathe he fell to the ground.

Elliott shouted, "Mr. Morgan, you may take your shot if you wish. The marquis has violated the rules and all weapons are permitted!"

Andrew, stunned, couldn't move. He raised his pistol, which was ready to fire, but his opponent was already mortally wounded.

Nobody spoke. Elliott moved over to where the marquis still struggled but was clearly near death. His face was blue but his feet kicked a bit. Blood seeped from the wound and stained his white shirt and blue silk coat. He wasn't able to breathe or to talk. Elliott then shouted, "Doctor, tend to his lordship!"

The doctor emerged from behind the marquis' armed guards. He came to the marquis' side and looked at the weapon piercing the marquis' throat. He tried to pull it out but the shaft was thick and the arrowhead an elongated stone triangle that couldn't be drawn out backwards. He asked Elliott to break the arrow so it could more easily be removed.

Elliott shouted to David who ran over to his side. "This is your doing. How do we get the arrow out?"

David said solemnly, "He likely will die of the removal. The arrow is keeping his windpipe together a bit. If I pull it out he'll stop breathing altogether."

Elliott looked at the doctor, who said, "Perhaps the other

young man could put the marquis out of his misery. He won't survive this in any case."

Andrew was now alongside the group and looked down at the marquis. The felled man's eyes were open and he seemed to be staring upward without blinking. His blue face had no expression and he hardly breathed.

Elliott said to Andrew, "He challenged you and you are entitled to one shot. He's dead either way. Do what you wish."

Andrew looked at Elliott. "If he were my horse, I'd put her out of misery. He doesn't deserve that kindness. I won't waste a pistol ball on him."

The marquis soon stopped kicking. Elliott suddenly remembered the previous encounter with the marquis' men. He asked, "David, do you want this arrow back?"

David wore a grim face and responded sadly, "No, sir. It belongs to the marquis now. Bury it with him, so he can take it to the next world. That way the heavens will know how he got there."

<hr />

Florence, the Marchioness of Northampton, saw everything but heard and understood nothing. The moment the arrow struck her husband, she knew her life had changed. But she expected him to recover and get up to fight again, as had happened many times earlier. If he were humiliated he'd take it out on her. She fully expected to be back at Ravensport within the next few days and to contend with an irascible marquis.

Sarah knew differently. She'd seen men mortally wounded in fights in and around Jamestown and she heard many tales from William Roscoe who'd been a sheriff. When Sarah saw the marquis fall, she knew he'd never get up. "My dear Florence, you must stay with us until everything is sorted out. You must think of yourself and Charley now."

"What do you mean? Is the marquis not going to survive this?"

"There's no way. The doctor can do nothing for him. Do you have close family nearby? Someone you trust? What of your parents? Will they come to comfort you? Who should be informed? You'll have to arrange a burial and church service. There will be lawyers to see to his estate and possibly papers to sign."

Florence couldn't believe what she was hearing. At seventeen she now held the positions of marchioness, widow, and protective mother of a three month old marquis. She knew she was totally unprepared for these responsibilities and she knew London well. She knew the lawyers and bill collectors wouldn't wait long until they came to hound her.

"My parents? They've never been of any help before. They'll probably be the only people in England to mourn for him along with his own mother, and they'll blame me for everything that's happened. I certainly can't trust them. What should I do, Sarah?"

"Right now, nothing. Come back home with me and we'll think about where you feel most comfortable. You'll have to make many decisions—where you want to live, how much of your current staff you want to keep. Don't you want someone you trust to come and stay with you a while?"

"No, not right away. I can't believe I won't see him again. Imagine that great house without him strutting down the stairs. I can't believe this." Florence didn't weep for her husband, but felt no joy in losing him either.

Andrew and David, both flushed with excitement and with hearts still pounding, climbed back into the coach and Colonel Elliott rode over on his horse. He bent his head to Florence and said, "Milady, the marquis has left this world. His body will be transported back to Ravensport, and arrangements need to be made for his funeral. Will you come with the guardsmen who'll transport him? We'll need you to offer some direction. His lawyers will probably have some idea of his instructions for funeral arrangements, but as his widow and guardian of the new marquis your wishes must be respected."

Florence looked at Sarah who quickly said, "Lady Northampton will return to Whitehall with me for a while. She won't be returning to Ravensport until she's met with the lawyers about the estate and his will. You may inform the marquis' guards that the house is to continue as before until they hear directly from the marchioness. You may also inform them that no property of any kind is to be allowed to leave the estate, no matter who is carrying it."

"That's wise. I'll station ten horse guardsmen at the entrances and tell them that nothing is to come in or out. The marquis' men will also help. The property will be sealed until the lawyers sort all of it out."

Sarah looked at Florence. She was younger than Sarah's youngest sister and had dutifully married the man selected for her by her parents. She likely never expected much happiness from the marriage, but she'd attained status and wealth and her parents were probably quite satisfied.

Florence was a caring and attentive mother, but now as a widow and marchioness she occupied an established place in the world of property and politics. She obviously felt abandoned by her parents. This wasn't a world of large extended families as in Virginia. This was a world governed by aristocrats, lawyers, and bill collectors.

Sarah said quietly, "Don't worry. Those people will wait. You're the marchioness and guardian of the baby marquis. We'll be happy to help you and want nothing from you. Consider us your family. You can ask for anything you like. We have lawyers and clergy nearby, and if you wish we can find others to help."

Andrew and David didn't know what to say to Florence. David appeared to be near tears and said, "I'm sorry, milady, but he would have shot Andrew in the back. I had to stop it." Florence looked at him, put her arms around his great shoulders, and then finally began to weep herself. The coach went back to Whitehall where James, James's brother William, and the houseguests awaited.

When the coach emptied, it was clear that Andrew and David had survived, but Florence needed to be helped. Sarah took her hand and led her into the house where Mrs. Goodman was ready with some tea. It was still early morning.

"Perhaps milady would like to lie down for a while?" Mrs. Goodman said.

"We have much to talk about and need good legal advice," Sarah said. "The marquis is dead, and funeral arrangements need to be made. Also, her ladyship needs representation on estate matters. Do you think Tom will be willing and able? Perhaps we need to talk to Cunningham to suggest a lawyer?"

"I've asked some friends from the Rolls office where I used to work before coming to Virginia," James said. "They came to our service this morning. They think Tom is a fine attorney and honest. Perhaps Andrew or David could run over to his house and see if he's there. It's still quite early."

Actually, all of the neighbors were still at home. Nobody was going to leave until they heard the outcome of the challenge, and they'd all been to church to hear the Blair brothers' preaching.

David knocked at the Adams door, directly across the street, and their eight-year-old son John answered. The boy lit up when he saw David and yelped. "Oh wonderful. You've survived. I wish I could be as big as you David."

David smiled at him and lifted him to his shoulders. "Well, first see how you like it up here." Emily and Tom came quickly, and Tom asked, "Is Andrew well?"

"Yes, quite well. The marchioness needs to talk to you, if you could come."

When Tom and David got to the Blairs' parlor, Marjorie and

Sarah were busy talking to Florence who now held baby Charley. Percy and Susanna stood nearby, along with Anne and Henry. The Earl of Exeter, Marjorie's husband, whispered to William Blair in the corner while James looked on. Andrew was outside playing with the three Exeter boys. The small parlor seemed to be overflowing with people, but conversation was muted.

Tom approached Florence. "Your ladyship should probably return to Ravensport to take possession of the house and govern the funeral arrangements. You needn't make any legal decisions right away, and I'll be happy to collect inquiries from lawyers and business people."

"Does Florence need to tolerate the presence of the marquis' three mistresses?" Marjorie asked.

Tom paced the room, thinking to himself. Finally he responded, "No, but she must be careful not to induce them to steal property from the house. She should move them into the same suite of rooms and the house staff should take an inventory of all furnishings. The mistresses shouldn't be permitted to leave with property that doesn't belong to them."

"If they have jewelry that's not paid for, who owns it?" Marjorie said.

Tom smiled. "Milady, if it's not paid for, the jeweler owns it. The same for gowns and wigs. We'll need to do a complete inventory, and that might take time. If your ladyship wants them out, you may order that and promise to let them have their property once that's determined."

"Florence isn't used to managing these kinds of things," Sarah said. "Florence, do you want these people to leave?"

Florence looked at Sarah. "Could you come with me to the estate? I feel so alone in this."

"Of course. Tom should come as well. You should think of what you'll give these people. Do they have some place to go? Perhaps you can give them ten pounds each and call it even. That should be enough to tide them over for a while."

Marjorie was indignant at the thought. "A proper wife shouldn't have to pay off three mistresses. What sort of world is this? What do you say Reverend Blair?"

James simply cleared his throat. His education hadn't prepared him for this problem, and he really didn't know what to say. He simply suggested, "Sarah's a good manager. She and her ladyship should go now and get the place under control."

Florence then stood and looked at James. "You know, Ravensport is quite a distinguished address. We have four wings and six freshwater ponds and an outlook over the river. If the Blair household isn't tied to Whitehall, you could all come and take over one of the wings. It's quite a good place for entertaining, especially to the Board of Trade. I'd be happy to help you in your visit to London."

Sarah looked at James who seemed indecisive and out of his element. She moved across the room to stand at his side. "We don't need to decide anything like that today. We'll go to Ravensport now and instruct the staff. We'll also see to funeral arrangements. Will the funeral be here or elsewhere?"

"Probably in the cathedral near his family seat in Northampton," Tom said. "We'll hear specifically about his will from his lawyers, probably tomorrow. Where does milady wish to spend the night tonight and what of the baby?"

Florence thought a moment. "I'll return here and don't want to be pestered by people I don't know."

"I understand completely. Take your time," Tom said. "These are important decisions that will be difficult to undo."

CHAPTER 12

Sarah, Florence, and Marjorie boarded the coach to return to Ravensport. Tom Adams went on horseback so he could arrive before them. The coach, now decorated with the black bunting of mourning, was escorted by four men of the horse guard, riding two ahead and two behind. Along the street now many of the neighbors, knowing what happened, waited to show their respect to the marchioness.

Once the coach left, Marjorie immediately said, "You know, Florence, once the period of mourning is over, and you can decide how long that will be, you'll be one of the most eligible widows in London. Dukes will call on you. Your mother will be busy sizing them up for you. Be prepared. You'll certainly be invited to court to meet the Queen."

Sarah was curious. "Does Florence's family have anything to do with her now?"

Florence, now finished with crying, said, "Anything? I pay for virtually everything of theirs. That's what made Edward so angry. He thought he was getting a dowry but ended up with greater debts than he ever imagined." Florence seemed determined and continued, "I've never been involved on the business end. I suppose the lawyers reading the will can at least summarize what I own and what I owe. I know we had large country estates that supplied wool to the textile industry here, but Edward never paid attention to that. He had business managers. I know he had large debts also. He brought his mistresses to Ravensport rather than set them up in their own places. That probably saved him money."

"Have you ever visited the country estates? Do you know the managers?" Sarah asked. "Now might be the time to call on them, just to meet them and see what they do for you. Managers, like factors, exist to serve you. You should know what you're paying them for."

Florence looked at Sarah and blushed. "I'm so glad you're here. I have a title and have already visited the Queen. I know how to entertain and visit with royalty and their hangers-on. I can read but can't follow legal documents, and I certainly don't understand accounts."

Marjorie agreed emphatically. "Who can? When I married Henry he was an earl, but our money is mine—and that's Culpeper money. Our wealth is from investments in Virginia and the Caribbean. We use Cunningham mainly but have used other factors and bankers from time to time. I'll introduce you, Florence, and you needn't worry. If a manager displeases you, you'll find another. It's no different than the dressmakers—they exist to serve you, so long as you have the money."

Sarah nodded in agreement. "Yes, money makes the world go round, much the same everywhere. We're smaller than you are, so we keep a closer eye on everything. My father and I still ride out to see the tobacco. What do you think about Edward's mistresses? What do you plan to say to them?"

Florence pouted. "I know exactly what to say and what I'll do. If Edward left them anything in his will, they'll get that and nothing else. If they have debts, they'll have to pay them. If their jewelry is unpaid for, they can make their own arrangements with the jewelers."

Marjorie looked at Sarah. "Well said, but they may not have places to go."

Florence was adamant. "We have debtors' prisons. Percy spent two nights at Newgate."

Sarah said nothing as they approached the house. The large mansion now carried black decorations and all the curtains were drawn. The lead guardsman helped them out of the coach and they slowly made their way up the ornamental outdoor staircase. As soon as they arrived, the door opened and four servants, liveried in black, took their outer garments. They entered a front parlor where Tom Adams and four men, all dressed in mourning black, waited for them.

The four lawyers for the estate stood up from their seats and took turns bowing and offering condolences to the marchioness. They showed the women to comfortable, soft chairs near a grand fireplace.

"I've agreed with these gentlemen that we should take some time in assessing the inventory," Tom said. "The marquis left only simple documents and made no specific bequests to family or others. He didn't expect to die so soon. Under the law, the widow will get one third of everything, while the heir—that's baby Charley—will get the rest. These four gentlemen will manage the estate for you and for Charley's benefit."

"Edward has two brothers and three sisters. He has several nieces and nephews. Do they get nothing at all?" Florence asked.

"No, nothing," one of the lawyers said. "All of his estate is yours. You can make gifts if you wish, but first let us do the inventory. Then you'll know better what you have and what you owe."

"Yes, I could give them some of Edward's personal effects and the like." Florence thought of all the relatives who likely would call on her now.

Florence straightened her shoulders and looked at Tom. "I'd like you to inform the three women my husband brought here that they are no longer welcome. They will receive no payments from me. If the marquis made them gifts, they need to show that they're paid for. Without such proof they will walk out of here with just the clothes on their backs. They may stay, if they wish, until the inventory is completed and the jewelers satisfied."

"Shall they stay in their present apartments?" Tom asked.

"Absolutely not! Send some guards to their rooms and put them upstairs in the main building, in the servants' quarters. They aren't to have any special privacy and all of their belongings are to be inspected. If they don't like the arrangement, they may leave. If I owe them something, they can leave an address where I can send what's owed them."

Marjorie and Sarah looked at each other. Finally, Marjorie said, "Do you know these women Florence? Have you ever spoken to them?"

"No. Why should I?"

"They may be nobody and then it doesn't matter. But Edward may have taken a duchess or a person of wealth who paid for her own jewels."

"Then she can leave. She needn't wait for lawyers."

"But you needn't poison the well before you've even taken a drink. They knew Edward, it's true, but mainly for the time you were carrying Charley. What's the point of inflicting more injury on them than Edward's death? Now that he's gone, they know they have no place here. Why make enemies for no reason?"

"You're young and nobody can tell you that you'll never see these women again," Sarah said. "You'll be living in the same city and meet many people who know them. Let them have a kind keepsake or two from the marquis. Make sure they know it's from you. There's nothing to gain if you make them hate you."

Marjorie continued, "Move them in together but not to servants' quarters. Move them to the main house, without special personal servants. Tell them to bring their personal effects, clothes and the like, and not items that are still to be paid for. Have your servants make a list of everything they bring for the inventory."

Florence looked at Tom. "Would that be possible?"

"Yes, of course. They already know that everything in the house has to be accounted for. Now, milady, to more somber decisions. The funeral will take place out of the city. The body is here in a wooden casket, in the library. The embalmer removed the arrow. What do you want to do with it?"

Florence looked shaken. "Can I see him in the box?"

Tom whispered, "Of course," and took her hand and led her across the great front hall to the library.

There in the wood-paneled room lined with books two stories high, the great casket sat on two large tables. The embalmers were still there and Tom signaled them to open the box.

Florence peered in. Except for the wound in his neck, the marquis looked in perfect repose. He had rouge on his cheeks and he wore his favorite red silk coat and white breeches. The arrow's shaft, broken in two pieces and blackened by his blood, lay beside him.

Florence looked at Tom. "Leave the arrow there. It should stay with him. He earned it."

Florence returned to the parlor, sat down, and spoke seriously to Sarah. "I know you have much business here in London, but I need your help over the next few months. If you and the reverend could come and stay in one of the wings, you'll be very comfortable. If you help me organize the household, there will be no rent to pay. I promise you'll meet every member of the Board of Trade and you can entertain them under fine conditions."

Sarah understood the heavy burden on the marchioness. In Virginia, a death of an important person would bring the support of large close families. Business partners normally were trusted family members. Florence had nobody.

Sarah took Florence's hand. "I'll give you a final answer tonight. First let me speak to the lawyers, and you have to prepare to attend the funeral. As it's to be away from here, you should make a list of everyone to be informed. Perhaps you should speak to the minister who'll give the eulogy. James could be helpful there. Meanwhile, I'll look around the house and grounds a bit. Probably the boys will enjoy the change, especially David. He loves a morning swim." Florence looked relieved; she thought Sarah was giving the change serious thought.

"I'll let your parents know, and Edward's brothers and sisters should be sent the message by coach right away," Marjorie said. "You need to bring the baby to his father's funeral but be circumspect. Tell the mistresses not to come. Tell them that if they do it will cost them."

"I feel that James and I should come, though we really didn't know the marquis. Andrew and David should stay away," Sarah said.

"I'd be very disappointed if you didn't come, and I want the boys to be there also," Florence said. "They've saved my life and Charley's, you know. You and the Exeters can come and stay with me in the country house. Andrew and David could stay away from the church during the funeral service. I'm sure they'll love the country and everyone will want to meet them."

"I just don't want one challenge to lead to another," Sarah said. "I know how ridiculous disappointed relatives can be."

With that, Sarah left the room to talk to the lawyers. She walked around the grounds and decided that moving to Ravensport would be good for the Blair household.

That evening Sarah and James discussed the offer of the marchioness to move to her estate at Ravensport.

"We haven't roots in London or Whitehall, and the marchioness needs us, James," Sarah said. "She's younger than my youngest sister, and she's left with a baby, an estate run by lawyers she doesn't know, and a household of more than a hundred servants. We could be a help, and she probably could get the Board of Trade to assist us."

"We're hardly here a week," James said. "I worry we're being a little hasty."

"But what would be wrong? If it doesn't work out, we could move again. Andrew and David will need some kind of protection now. Every young hero in London will be looking for a way to challenge them."

"Why do you think that?"

"Young men want to impress people, and London rewards winners. How better for a young man to show off before his peers or his ladies? The boys aren't from here, and they'll get no special sympathy. The marquis probably had some close friends who especially will look for revenge."

"I think you're exaggerating. The Queen resides here. There's a militia and horse guards. Dueling is technically against the law."

"But the laws aren't enforced. Colonel Elliott of the horse guards spends a lot of time being a second in duels around town. It seems to be a business of sorts."

James shook his head and thought again. "Well, it would be quite a step up for a lowly Scottish minister and his Virginia wife, and no rent?" He smiled at the thought.

"We can tell her tonight as she's still here with us. I've walked around the grounds and there will be plenty of room for everyone. The estate isn't as big as King Carter's, though his house is smaller and he has far fewer servants."

"With all the servants, we'll have the time to devote to the reasons we're here. I haven't managed to put my arguments together for the board yet."

"First find out who they are, then do the arguments!"

James knew he had no choice now. He and Sarah went down to the sitting room and there found the marchioness, Marjorie, Henry, William Blair, Andrew, David, Colonel Elliott and his wife, and Tom Adams and his wife. Sarah immediately went over to Florence and said, "We've discussed the matter and will be happy to move the household to Ravensport. It won't be difficult, as we've barely unpacked. You should decide where you want us to reside."

Florence embraced Sarah. "Oh, thank you. I think the west wing with an outlook on the river would be most pleasant for you. The rooms get plenty of sun. Ten to fifteen servants serve each of the wings. Come and see where you'd situate people."

Marjorie, overjoyed, leaped up. "How wonderful! Sarah will figure it all out, you'll see! An estate is something like a business, isn't it?"

Tom laughed. "A business that doesn't make any money. A hard bargain to organize. Are you sure you want the responsibility, Mrs. Blair?"

Sarah responded in her softest Virginia accent, "Mr. Adams and Colonel Elliott, I can't thank you enough for what you've done for us already. We're all in your debt, and for me this is the least I can do. I think I can help Florence through these next few months, which will be very difficult for her. I hope I may ask you for additional assistance if the necessity arises."

Everyone in the room spoke at once. There were shouts of "Of course! Just ask!"

Then Sarah looked at Colonel Elliott. "You especially, Colonel, are to be thanked. I'm sure Andrew and David wouldn't be here and so healthy if it weren't for you. All of this is my fault.

I pulled the pistol on Percy and sent him to Newgate. I sent the boys to see the marquis and told them to stand their ground because they spoke for me. Now, sir, would you be able to assist us in determining how large a guard we should keep and which men can be trusted?"

Andrew and David listened carefully to this conversation. "Colonel Elliott, can we help with this? We'd like to see the weapons you use and how they're made," Andrew said.

"I'd be delighted to come out with you to see who the guards are and to assess how many you really need," the colonel said. "The marchioness must trust those around her who are there to protect her and her household. She must be present. Can you come tomorrow, milady?"

"Of course," Florence said. "But I must prepare for the funeral. I expect relatives to start arriving soon also. I'd also like some protection from them."

William Blair, a prelate with a booming voice, said, "Milady, I'll be delighted to greet whoever comes to your door and to seat them where you will and keep them occupied with holy stories. Will that be alright?"

Florence smiled. "Thank you. I can't believe how kind all of you are. You know I'll have to be in mourning for a few weeks at least, but my first invitation to Ravensport will be to the neighbors on this street. I hope I can at least entertain you with a decent meal and some drinks."

"I'll help wherever I can," Marjorie said to Sarah, "but tomorrow I want to take you down to the city to meet some bankers. Reverend James can organize the household and think about repacking. Florence will be in good hands with two reverends to rely on. We'll all be going up to the funeral in two days, so there's little time to waste."

"A good idea to get away from all of this for a day," Sarah said. "Marjorie and I need to talk quietly some place far away from people and this will be our chance." Sarah looked at the boys. "We need to prepare ourselves. Andrew and David, you'll accompany Colonel Elliott to the house tomorrow, and I'll visit Cunningham and see a few bankers in the town. We'll all be back tomorrow evening here for supper and prepare for the funeral."

⁕

Marjorie and Sarah arose early. Henry had prepared a small covered cart drawn by two dappled horses with enough room for two passengers and packages. He provided the protection and Percy accompanied them to show the way. Sarah made sure her pistol was loaded and she took some extra powder and shot. She carried the pistol in a pocket hidden in the inside of her outer cloak. The extra shot and powder were in a leather bag. The bag also held a piece of muslin, some scent, and a sheet of parchment.

They took the shortest route to the old city, an area where the largest factors and bankers kept offices. As they made their way, streets became narrower, busier, and crowded. They could hardly hear each other as street shouts and the sound of the horses' hooves created a loud din. The cart rumbled and shook over the heavy cobblestones, but Sarah never drew her pistol.

When they arrived at the offices of Cunningham and Company, Henry helped the women out of the cart. An officer in an elaborate navy-blue coat and breeches opened the door and admitted the two women into the building. Henry and Percy waited outside.

After the officer took their outer cloaks, Sarah asked to see David McAllen. The officer left them for a few moments and soon returned. He then led them up a tall, spiral stairway decorated with elaborate iron railings to McAllen's office. When they entered the room McAllen stood at his desk and in a warm and friendly voice said, "Greetings." He motioned to seats in front of a large marble fireplace, and the three of them sat down. Tall glass windows lit the high-ceilinged room and large paintings of former Cunningham executives and ships at sea hung on the tall walls.

"You've had a most extraordinary introduction to London, Mrs. Blair. I hope all will be calmer for you now and you'll be able to relax a bit," McAllen said. "I've heard the news about the marquis. Indeed, it's the talk of all London."

"Our household has had quite a shock, Mr. McAllen. The marchioness is staying with us for now but has invited us to relocate to Ravensport. She's asked me to help her reorganize her household."

"Well, if there's anything we can do to assist please feel free to call on us. Will you be moving from Whitehall soon?"

"Yes, probably after the funeral. We go to Northampton day after tomorrow. Do you think Mrs. Goodman and John would like to move with us? I've asked them and they're both willing to come. We won't take any of the Whitehall furnishings."

"Don't worry about Whitehall. We'll have another tenant in before long and bring in new staff. Now, I want to tell you about your two tobacco ships. The cargo brought a very fine price as few ships are making deliveries, what with the war and increased piracy at sea. We have kept your account up to date. I'm sure you'll want to make purchases to take back to Virginia with you when the time comes." He lifted an account book from his desk and turned to a page that he showed to Sarah. Both of them smiled at each other.

Marjorie looked up at McAllen and said, "Sarah will need some spending money for household needs. Can you give her a bank draft? We'll be visiting some city bankers to make life a little easier."

"A very good idea! Who do have in mind?"

"I thought one of the Jewish bankers would be suitable. They have investments in the New World and are quick to respond to requests. I thought possibly Gideon or Seixas?"

"May I suggest Mendoza? Some Dutch Jewish bankers also

are quite reputable, particularly Levy and Cohen. Let me know whom you choose. We'll be happy to work with you."

Relieved, Sarah sat in a quiet place and felt pleased with the profits now in her account. "Mr. McAllen, I'm sure I'll be coming to the city regularly with the marchioness over the next few weeks and months. I'd like to set up my accounts today and maybe engage a dressmaker for my basic needs."

McAllen stood and smiled at Marjorie. "Well, I'm sure the baroness will be helpful in the dress department. How large a draft do you need for now?"

"Let me have ten percent for now. That should be eight hundred pounds or so."

McAllen smiled. "Mrs. Blair, this is war time. Ten percent of just the profits from the last two shipments will be over five thousand. Of course, you have much more than that in your full account. How much do you need right now? If you leave it with the bankers, make sure you get at least eight percent interest. We can handle major purchases directly from here—that is, for furnishings, cutlery, and all the rest. We can get a better price than most, so interest shouldn't be an issue. How long do you think you'll be in England?"

Sarah smiled with relief. She sat back in her chair and looked at the ceiling trying to remember everything she intended to buy for herself and friends. "We'll probably stay a year or so, perhaps a little longer than that. I don't worry about interest as much as making the necessary purchases. The merchandise will be re-sold at a profit when we return to Virginia. This time I want good quality. I'll want to see the items I buy while I'm here."

"Of course," McAllen said. "You also may want to have a portrait done now that you're here. We can recommend painters around town, though I'm sure the baroness will be helpful there as well."

Marjorie laughed. "How do you want to look when you're hung? We've got quite a range to choose from."

McAllen wrote out a bank draft against Sarah's account and gave it to her. He signed the draft with his name for Cunningham and Company. She looked at it carefully, smiled, and said, "I trust if I need more I can call on you again?"

"Of course, you are most welcome whenever you need anything. Please, feel this office is yours. You're a most worthy client, and I feel personally responsible for the recent troubles. Don't hesitate, really."

With that, the two women rose and took their leave of McAllen. As soon as they sat in the cart, Marjorie said, "I doubt we'll see dressmakers today. We'll need to size up a few bankers. Perhaps you should have more than one account?"

"Yes, one for me and one for investments!" Both women laughed.

Marjorie said, "Well, yours should be the bigger one, as you'll only be here a year!"

The cart drove off to the bankers. London was a trading city, and different parts of the town were devoted to specialized trades and held different people. London had breweries, ship building sites, and a large silk industry. London craftsmen dyed and pressed textiles shipped there from all over the country.

They crossed the Strand, the main shopping area for the wealthy, drove down Fleet Street and Cheapside, where virtually every building held some sort of shop. Sarah saw large, gilded signs announcing ironmongers, furriers, tobacconists, milliners, haberdashers, lamps and lanterns, apothecaries, paperhangers, and goldsmiths.

Marjorie knew Sarah loved what she saw. "You know many of the aristocracy don't bother with bankers. They simply deal with their goldsmiths. They exchange their jewelry for what they need. We could visit a goldsmith for your personal account.

What do you think?"

"Is that what Florence does?"

"Possibly. She might need another account herself now. She's really just a baby and hasn't settled into London. She was married only a little over a year ago and the marquis didn't take her into town that often. She was pregnant most of the time after all."

"She seems to know her business now."

"When the marquis ordered Percy and Susanna from the house she was left alone there. She sent me a message and I came by every afternoon. You mustn't feel responsible for anything, Sarah. In some ways Florence is very fortunate. With you around, she may even learn a little more about how to handle finances."

The cart stopped at a two-story building with a sign saying Mendoza and Brothers. The street was shabbier than the Strand, but the buildings appeared old and sturdy. Large parts of the old city they'd driven through appeared newer, having been rebuilt since the great fire of 1666. The buildings they saw now were of brick and stone and blackened with soot. Across the street and down a bit stood very similar structures, all devoted to banks, under the names of Nunes, Seixas, Salomon, and Levy.

Henry helped Marjorie and Sarah out of the cart, and again he and Percy waited while the women entered the building. The street had little traffic as it held few shops, but a tavern stood on the corner.

When the women entered the building they were surprised to see children playing in the lobby. Soon a middle-aged woman, quite well dressed, came down a flight of stairs shouting, "Children upstairs! Birthday cake for everyone!" Two small boys and three girls raced up the stairs at the announcement followed by the woman.

The lobby suddenly seemed silent, but at that moment a dark, burly man appeared from behind the stairs. He walked up to the two women and bowed. "My name is Samuel Mendoza, my ladies. How can I help you?"

Sarah smiled and introduced herself and Marjorie, mentioning McAllen and Cunningham. She mentioned her family and their trade in tobacco and that she'd only recently arrived in London.

Mendoza, a man of about forty with very dark hair and dark, bushy eyebrows, asked, "My goodness, Mrs. Blair, you are here all the way from Virginia? I'm so happy to meet you. I know many seamen and ship owners who trade between Virginia and the Caribbean. It's really an honor to meet the owner of such a commodity as Harrison tobacco. Harrison is a name well known to tobacco traders."

Sarah, impressed that Mendoza knew the Harrison name, smiled. Marjorie then said, "Yes, Mrs. Blair would like to open a temporary account and to be informed about proper investments and where to make major purchases. Mr. McAllen recommended you specifically."

Mendoza was pleased with the mention of McAllen. "Yes, I've sometimes helped David and advised him on the sugar trade. Are you interested in some Jamaica investments? I have a visiting captain arriving any day. He'll be happy to tell you all the details. Where will you be staying, Mrs. Blair? I'll be happy to send a messenger when he arrives. He'll probably stay with us a while, until he gets tired of the children."

"How many children do you have?" Sarah asked. "Is it normal for visiting seamen to stay with you?"

"He's a dear friend of many years. Yes, my wife and I are blessed with nine children. The oldest is already sixteen and soon to join the firm. He's upstairs right now, celebrating his birthday."

Marjorie gushed. "Happy day to all of you. A wonderful occasion. We wish him long life and much success and happiness. I hope we're not interfering."

"Of course not! I'm honored to have you. And because this

is a special day, I offer you nine percent interest on any moneys you leave with me. I guarantee you'll not find a better deal anywhere in the city!"

"That's very generous of you, and I'm most interested in meeting your sea captain," Sarah said. "What's his name? I own several ships and know many captains who trade in tobacco."

"Yes, you may have heard of him. He's Simon Grey and sails the *Sweet Susan*, a ship that carries many cannon. He's made quite a profit in running guns from Germany recently."

"I believe I've heard of him. Does he sail out of Charles Towne in Carolina?"

"I believe so. You can see him soon and talk over old times when he gets here."

Sarah and Marjorie whispered to each other, and Sarah took the Cunningham bank draft out of a leather bag she carried. "Let me leave half of this with you now for a new account. I'd like the change in currency. When we speak again, it will be about investments. Will that be sufficient, Mr. Mendoza?"

Mendoza looked at the draft and obviously was impressed. "Half of this is a grand amount for a new account, but I doubt you'll need so much in change. Anyway, it's dangerous to carry too much gold coin with you. You should see Mr. Levy down the street. He's Dutch and carries on trade in diamonds and gold. You can set up an account with him, as he knows the trade with northern Europe very well. He'll set it up so you have ready cash for today and impeccable credit with everyone in London. You could treat yourself to some nice jewelry at the same time."

Mendoza sat at his account table and made a note of Sarah's transaction in his account book. He wrote out a receipt, which she then put in her leather bag, along with the pistol shot. While doing this, the women heard loud shouts from upstairs. The women smiled and Sarah said, "Thank you so much, but I think they need you upstairs now."

The women visited Levy and both opened new accounts.

Sarah bought Marjorie a gold bracelet.

"Why do that? You should be careful you don't spend too much too soon."

"You've been too kind to us," Sarah said. "It's our custom to bring gifts to friends when we visit. Keep this as a keepsake of Jane Parke and me. She'd want you to have it."

"Well, then let me treat us all to lunch." Marjorie, Sarah, Henry, and Percy then went back to the tavern for lunch and a few beers.

⁕

Florence, the Marchioness of Northampton, now widowed and about to come into a great inheritance, had many family members who needed her support and some who felt entitled to it. She'd been an obedient daughter and married Edward at her father's command. Her father, the Earl of Scarborough, a baron with business interests in the textile trade, believed it would be a good match from a business perspective. Her mother, the Baroness of Scarborough, loved the idea of having a marquis for a son-in-law and spent lavishly on clothes and entertaining. The baroness looked forward to being presented at court and constantly encouraged Florence to do the same.

Florence didn't care for court intrigues and while she enjoyed the large houses, jewelry, clothes, and entertainments that came along with marrying a marquis, she often felt quite lonely. She'd hoped that having the baby would bring Edward closer to her, but instead it drove him away, mainly to gambling and a parade of mistresses. She'd been presented at court and already had lunched with the Queen, but she really wasn't enthusiastic about the prospect of court life. Now Edward was dead and she wanted to get away from it.

The funeral, because the death was so unexpected, wouldn't formally be held for another two weeks while Edward lay in state in his ancestral home, Castle Ashby. His body, already embalmed, would have to be put on display in his coffin. She'd have to play the mourning widow in black and wear a peaked, black headdress. She was expected to act as if she was receding from the world. She thought it was a farce; she didn't mourn the loss of Edward who'd mistreated her from the day they were married and threatened her repeatedly.

When Marjorie and Sarah returned from the city they found Florence in the parlor surrounded by a mother, father, mother-in-law, and half a dozen younger people, all obviously siblings and spouses of siblings. Almost everyone was speaking at once, and several were shouting at each other. Colonel Elliott stood in a corner of the room with four armed guards. Tom Adams stood next to him and said nothing.

Mrs. Goodman and Anne had provided refreshments, and the two Blair brothers had tried to calm the people, mainly with soothing reminders of the inevitability of sorrow and God's will. Florence sat on a soft chair near the fireplace with her head in her hands, weeping.

Sarah, seeing the chaos, immediately went to Florence. "You shouldn't be in public like this. Come upstairs and lie down." Sarah looked at James who immediately bowed to the company.

James said, "My wife, Mrs. Blair, and the Baroness of Exeter. Please excuse the marchioness. She's in distress just now and needs a rest." Sarah and Marjorie helped Florence stand and escorted her out of the parlor and up to the Blair bedroom.

Downstairs Colonel Elliott stepped forward with his men. "Please let us escort you to your carts. It's time the household had some peace. We leave for Northampton in a day and all matters can be attended to there when everyone is a bit calmer."

Florence's mother refused to move, as did Edward's mother. They looked adamant and clearly didn't like each other. Soon two younger women stood and said almost in unison to the baroness, "Staying here won't improve your inheritance,

Mother. Florence will see who she pleases now." A young girl of about fourteen stood behind them, looking at her feet and saying absolutely nothing. Sensing that nobody would soon do anything she quickly left the room and followed Florence up the stairs.

Florence sat on the large four-poster bed breathing deeply. She no longer wept, but the stress of the last few days had unhinged her. "Florence, take care not to say anything to anyone except in the presence of your lawyer," Marjorie said. "Did you promise anyone anything?"

Florence began to weep again. "I think not. They all demanded so much at one time, and I don't even know what I have to give them. The lawyers haven't read the will out and there needs to be an accounting of the estate. Nobody expected Edward to die like this. Everyone's worried, although I don't understand my mother and mother-in-law. They're both well provided for."

"Darling, it's the prospect of getting more that excites them."

The door opened a crack and Florence looked up and murmured, "Sophie, I didn't know you were here. Come here and sit by me."

The young girl entered the room and curtsied to Sarah and Marjorie. Marjorie immediately embraced her. "Finally, someone Florence really wants to see. You stay right here with us." She looked at Sarah. "This is Florence's younger sister, the last left at home. All the rest are married or away at the wars."

Florence looked up and said, "Stay with me, darling. Yes, I have three brothers in the Queen's army and two married sisters and this lovely Sophie." She hugged Sophie and seemed to calm down.

Sophie whispered to Florence, "Robert came. He's hiding behind the horse guardsmen. He'd love to say a few words to you." She looked up at Sarah. "Robert is Edward's brother. He's a minister of the church and my parents don't like him much. His mother hardly thinks anything of him either, since he's only a second son. He was Edward's only civilized friend."

"Would you like us to send for Robert?" Sarah asked. "It would be no trouble."

Florence nodded and grasped Sophie's hand as they sat on the bed. Sarah promptly called for a servant to bring Robert. Sarah could see that the two sisters looked very much alike—both young and blond with light-blue eyes. Their ages were little more than three years apart.

Robert was in his early twenties and wore the black attire of the clergy. He stood shyly at the door once it opened, apparently too embarrassed to enter the room. Florence called out, "Robert, don't be silly. Come in. I want to talk to you."

Robert entered the room, the only man there. Marjorie pointed to a chair and he brought it over to where everyone else was sitting. "Please forgive us all, Florence. It's been a great shock. Your father was away when your mother heard of Edward's demise, and that's why everyone is here. Your father wouldn't have permitted this performance."

"You're kind to come, Robert. Edward's never been very good to you."

He laughed. "The lot of second sons who don't want to kill people. I'm honored to be here, Mrs. Blair, and to meet the two reverends. We've been talking about funeral orations."

Sarah nodded. "Yes, we have to be used to death, a natural follower for those who fight duels."

Robert pulled up his shoulders. "Florence, I want you to be aware that the lawyers will tell you things that only your father knew before."

"What do you wish to warn Florence about?" Sarah said.

"Well, it's the title. There's really been no Marquis of Northampton since the time of Queen Elizabeth. We're all Comptons, descended from one of our ancestors who served at the trial of Mary, Queen of Scots. There's always been the belief though, that if we could reestablish our finances, we could get the title of marquis restored. Comptons always call themselves *Marquis* out of habit, as it's an old title created by the last King Henry."

Florence laughed. "Is that what worries everyone? The Queen had me to lunch and was very kind to me, and plenty of baronesses come and go at the royal court. I expect once my mourning is over, I'll be asked again. Everyone addresses me as marchioness, whether they know the truth or not. I'm sorry I can't tell you about our finances, but I plan to see to that problem myself. I won't throw it away, and I care for my brothers and sisters and cousins. We'll just have to wait a bit."

"I hope I can stand at your side at the funeral, Florence," Robert said. "You'll be badgered by many people and you don't deserve that. You should keep the baby, as it's his father's ceremony, but leave the services as soon as you can."

"Thank you. Yes, stand by me along with Sophie. I'll have at least two nurses along with the baby. Try to get the bishop not to take too long."

"Not much chance of that," Marjorie said. "That will be his moment of the year. He'll stretch it out as long as he can. The crowd will be a captive audience. Robert, please go down and tell everyone they'll be received at Ashby. Make sure they leave us now. If Sophie wants to stay here she can. Florence has to see to choosing the pallbearers and all the other funeral arrangements."

"Oh, Florence, can I stay with you?" Sophie said. "Mother is in such a temper, and I don't know how it will be when Father returns."

"There's enough room. You can stay with me and Charley."

The next day a great funeral hearse arrived at Ravensport to transport the marquis back to Ashby Castle where he'd formally lie in state. Florence decided to bury him in his red coat alongside the arrow, though she'd been told that proper funeral attire would be white linen. Florence knew that Edward would have hated to be buried in white. The hearse carried the coffin and the marquis as Florence directed. The Blair household followed in two great coaches.

When they arrived at Ashby Castle the building was swathed in black cloth. Inside all mirrors were covered and all servants dressed in black. Florence wore black silk crepe made for her by a French Huguenot weaver from Spitalfields in London. She expected four to five hundred people for the funeral, and almost all would pay respects to the body as he lay in state in the great downstairs ballroom of the castle. She'd ordered some two hundred mourning rings she'd give away, all bearing Edward's name and crest. The rings, made of gold and black enamel, were an indicator of the wealth and status of the marquis, and its inscription announced that death came for everyone.

Florence knew Edward's closest friends and gambling partners. His two brothers and Florence's three brothers would serve as pallbearers along with three friends. The eight would move the coffin from Ashby to the hearse, then from the hearse into the church where they would hold up the black pall cloth draping it. After the service they would bear the coffin down to the church vault where the marquis would be interred next to his ancestors.

Ashby Castle was ready for the arrival of hundreds. Drinks were provided for everyone. Visitors could sit and commune about the departed in various quiet corners. Edward lay in state for fully ten days until all the pallbearers arrived.

⁂

Andrew and David spent the ten days in a hunting cabin out in the woods on the Ashby grounds. They swam and fished in wide streams and steered clear of invited guests as much as possible. They were, however, now famous. Edward's friends were anxious to meet the giant who felled Edward with an arrow. One of these friends turned out to be Daniel Parke of Virginia, an old acquaintance of the Blairs.

On a sunny afternoon, the day before the funeral service, Sarah and Marjorie rode out in a small cart with a picnic lunch to see the boys. Ashby Castle had been full of visitors and people from everywhere for more than a week, and they were ready for some peace and quiet. When they arrived at the hunting cabin they could see several great horses grazing in the nearby meadow.

They made their way to the rear where five men, including Andrew and David, were enjoying some beers. Daniel Parke stood holding David's bow. He was the only one in the company near David's height, as he was six feet four inches himself. A dark-complexioned man with high cheekbones, he had a contemptuous look on his face and an arrogant bearing, much as Sarah remembered him. She and Marjorie advanced to the table and put down the picnic lunch, enough for everyone.

When he saw Sarah, Parke bowed from the waist. "I'm honored, Mrs. Blair. How odd that fortune brings us together again."

Sarah remembered well when Daniel Parke had grabbed her by the arm and forcefully pulled her out of a church pew in Jamestown. "Yes. Odd. And somehow always to do with the church. I bring you greetings from a loving wife and two lovely daughters in Virginia. They hope their father keeps well." Sarah tried hard not to sound sarcastic.

"Yes. Of course. Have their husbands yet been chosen?"

"So, you know their ages. How thoughtful of you," Sarah said. "Have you something you wish to tell them when I return? Do you have an interest in your own flesh and blood?"

Andrew stood. Sarah seemed to be looking for an argument. The bad blood between her and Parke was obvious. Marjorie moved over and softly said, "Colonel Parke, I'm sure you don't remember me. I'm the Baroness of Exeter and I stayed with the Ludwells in Virginia for a few years when I was a child. I know Jane well and keep a close correspondence with her."

Parke smiled. "Yes, so I understand. I have a correspondence with Philip Ludwell myself. He's pleased with my work for the Duke of Marlborough."

"All of Virginia must be proud of you," Marjorie said.

"Of course I care for my girls," Parke said. "When they marry I hope they'll remember me and name a child after me. My duties here overcome me as we fight a great war in Europe. I leave for the continent soon. I hope you'll let them know that I care for them."

The next day Edward, Marquis of Northampton, took his place in the vault of the church. Florence stayed at the service for an hour; the sermons continued for four hours after she left. She stood next to her sister Sophie and Edward's brother Robert, and when she left they left with her.

The following week Daniel Parke left for his regiment, and the Blairs moved to Ravensport.

⚓

The marchioness wore mourning dress for three weeks after the funeral. That ended when she received an invitation to lunch with the Queen. She had a week to prepare.

"Well, I must visit the dressmakers," she said to Sarah. "I think you should come with me and order some clothes. We should start to invite some members of the Board of Trade, however discreetly. What do you think?"

Sarah was delighted at the prospect of visiting the city again. She'd spent the three weeks going over the estate's accounts and speaking to the lawyers and Tom Adams. She'd arranged to pay off the marquis' most prominent debts and sold off some of the furnishings in the Ravensport wings that had been occupied by his mistresses. She'd also supervised moving the Blair household. Marjorie and her family had left for Exeter but would return to their town house in the city in the next few weeks.

"I think it's time," Sarah said. "Let's visit the bankers while we're in the city and set up an account for you to use for regular purchases. I've left the estate lawyers in charge of your main business, wool and textile manufactures. You should get to know where your profits are being invested, but you may want to talk to the lawyers and accountants yourself. You can do that later and see which of Edward's things should go to his family members."

"Yes, yes. But I have lunch with the Queen and will probably see some useful people at the palace. We can talk about accounts later."

Sarah would have seen to the accounts first but this was London. Florence knew her way around, and Sarah was tired of talking to lawyers and accountants. She looked forward to a relaxed day of buying things. She asked Henry to get the cart ready, and soon they were off to the city. Andrew rode up front with Henry to provide protection. David stayed at Ravensport with Colonel Elliott and helped to review the thirty to fifty guardsmen who protected the great house.

Florence still wore black crepe and hoped her dressmaker would have a better understanding of what was needed for a lunch with the Queen. She ordered Henry to take them straight to her French dressmaker in Spitalfields. They drove through the town and on the way she decided to stop at her goldsmith, Pierce and Company.

Mr. Pierce was well known to London aristocrats and he'd known the late marquis very well. Florence had confiscated some unpaid-for jewelry from the three mistresses and added a few items of her own. As far as Florence knew, Pierce had never been fully paid for the items.

"Why deal with Mr. Pierce? Edward's dead and the mistresses no more. You don't have to keep reminding yourself of your days of unhappiness," Sarah said.

"I know, but Pierce didn't ask to be paid, and I was told they were unpaid for. Something seems not right there."

"Does he have a reputation?"

"Only that he's safe and expensive and will keep his mouth shut when necessary."

"You won't need his safety and keeping his mouth shut, will you? Why pay for something you don't need?"

"Well, it helps to have him as a sort of gossip. He knows what goes on, for a proper price of course. If you really want help with the Board of Trade, he can be of some service."

They entered Pierce's shop and were greeted by a small, dapper man of about fifty, dressed in fine green silk.

"Welcome, my ladies. I'm John Pierce, goldsmith. How can I help you?"

Florence extended her hand. "I'm pleased to make your acquaintance, sir. I'm the Marchioness of Northampton, and this is Mrs. Blair of Virginia. I've some jewels that were in my husband's possession when he died. I believe they're yours."

Florence gave Mr. Pierce a small leather bag, and he emptied it on a table. On the table sat a small diamond tiara, five gold rings, and four gold bracelets, one with diamonds inset, another with emeralds. Mr. Pierce looked at each item carefully and soon looked up at Florence.

"Yes, milady, I recognize these things. You have my sympathy for your recent loss. I thought it improper to ask for payment so soon after his lordship's unexpected demise."

"Well, thank you for your consideration. I have no personal use for the items, but perhaps I could open an account?"

"Let me see my account book. I believe the marquis may have opened one, though I may be mistaken."

Pierce walked over to a shelf on the wall and brought down

an account book. He turned some pages. "My lady, these items have been paid for partially. The marquis was here only a month ago and claimed he'd won a great deal at the gambling table. The emerald bracelet is all paid for and he owed a little on the rest."

Sarah looked around the jeweler's front room. He had a guard at the door, sitting on a chair at the entrance. The guard, a tall, muscular man with a full, black beard, wore a military-style tunic and was armed with knife and pistol. Other than that, there seemed to be very little security.

"Mr. Pierce, how do you keep your business safe?" Sarah said.

Pierce looked up and smiled. "Yes, this isn't Virginia, madam. We have a local militia that provides safety for the shops on this street. The goldsmiths are important to the life of the city, and we aren't bothered very much. I keep my best pieces in a very secure strongbox, which I've properly hidden."

"Mrs. Blair is of the Harrison family and may want to see some nice things to take back for friends and family," Florence said.

Pierce smiled broadly. "How wonderful you've come to London. I'll be happy to help you."

"No, no, not today. Help the marchioness with her account. How much are these items worth in trade?"

Pierce took a piece of parchment and began to write in pen and ink. He came up with a total of two hundred pounds. Sarah asked, "Is that for all pieces with precious stones included? I think Levy might give a better price for diamonds."

"So you've been to Levy? Yes, the Dutch favor diamonds above all else. I have a higher cost to maintain here, but I think I can handle two hundred fifty, if that's all right?"

Sarah and Florence walked to the edge of the room, and Florence laughed. "Do you think it's normal to bargain like this? It might be beneath the dignity of a marchioness."

"I imagine kings and queens bargain the same. It's nothing

to be ashamed of. There are goldsmiths all over London."

"Yes, but Pierce knows Edward's friends and Daniel Parke, as well as the Duke of Marlborough. He can be helpful for my luncheon and when you start to entertain the Board of Trade."

Sarah didn't know what to say to that. Florence knew the politics, the court, and what to expect at a queen's luncheon. They turned back to Pierce, and Florence said, "Two hundred fifty will be fine, Mr. Pierce. I know you depended a bit on the marquis, and I have no wish to harm you and your family."

"Well, thank you, milady. Can I offer you something, just as a gift, for continuing the account?" He held up two pearl earrings, and Florence smiled. "I can't accept a gift as lovely as this, but I'll be lunching with the Queen soon and I suppose pearls will be proper to wear for that."

"Oh yes, milady. I've heard about the luncheon."

Pierce proceed to tell Florence everything about the lunch, including everyone who'd been invited, what the Queen would likely be wearing, and the latest gossip about the ladies of the court. Florence thanked him profusely and looked happy for the first time in weeks. She decided to keep the pearls.

They left and ordered the cart to Spitalfields. "Do I have to still wear black?" Florence asked. "They know it's only a month since Edward's death. I don't want to shock everyone."

"The Queen invited you. How can it be shocking to accept the invitation of a queen?"

Florence looked worried, but soon they arrived at the shop of Pierre Bouquet, dressmaker to the London elite. Henry helped the ladies out of the cart, and Florence turned to Andrew and Henry. "This will take some time. Give us a few hours. Why don't you find something to eat and bring some food back with you?"

Henry and Andrew drove away, and the two ladies entered the dress shop. Florence saw Bouquet and immediately embraced him. "Oh, Pierre, what a performance a funeral is! I missed you and need your advice."

Pierre had made Florence's mourning clothes of black crepe. "What is proper for a widow one month after her husband's death at a queen's luncheon?" she asked.

Pierre bowed. He was tall and dark and not more than thirty. He wore a finely fitted burgundy, silk coat and breeches and sported a sharp, small mustache.

"Please accept my condolences, madam. I know you've suffered a great loss and have much to be anxious about."

Florence looked at Pierre and covered her mouth to hide a smile. Sarah saw everything and knew that Florence missed more than the clothing. Florence and Pierre were obviously good friends. "Let me introduce Mrs. Blair who's here from Virginia and will need a few things for her stay in London."

Pierre bowed to Sarah. "I'm at your service, my lady. What have we to do first?"

Florence went into the back room where three seamstresses sat sewing. Pierre took out some bolts of silk cloth and placed them on the main table in the front of the shop. He said to Sarah, "Please look at these and tell me what you'd like." He also placed some dress patterns before Sarah, who sat and started to look through them.

Over the next four hours Florence and Sarah chose patterns and fabrics, were fitted and refitted, and changed their minds many times. They enjoyed every minute of it and Pierre kept the conversation going throughout. When Henry and Andrew came back with the food, they were told to go out again and bring in more.

Finally, they made ready to leave. Florence would wear navy blue to the Queen's lunch, with some black crepe trim. Sarah ordered five gowns of different colors and patterns, all very modern and very French.

Florence went to the Queen's luncheon in her magnificent new gown with a black and navy-blue cap over her newly adorned hair and in a coach drawn by four white horses and accompanied by six footmen who had been militia for the marquis and were well acquainted with the royal court.

Sarah, amazed at the extravagance of simply attending a lunch, decided that it was time to see to her other shopping. She told Henry to get the cart ready and to call both Andrew and David. James had arranged to see some church friends in the city and took his own cart, driven by two Ravensport guardsmen.

When they were off Sarah told Henry to take her to Mendoza. Andrew was curious. "Where do we go today?"

"To see things you may want to bring back with you. I need to buy furnishings, cutlery, and ironware, and you need to see a proper forge if you're going to outfit your own. What would you like to see, David?"

"Well, I think we could use some knowledge of the firearms in use here. England's at war and the English have bought the best according to Colonel Elliott. The guns come from Germany and Switzerland he says."

"Well, we need to get an idea of how best to buy armaments. Perhaps Mendoza can suggest whom we should see. I'll want to negotiate prices, but first let's decide what we're buying. We'll need advice and visits to a few places."

On the way to Mendoza, they stopped at two ironmongers and bought some pots and pans. They asked where the goods were manufactured and asked for the names of nearby forges. The retailers recognized Andrew and David, whose reputation now had them as two giants from Virginia who angered very easily. They drew crowds and raucous shouting wherever they went.

When they finally made it to Mendoza, they had a claque of people on their heels asking for favors or offering a drink. They could hear "*Fee-Fie-Fo-Fum*" and "*Have a beer on me!*" The rest was hard to interpret, but they didn't feel threatened. They had to elbow their way into Mendoza's shop.

Samuel Mendoza looked very nervous at the sight of such a large crowd but welcomed Sarah and the two boys into the shop. "I'm afraid you're getting to know all sides of London, all except the kindness and forgiveness of people. Let me ask the crowd to move or we'll have to call the militia."

When he emerged from the shop, a dense crowd occupied fully half the street. Horses and carts had no room to pass. Mendoza shouted, "We're open for business, but we need an open street. Please calm down and let the people be. I don't want to call the militia."

He heard a generally grumpy mumble, and then the tavern on the corner sent out two tavern maids. "First beers on the house!" they shouted while waving at the tavern. Inside of ten minutes the crowd dissipated.

Mendoza returned to his shop smiling. "There you have London. You see, we manage and we're in it together."

"Yes, we're all in it together whether we like it or not," Sarah said, smiling. "You've got fine neighbors."

Mendoza shook hands with each of the boys, unbelieving of the height of both of them. "Let me introduce you. I have a houseguest from the New World, Captain Simon Grey."

Standing in one corner of the shop was a very tall, blond man with a moustache and hair down to his shoulders. His face was ruddy from being out of doors. Sarah recognized the look of a Virginian, either a farmer or seaman who spent most days in the sun and wind.

Captain Grey came forward and bowed. "Very pleased to meet you, Mrs. Blair. Samuel has told me about your arrival, and I'm afraid all of London thinks it knows all it needs to know about you. I'm sure it's much more interesting than tavern gossip. Also, I believe we have mutual acquaintances. I got to know Sheriff William Roscoe very well on his journeys to Charles Towne."

Sarah shook Grey's hand and looked at him, remembering her lover, William. They were nearly the same height, and there was something similar in the way they stood, erect and very tall.

Mrs. Mendoza and her son Israel came down with a tray of food and drink. Israel was a thin sixteen-year-old. Tallest in his family, he'd also heard the stories. He stood next to Andrew, who at six foot three was fully six inches taller than Israel. David, at six foot eight, could barely stand up in the shop. Israel laughed when he saw him and shouted, "I heard the stories and didn't believe. Now I believe everything!"

Mrs. Mendoza looked at her son. "These are our valued customers and deserve some peace and respect. Please, Mrs. Blair, sit and take some refreshment. We're delighted to see you and hope all is well."

"Thank you," Sarah said. "It's been very strenuous for us today. We can't seem to make much progress as the crowds follow wherever we go."

"Yes, unwanted celebrity can be tiring," Captain Grey said. "But you'll have fun with it. Have you selected a portrait painter? Now would be a good time to choose one. They'll be fighting all over themselves for a chance."

Sarah laughed. "The last and least of my current worries, Captain. If you have someone to recommend, I'd be interested. I'm here for other matters though."

Mendoza gave Andrew and David cups of tea and brought out chairs for them. Israel sat between them. "How can I help?" asked Mendoza.

"Well, we'd like to purchase some heavy equipment as well as furnishings. We'd like to build some forges and need the proper firing materials. Also, there's need for arms in Virginia. As you say, when you're on your own you have to see to your own safety."

Captain Grey nodded. "I know your difficulties well. The French send their Indian friends on raiding parties and slaughter whoever they find at home. I think I can suggest where you can obtain decent muskets and rifles."

"Mrs. Blair, while you're in the country, please take the time to see it," Mendoza said. "Go to Sheffield to purchase the cutlery. Go see the china makers and decide on your patterns. Go to the furniture manufacturers and make them show you what they're building right now. You'll enjoy the cleverness of the makers of things."

"I'm moving to an apartment not far from some furniture and portrait galleries," Captain Grey said. "I'd be happy to take you to see them."

Sarah said, "I believe Cunningham can negotiate decent prices on large purchases, and I'll need to make some for myself and some neighbors. We have so little manufacturing that almost any furniture, carpets, mirrors, and the like will easily be sold for a decent profit. I suppose it's a good idea to see what's being purchased and for what price before I tell Cunningham of the order."

"Let me give you the names of two importers of arms into England," Captain Grey said. "They come from Germany and Switzerland. Perhaps the boys can see them on their own or take some of their guard friends to look the materials over. I'm sure they can see to buying up forges on their own too." He laughed saying this, looking directly at David.

"Sir, I don't know what you've heard about us, but I can assure you we've never been the aggressor," David said. "We've merely defended a lady and her baby and ourselves when under attack."

"Perhaps you should tell us the whole story. Israel seems anxious to hear every word."

Andrew began and David interrupted every now and then.

They stood up to demonstrate and strutted around trying to show how the weapons were held and where they were located. The rest of the Mendoza children, a few of their friends, and some nursemaids soon occupied the stairs where they could hear the whole story.

Captain Grey applauded when they finished. "You can go on the stage with a story like that. I'm not joking. There are story tellers here that sell themselves with much less."

Sarah laughed. "Only in London can one live by selling stories."

Mendoza smiled at Sarah. "But we both know well, selling's the thing and whatever we trade it keeps us living. Now that we talk about it, you asked me to keep an eye for investments. I have a sugar plantation in Jamaica and perhaps some real estate in commercial property here in London. With the war, real estate will do well, though the Jamaica trade is somewhat more risky."

"Well, there are privateers and warships in the Caribbean, but a clever captain can find his market," Captain Grey said. "Sugar, after all, is a necessity."

"Do you have some descriptive materials I can look at?"

"Better than that for the London properties! I'll give you the address and you can see for yourself."

"Are you staying at Ravensport?" the captain asked.

"Yes, it's a help to the marchioness right now and we can better entertain the Board of Trade there."

"But it's a long drive if you're busy with matters in the town. Do you have anyone in the city with a place where you can stay?"

"I'm sure I could stay with the Baroness of Exeter, though I'm not sure where her town house is located."

"Oh, their house is near the Strand, very convenient," Mendoza said. "That would be very helpful if you could stay there while shopping. Really, think about it."

They spent the rest of the day going from shop to shop. Crowds still followed, and Henry struggled to keep people away from the two horses that pulled the cart. They began to get used to the noise level, and when they returned to Ravensport, David announced, "I'm going to the river for a swim." Andrew joined him. For over an hour they swam, trying to get the sounds of the city out of their heads.

CHAPTER 13

Over the next several weeks everyone buckled down to a normal routine. In the morning, Florence spent time with the baby and her younger sister Sophie who'd elected to stay at Ravensport. William Blair returned to Scotland, but James spent a few hours in the mornings providing lessons in reading and literature. He taught David, Andrew, Sophie, and a number of guardsmen and servants.

Florence had her hairdresser and dressmaker out three times a week and began to plan some small entertainments. She had some friends for lunch at least three times a week, and these small gatherings gradually began to grow into more elaborate meetings. Robert Compton also visited several times a week and assisted James in providing the lessons to the staff. Florence's parents stayed away; her father knew she didn't want to deal with her mother at this time.

Sarah, Andrew, and David continued shopping forays into town, and sometimes Sarah stayed with Marjorie at her town house. She often saw Captain Grey when in town and began sitting for a portrait with John Hargrave, a painter who lived a few houses down from Grey's rooms. Marjorie often invited Sarah and Captain Grey back to her place for supper.

Andrew and David stayed pretty much on their own or with some of the other guards or Colonel Elliott. They enjoyed London, visiting theaters, watching sports, and meeting other young people in taverns or at fairs. They found some friends in the town and often stayed overnight with them. Andrew still had his heart set on Suzanne of Charles Towne and wrote her long letters in his new London handwriting, much improved by the lessons of James Blair. David became very interested in a tavern maid named Penelope. She was dark and small and claimed to be Greek.

Over several weeks Florence and Sarah invited to Ravensport for lunch either the wife or current mistress of every member of the Board of Trade. Sometimes, when Florence knew the people, she invited both the wife and the mistress. Florence, because she had the ear of the Queen and had lunched with her, was more than popular—she was very much in demand. Everyone had a nephew or uncle for her to meet. Every eligible duke in the kingdom was sized up for her. Florence simply smiled calmly. She wasn't ready to marry again so soon, but she was getting ready to broaden her invitations to include some men.

One morning Florence said to Sarah, "Are you ready to meet the board? They certainly will be ready to meet you. Between the wives, the mistresses, and the street stories you are quite a celebrity!"

Sarah laughed. "What a disappointment I'll be! I'm only the minister's wife you know."

"Everyone knows you're the Harrison and that you've got Ravensport back on its feet. They'll be kind and respectful. I think you should meet them while they are talking about you, and I'm sure they're talking about you."

"Have you been saying things about us and Virginia?" Sarah asked.

"No harm, I assure you," Florence said. "Let's do a list and send out engraved invitations. How about a late afternoon supper? We could have musicians in front of the pond and tables set with delicacies outside or under tents. And of course, cards for playing and wine to drink."

"Remember James is a man of the church. He wouldn't like us to push gambling."

"No, but people have to have varieties of entertainments. Would Andrew and David like to show off some archery tricks? They're such famous archers now. We could invite the families, including children, from Whitehall?"

"That sounds better, much less formal. We can certainly get into conversation as to why we're here, but everyone will be boisterous and entertained at the same time."

By the time Sarah and Florence presented James with the invitation list, fully eighty people were included. Because the supper was so large, Florence decided on a head table that would include special guests. They'd include members of the Board of Trade and spouses—Lord Dartmouth, the Earl of Stamford, Lord Weymouth, Sir Philip Meadows, and John Pollexfen. The table would also hold herself and Robert, the Blairs, the Exeters, Captain Grey, Colonel Elliott, and Tom Adams.

"That gives us a head table of twenty-one," said Florence.

"Not very intimate for conversation," Sarah said. "Maybe the Exeters, Captain Grey, Colonel Elliott, and Tom Adams could be mixed with some of the others from Whitehall? Maybe Robert and Sophie could sit with them?"

"Sophie's very excited and has a lovely gown already. We need to get some young militiamen so we can have some dancing. I'll have the colonel select six for a special award." Florence enjoyed this part of the planning. She wanted her young sister to enjoy the party.

Sarah asked, "Should we invite Daniel Parke?"

"Certainly. He'll be here for the Duke of Marlborough. And the representative of Virginia here is Mr. William Byrd, who's quite renowned for repartee at parties. Do you know him?"

"I've met him and his family back in Virginia. His father isn't keeping very well but is highly respected."

"Well, that sounds like a good start. I think we've kept it under a hundred."

"I'm getting a little excited myself. I think it will be lovely. Thank you so much, Florence."

"Don't be foolish, Sarah. It's a sensible way for me to get back to seeing people without being too flagrant about my lack of grief."

"I'll ask the reverend to prepare a special toast to the hostess for her kindness, and we needn't mention much of anything else."

Two weeks later the guests started arriving in early afternoon. They were announced by four trumpets, and once they came down from their carriages six guardsmen, Andrew, and David greeted them and then invited them to the lawn to witness an archery contest in the medieval style.

The day was cool and sunny with a slight breeze as Ravensport had a high outlook over the river. As the guests gathered they could smell the slow roasting beef, the fine wine, and the additional complements to a sumptuous feast.

When the guests assembled, James welcomed everyone to Ravensport, mentioning the kindness of the marchioness and the warmth and support of the neighbors from Whitehall. Colonel Elliott, who announced the archery demonstration, followed his brief remarks. He assembled the archers, introducing each one by name. All, including Andrew and David, were wearing the uniform of the marquis' guard, dark green and gold. Targets were set up and distances measured. For the next hour the contest pitted the archers against each other. A large number of children watched and cheered, and after the demonstration they were allowed to hold the weapons or jump up and be carried on David's shoulders.

Florence introduced Sarah and James to the Earl of Dartmouth and Viscount Weymouth, Board of Trade members. Both of these aristocrats understood that they made money off trade, but neither had any sense of where Virginia was, how hard it was to raise a crop and ship it, and how dangerous war with France was for Virginians. Viscount Weymouth seemed more interested in gardening and had a keen interest in trees. The Earl of Dartmouth had a military background but had never visited the New World.

John Pollexfen, a man of about sixty and quite a bit older than the other two members, introduced himself after Weymouth and Dartmouth had wandered away.

"Let me introduce myself to the Virginians. I'm a son of a haberdasher myself, but I know how trade comes and goes and what war can do for and against it. I hope I can be of service."

James was delighted to meet this jolly fellow, who'd been elected to Parliament several times but now was on the board.

"We'll be making a presentation to the board soon. Our governor, Mr. Nicholson, has lost the support of many of the planters and has building plans that will bankrupt the colony."

"Yes, Nicholson is known for his arrogance," Pollexfen said. "He's already been recalled at least once I think. We'll be attentive I assure you. It wouldn't be a bad idea if you could come up with a name for a replacement. Have you thought of Edward Nott?" He pointed to another man of about sixty standing near the wine table. "Please let me introduce you. He's quite a fine fellow. You'll like him."

Sarah stood back while James and Pollexfen walked over

to Mr. Nott. She turned slightly and saw a well-dressed, young man bow to the waist and say, "My lady from Virginia, I'm your representative here, William Byrd!"

Sarah laughed out loud. "Oh, William, it's wonderful to see you again. Have you heard from your father?"

Byrd looked saddened. "He's not doing well. I'm afraid my days here are numbered as I'll have to go back to help out with the estate."

"Is there a Mrs. Byrd yet?"

"No, not yet for me at least. I'd hoped to meet a proper English lady but have yet to find the lady for me."

"Well, I wish you good fortune William. We may see each other again on the other side."

The dinner was warm and cordial and James felt ready to make his presentation. Pollexfen had recommended that he wait a few more weeks and what he should say in his remarks. For James this had been a fine supper.

⚜

James Blair took the advice of John Pollexfen very seriously. At the dinner he had a long talk with Edward Nott, and James felt he'd be a fine replacement for Nicholson as governor of Virginia. Sarah Blair sat next to Pollexfen at the dinner, and their conversation ranged from trade to politics to families. At the end of the evening Sarah and Pollexfen felt they understood each other very well.

Pollexfen asked, "How is it you're here, Mrs. Blair? It's most unusual for us to have the honor of meeting the spouses of those who come on business."

"Well, sir, my father, Mr. Benjamin Harrison, a great tobacco planter and shipper, asked me to come. I know more about the tobacco business than James. I handle our shipping and own several ships."

"Most ingenious. And are you enjoying London? I trust you find the shopping to your liking?" He smiled knowingly when he said this.

"Oh, very much, and Florence has been very kind and very helpful. It's quite the accident that we met in such peculiar circumstances."

"Yes, we've all heard about your brave young men. Make sure you take them home alive and in one piece."

"I've promised their parents as much. Do you recommend any particular goods or investments just now, Mr. Pollexfen?"

"Why, Mrs. Blair, I always say stay with what you know. If you wish to invest, why not buy a few more ships? They'll take your goods back for you and then you'll have the use of them later. Do the planters not own their own piers?"

"We're only beginning to move up to the James. My brother has the patent on some land but father is very frugal. I think the younger generation will do things differently."

"Well, no doubt the patriarch has to see to the health of the whole family. I, for one, have built myself a large London house, though for years my family occupied rooms above a wool shop down on the peninsula. Life's too short. In London, we enjoy what we can, whenever we can."

Something in Pollexfen reminded Sarah of her father. She was sure she could talk her father or her brother Benjamin into building a pier to hold ships. Both had taken on public duties and moved away from thinking of business. So had Pollexfen, whose Board of Trade duties seemed to subsume his interests in his own business.

Pollexfen recommended to James that he wait until the winter convoy of ships for Virginia left London before making his appeal to the board about Nicholson. Until then, the members of the board would be occupied with numerous small matters and the convoy would be taking much board correspondence back to the colony. Pollexfen believed that the board would be predisposed to hearing what James had to say—if he waited for the right moment to say it.

On March 4, 1704, James Blair submitted a petition to Queen Anne from six members of Virginia's Governor's Council asking that Francis Nicholson be removed as governor. Affidavits from a number of plaintiffs against Nicholson accompanied the petition. James had worked on the petition for six months.

James prepared to present the case for Virginia's Council at a full meeting of the board in its elaborate hearing room located in Scotland Yard on Whitehall Place. The Board of Trade and Plantations, formerly known as the Lords of Trade and Plantations, had evolved from a committee of the monarch's Privy Council to a permanent advisory board. In legal terms it only advised the Privy Council but was highly respected because of the long service of its members, some of whom had already served over twenty years. The board had a permanent secretary, Sir Robert Southwell, and an assistant secretary, William Blathwayt, who kept up a constant correspondence with all of the colonial governors and their agents. The board had become a clearinghouse of colonial information, and it recommended appointees as royal governors and prepared their instructions and commissions. The board also exercised a power of judicial review over cases starting in the colonies and appealed to the Privy Council.

The meeting on March 4 held a quorum of five board members: Viscount Weymouth, the Earl of Bridgewater, John Pollexfen, and Lord Dartmouth along with the presiding officer, Sir Philip Meadows. William Blathwayt acted as Secretary. Nicholson as a sitting governor could not attend but was represented by John Thrale, his agent for the colony in England. The meeting began with a welcome from the presiding officer. All of the members sat around a rectangular table in an ornate room that held a high, elaborate plaster ceiling. A large marble fireplace was lit and warmed the room. The boardroom didn't hold elaborate furniture other than bookcases full of documents and maps in every empty space and all corners of the room. The lords were attired in fine silks, wore elaborate perukes, and held their pewter pens above pieces of parchment. They were serious in their demeanor.

James stood and addressed the members. "We've divided our complaints into two categories—public issues that deal with the public order and private matters, which include matters pertaining to the Church of England.

"My lords, Governor Nicholson has abused his powers with respect to his council. The planters are concerned that his actions will endanger the health of the colony. Specifically, he altered county courts without advising the council; he appointed sheriffs without advice of the council; he chose county militia commanders from other than councilors; he avoided a fair audit of revenue in council; he convened the burgesses when spring planting required them on their farms; he refused to make college lands available for sale; and he kept from the council the instructions sent by the Board of Trade to guide Virginia's government."

Thrale stood and asked to respond. He said, "These are improper proceedings. The governor is entitled to see charges against him and to be able to respond accordingly."

Lord Dartmouth said to Thrale, "A sitting governor must see to his business. He may not leave the colony without permission, but you as his agent may represent his interests. Do you deny the specific facts, cited by the reverend? He's produced sworn affidavits by witnesses, all available for you to read. Do you have conflicting testimony?"

Thrale began to cough and eventually stood. "I request that these materials be sent to Virginia for the governor's response."

Sir Philip interrupted, "We are holding a full hearing and

the governor will receive all materials in due course. Mr. Thrale, how long has Colonel Nicholson been governor of Virginia?"

"He arrived in 1698, my lord. He was previously lieutenant governor some years before that."

"Well, he should by now know how to get along with the people who make up the colony," said Pollexfen.

Thrale responded, "My lords, these affidavits show that many of the complaints mischaracterize Mr. Nicholson, who is simply a faithful servant of the Queen, seeking to carry out your lordships' instructions."

"He has gotten along with almost nobody, and his current behavior frightens people," James said. "I've heard him often debase and vilify the gentlemen of the council, using to them the opprobrious names of rogue, rascal, cheat, dog, villain, and coward. I have heard him say they got their estates by cheating the people and swear that he valued them no more than dirt under his feet and that he would reduce them to their primitive nothing."

James decided to give his full presentation. He described Nicholson's "high, haughty, passionate, and abusive way of browbeating, discouraging, and threatening all that do not speak and vote as he would have them." He quoted Nicholson as threatening to ruin councilors and cut their throats. He accused Nicholson as having abused the whole assembly and of stirring up trouble between individuals, creating factions, spreading rumors, and belittling colonists.

All of these charges repeated the words of his written affidavit.

James criticized Nicholson as being unfaithful to England's parliamentary principles and the dictates of the Magna Carta. He noted that Nicholson accused the colonists as "very unjustly and disadvantageously grown rich and haughty, tainted with republican notions and principles, uneasy under any government, and ready to shake off their obedience to England."

Thrale never disputed James Blair's accusations, having no evidence or witnesses to the contrary. He took his leave that day, and a week later he died.

Nicholson sent no other representative to the board, which decided to send Nicholson the indictment submitted by Blair. These were transcribed and sent by ship in June. They didn't arrive in Virginia until December.

CHAPTER 14

Once James made his presentation to the board, he and Sarah began to think about returning to Virginia. His formal presentation had been well received, but business couldn't be considered complete until Nicholson was formally removed and replaced. James believed he'd made a strong case, but a little extra lobbying couldn't hurt. He talked to Sarah and they decided to stay in England until the board formally made a decision, and that meant waiting for Nicholson's written responses and the appointment of a new governor.

Sarah wasn't quite ready with her purchases and her portrait was still incomplete and the weather was warming. After a cold, gloomy winter, Sarah looked forward to seeing more of the country. James thought they should visit his brother William in Aberdeen before they left the country.

Florence also looked forward to the warm weather, and by the spring she had difficulty keeping her mother away. Every time relatives came, she heard the same commentary. "What a lovely little marquis! Have you thought of getting him a proper father? How long can you wear widow's weeds, with every duke and earl making you offers?"

The only calm Florence enjoyed came when Marjorie and Sarah informally lunched in the back garden next to a pond at Ravensport. One warm April morning, the three put together a picnic and sat on the grass next to the largest pond. They had a wonderful overlook onto trees and the river. Florence held baby Charley while a nurse stood by; servants carried the drinks and blankets. Charley was now eight months old and everyone's favorite. He giggled all the time, crawled on the blankets, turned over, and was beginning to say some words.

When Florence held him he said, "Mama," and laughed.

"Oh dear, I'll soon have to teach you *Papa*, I'm afraid," Florence said.

"Are you serious?" Marjorie quipped. "It isn't yet a year."

"But it will be by September. Between mother and the Queen I'd better figure Charley's future or they'll have my head. You're very kind to give me this space, but it can't work forever."

"Has the Queen spoken to you about it?" Marjorie asked.

Florence shook her head yes. "One of mother's friends is a lady of the court and keep's up the whispering to the Queen. The Queen herself is very kind and usually stops the talk of dukes and earls before it gets out of hand. You know, I'm a baroness or a marchioness and I don't think much of a title. Look at Pollexfen. He and his family live as well as anyone in England and without a title. I think I can marry whom I please and have title enough. I don't want a drunkard or a brute, and that eliminates a lot of our so-called aristocracy."

"Are you thinking of anyone in particular?" Sarah asked. "What about Robert? He adores you and the baby, and he's certainly no brute or drunkard."

"You know, I always liked him better than Edward, but Edward had the title and mother insisted on the title. Oh, how silly it all seems."

Marjorie thought a moment. "Have you been talking to Pollexfen? I'm sure the Lords of Trade have some suitable suggestions for you. Florence, you're very popular, so long as the debts are paid and the woolens being sold."

"And the ships, don't forget them. I apparently own two dozen, after selling five to Sarah. You know, I don't understand the gamblers. Why would you play games with all the property it took generations to put together? I never could understand Edward, or Daniel Parke for that matter."

Sarah thought about it. "You're doing well now, but investments are to help when things go poorly. My family made their fortune in tobacco and now shipping. My father is very like Pollexfen though. He leaves the business to others and worries about public affairs. The aristocrats would rather drink and gamble. Why do their families tolerate it? They should be leaders, not falling-down drunks."

Florence seemed stymied. "You know, you get the second sons. We make no place for them though we educate them. Look at the difference between Edward and Robert, only five years apart and looking very much alike. Edward thought more about having the reputation of an aristocrat than anything else. He always cared about how he looked and strode into a room. He wanted to be the talk of London society, and he didn't really care what they were saying. He had no serious interests and hardly ever looked at Charley. Robert loves to read and to teach, and nobody is better with Charley. Robert's not happy unless he's learning something new, and Charley's certainly new. Robert loves acting like an uncle."

"May I invite you all up to Exeter for a weekend?" Marjorie said. "I've already asked Captain Grey, and the boys will love it there. Won't you like to be away from the city for a bit?"

"James likes to visit with church and college people, and you have them up at Exeter," Sarah said. "I think it will be fine for us, whenever you want us. Perhaps we'll start our way up to Scotland at the same time."

Florence became enthusiastic. "We should plan your visit to Scotland. You have many friends and relatives to visit, and you could stop by Northampton on the way as well. We'll all have letters to write. Aberdeen is quite far. It takes weeks to get there. You might want to use one of the new ships and hug the coastline for part of the way, though I hate that kind of travel. It makes me seasick. The North Sea is rough all year."

All agreed that they should go soon, as the summer warmth disappeared so quickly. The Blairs planned to be back in London by September. Starting the visit to Scotland in May seemed the logical thing to do. It occurred to Sarah that it was last June when she began her voyage to London; she'd been away from home nearly a year. She'd written a number of letters home and received a few in return, but she missed her farm and family. She looked forward to the rest of the year, but she was already looking forward to Virginia.

❦

Three weeks later the large party from Ravensport arrived at the Baron of Exeter's country estate, a large, sprawling, stone home that abutted the town. The whole party was festive and included many of the household, including four nurses, a dozen guards, Andrew, David, Florence's sister Sophie, and Robert. Marjorie had tents up for shelter, as the weather was warm and beautiful.

Florence and Robert took Charley for a walk every morning, while James went into the church to talk to the ministers there. Sarah and Captain Grey either canoed around the ponds or found a path in the woods where they could take a picnic. Andrew and David hunted in the woods and tried out some new shotguns.

After a week in Exeter, on a lovely spring evening, the whole party assembled for a late supper. Florence spoke to the crowd.

"Robert and I have an announcement. We've decided to become engaged, when my year of mourning is complete. That will be September. We will marry this year, perhaps in October. I hope everyone here will be in attendance."

There were loud cheers of congratulations to the couple. They'd obviously thought about their situations for quite a while, and nobody was surprised. Florence's mother and mother-in-law would have to be informed, but Florence had matured over the last few months and could handle delicate diplomacy very well. Robert and she talked all the time and began to make decisions together. For now, he planned to stay in the ministry and teaching, but he'd eventually interest himself in some public office. Florence wanted to see him with ambitions she could support. They both were still young—he was twenty-two and she was eighteen—and still had most of their lives ahead of them.

Soon after the announcement, Andrew and David asked to talk to the Blairs. David asked to be excused from the trip to Scotland. He wanted to stay in London near Penelope, his small, Greek tavern girl. He'd agreed to help out at the tavern during the summer months, and London would be full of fairs and festivals. Andrew, on the other hand, still spent much of his time writing letters to Suzanne in Charles Towne. He was now making up poetry and including a French word or two. Like Sarah, he looked forward to returning home. He decided to accompany the Blairs to Scotland.

The Blairs agreed to the boys' plans. David would stay in London, at Ravensport, with Robert, Florence, and the rest of the household. Andrew, Henry, and Anne would come with the Blairs to Scotland. They wouldn't return to London until September, in plenty of time to help with the wedding and reception afterward.

Florence planned the wedding carefully. It was to be small but elegant. There were three hundred invited guests, and the archbishop of Canterbury in the cathedral at Westminster would perform the service. The Queen would stop by to offer congratulations. Florence was delighted that the Duke and Duchess of Marlborough and the Earl of Orkney would also attend. These were the Queen's leading generals in the current war with France.

<hr />

The wedding was held in early October, just as the leaves were changing color. Florence wore a gown of bright sky blue with gold trim, embellished with pearls and precious stones. Robert wore a dark-blue coat and white, silk breeches. They looked very handsome together and obviously were very happy.

When the Queen arrived for the ceremony and stayed for a few minutes to offer her best wishes, the wedding took on an atmosphere of kindness and good cheer. Everyone wished the bride and groom happiness, and the Queen spoke for everyone when she wished them well. Even the mother and mother-in-law looked happy, though most of the women cried when the final vows were spoken. Sarah stayed dry-eyed, but she felt great happiness for the newly-weds.

CHAPTER 15

Florence and Robert left for a month-long honeymoon, leaving Ravensport to the Blairs. After a year living on a great estate, James and Sarah now owned a great deal of personal property. They became serious about the journey home.

"Do we need all the books and manuscripts, or can we leave some for Robert?" Sarah asked.

"Well, we'd have to build a house with a library to keep all of it. I can sort through it. We can probably return some of it to the booksellers for credit. We can write for more books when we get home. Have you finished with the purchase of things for King Carter?"

"Hardly." Sarah laughed. "I think I've gotten him some large pieces he'll really admire, but I want to add a few more elegant things, like mirrors and Turkish carpets."

"We should be ready to go by the spring convoy, next April or May. Do you think you'll finish by then?"

"Well, I'll have to spend more time in the town and do some

visiting to manufacturers. There are furniture makers every-where, and I know the good quality importers now. I'd like to take Andrew out to see to everything he needs for his forge, though he has most things now. We need the finishing touches."

"Well, let's do this methodically. I think we won't hear of the board's final decision until early next year. They sent Nicholson our complaints in July. He should have received them by now, and he'll likely respond. I might have to make another presenta-tion."

"You needn't worry, the board's on our side. They want to keep tobacco flowing, just as much as we do. We've been very fortunate, James. All of our ships this past year got through in spite of brigands and warships. Now the war is winding down, and we have a fortune in credit that we can spend. Also, I have five more ships to carry the goods. We can sponsor many new businesses in Williamsburg after Nicholson is recalled."

James anticipated that Nicholson would send, along with his responses, a counter-attack charging him with neglecting his duties as commissary of the Anglican Church in Virginia. Many parish ministers in Virginia detested him, and James knew this. Nicholson could file complaints from witnesses with com-plete affidavits.

James also worried that the church now considered send-ing an Anglican bishop to Virginia. Such a functionary would be superior to James, and having a bishop would be a great honor for the Virginia colony. James heard that the church was con-sidering a well-known author who'd angered church authori-ties, Jonathan Swift. Swift had a wide following and served as an Anglican minister in Ireland. James meant to spend his last few months in London protecting himself from threats to his livelihood, wherever they might come from. He planned a full campaign of lobbying against Swift with friends in the church and on the Board of Trade.

Sarah began final preparations in November, spending every weekend with Marjorie, and making final purchases. She also visited John Hargrave whenever she could to have him finish her portrait. Often Captain Grey accompanied her on the shopping trips, as he was preparing to return to Carolina in the spring. He valued Sarah's taste in furnishings and fabrics.

When December came, the Blairs were still very busy. Sarah arrived at Marjorie's as usual but was greeted by a servant. "The baroness is delayed but left a note for you."

The note indicated that Marjorie had some shopping of her own in the town but that she'd invited Captain Grey for supper. She begged Sarah to make herself comfortable until she returned.

Sarah climbed the stairs to her usual room and heard a clicking noise. Someone down the hall had opened the door to see who it was. It was Simon Grey.

He smiled when he saw Sarah, "Our hostess wants our comfort and maybe a little match making besides."

"She has a romantic bent about things. Why don't you come down here to my room and make her happy while I sort out my things? Do you have much to do this weekend?"

"Well, Christmas is coming, but I won't have much celebration. When do you expect the return of bride and groom?"

"Not until the new year. We'll be quite on our own."

"Why don't you do something naughty and visit me in my apartments? I'm very near Hargrave, and we can decorate and celebrate New World style. We could invite some people if you wish."

"Oh, Simon, what a wonderful idea. I'd so like to spend a quiet evening or two, without going over lists and accounts and who knows what. Filling up seven ships isn't as easy as it sounds."

Simon laughed. "Yes, seven is quite a bundle, but there are so many people in Virginia. Are you sure you've got everyone covered?"

"What I don't know is whether James has Nicholson covered."

"I wouldn't worry about that. Nicholson can be moved without insulting anyone, and the board respects Virginia's planters, especially the Harrisons. By the way, where is James?"

"He's spending the week at the country place of the bishop of Salisbury. I think it's a reunion of old church friends. No ladies allowed." She laughed when she said this.

Sarah took a deep breath and looked at Simon. She saw so much of William in him. He was tall with broad shoulders and in his early thirties, as William would have been. She said, "It's been wonderful to know you, Simon. Do you have a family in Charles Towne?"

Grey looked at Sarah and took her hands. They sat next to each other on the bed. "Yes, I have a wife and three children, a boy of eight and two girls, six and four."

"What a lovely family. How well did you know William Roscoe? He used to take our ships down to Charles Towne every year."

They'd been waiting all these months to have this conversation, and both were ready. Grey knew William quite well and had traveled with him on occasion. He knew of Roscoe's seizing a prize, but he didn't know William had died soon after. Sarah no longer wept when she spoke of William, but when she spoke about him Grey knew she'd had a great loss.

"Mrs. Blair, am I being to forward to ask you to come to my quarters for the pleasure of an evening or two?" They both looked at each other, with so much in common and having shared so much over the last year. "Why, we have so little time left to spend together. We should take advantage of what we have, don't you think?" Grey said and pulled her close and kissed her.

Sarah soon stood, hearing loud noises from downstairs. Marjorie had obviously returned carrying many packages. She and Grey exchanged smiles and walked down together.

Marjorie made them sit next to each other in the parlor while she pulled out all the little items she planned to give away as gifts to family and friends. "I know you both must be planning your journeys back, and this past year has been a fright and a mess of work. This Christmas I want to see you both with some happiness, and I don't have proper gifts for you. I'll be going back to Exeter for the holiday. Would you like the use of this house while I'm away?" Marjorie had noticed the change in mood between Grey and Sarah. She smiled. "We really have so little time and so few are the chances for happiness. I want you to use this place."

Sarah spoke first. "You needn't worry your head about us. You've already been too kind. I don't know if I've ever had a better friend than you, Marjorie, and I wouldn't want to cause problems or have you subjected to embarrassing questions. We'll do fine, you can rest assured. Thank you for all your kindnesses."

Marjorie understood Sarah's meaning and smiled. They all went to bed that night in separate rooms, but Grey soon knocked at Sarah's door and ended up in her bed.

Over Christmas and into March, Sarah and Captain Simon Grey spent as much time together as they could. They never went out together except to shop. One of their favorite stops was to the artist Hargrave.

<hr />

Throughout 1704, the Board of Trade heard nothing from Francis Nicholson, though he did prepare responsive affidavits and sent them to London. The board had heard that Nicholson's affidavits were thrown overboard at sea to prevent them falling into the hands of the French.

By 1704, Nicholson had served as lieutenant governor of Virginia for nearly seven years. The Board of Trade decided not to get into legal arguments or discussion of personal affronts and insults and made its decision. It drafted a simple letter of recall to Nicholson, stating that the decision was based "not on any information or displeasure against you." Instead, the board believed that timely change was good for England's colonial service and that Nicholson's time had come.

Sarah and James Blair made their good-byes and sailed back to Virginia in March 1704. The new governor, Edward Nott, was expected to arrive on the summer convoy, in August 1704.

⌖

The months leading up to their departure were busy and at times hectic as Sarah packed and made an inventory of what was being shipped home and what was still needed. There were also lots of goodbyes.

Sarah's ships were laden with the finest European manufacturing. She'd been impressed with the loveliness of buildings and furnishings in London but became very selective about what she brought back. After fulfilling the wishes of friends and neighbors, and buying a few things for herself, what was she buying for? Williamsburg, after all, was only an idea in the mind of Nicholson, a governor who'd just been replaced. If it was to become a city, Sarah didn't want another London. Williamsburg wasn't a natural commercial place, like London, or for that matter, Charles Towne. She wanted to build a Virginia town, a place that Virginians would enjoy.

She spoke long hours with Grey about the logical purchases. "We like the life and the joy of having people from everywhere coming and exchanging ideas and pleasures. London has so much of that. Every kind of person lives in London—rich, poor, Anglican, every kind of non-conformist. Williamsburg can try for that, but we're so small. We don't need walls and private armies. We get along fairly well."

"You don't know what you're a capital of, but you'll be a capital," Grey said. "You'll have the college, the burgesses, and the governor. Think of what to build on that. Also, don't think so much of London. Virginians really don't face the ocean. They face the west—the mountains, the rivers, the land. That's where they'll be building."

So, Sarah brought what she thought would be handy for building a town, and she engaged some people and craftsmen to come and start their small businesses along Duke of Gloucester Street. She paid their passage, provided cash to bring their tools and materials, and took a fifty percent interest in their businesses. If they succeeded, she would gain from it.

Sarah brought an apothecary, a basket maker, two cabinetmakers, and a cooper, a milliner who was married to a tailor, a shoemaker, and a wheelwright. She knew some would end up on the plantations, but if the city was to become a real city, she favored being ahead of the game, not chasing after it. She didn't worry about the risks. Skillful people willing to work would always be a gain to the colony.

⟨⟩

For two weeks, Sarah packed and shopped for last minute items. She also said her goodbyes. She made a last visit to Marjorie at her town house. When she got there, Simon was there and greeted her warmly. He was leaving on his ship, the *Sweet Susan*, and would be part of the same convoy as the Blairs.

"Have you got the painting?" Simon asked. "I saw Hargrave at the gallery, but didn't see it."

"I thought I would say my goodbyes to Marjorie and then go over and get it. I'd like to make stops at Mendoza and Levy on the way."

"I have a cart here. I'll take you, if that's all right."

"That would be wonderful." Sarah looked at Marjorie and said, "Thank you for everything. I'll write you when we get home. The captain thinks it will be a short but rough crossing, about six weeks or so. We'll be home by end of April."

"I'll miss both of you," said Marjorie, near tears. "I hope you'll remember us for the good things. Florence and Robert are in your debt, and so is the Board of Trade."

Sarah blushed. "You've given me more than I ever expected." Then she looked at Grey. "And so have you. I'd been in sorrow and despair for quite a while until I met you, Simon. Now I can look forward again. I hope I haven't been a burden for you. I know I've taken up a lot of your time."

"I wouldn't have had it any other way, Sarah. You know how I feel about you."

They embraced, took their goodbyes, and then took off on their last errands.

Sarah kept her account with Mendoza and promised to write him either directly or through Cunningham. She bought a few pieces of jewelry from Levy to use as gifts. She then went to Hargrave and picked up the portrait.

Sarah spent that night with Grey at his quarters. They had a light supper and went to bed early as both had much to do the next day. They made love, and though Sarah thought she might be pregnant, she decided not to say anything to Grey. He had a wife and family to whom he'd return, and she didn't want to give him something to worry about.

⸻

Just two weeks before they left London, David informed Penelope of his decision to return to Virginia. Penelope's parents adored David and wanted him to stay in London. The parents, Alexander and Lydia Paulus, were well established in London's

Greek community. Over the previous six months, they tried to entice David with offers of a tavern of his own, a restaurant, or an inn. The Greek community in London dated back hundreds of years, and David had become a heroic figure to Penelope's family. His job at the tavern over the summer had primarily been to keep the peace and evict troublemakers. Penelope's parents thought of David as an ancient Greek of legend, and they knew that Penelope was in love with him.

Penelope knew that David wouldn't stay. He missed the open woods and fields of Virginia, and as his parents' oldest son, he felt obligated to return to help them with their small tobacco plantation. London had kept him busy and amused, and he loved Penelope, but he couldn't stay in London. He needed the outdoors.

When he told them he would soon leave London, Penelope's father said to David, "We should have a long talk. You mean too much to all of us for just a simple goodbye."

Penelope's mother started. "I can see that both of you love each other and want a life together. We want your happiness more than anything, and for me, I would be proud to have you as son, David."

Then Penelope's father said to Penelope, "If he can't stay here, do you want to cross the ocean and live in Virginia?"

Penelope was ready for the question. "Not unless he asks me to come."

The parents looked at David and then moved to a corner of the tavern to give David and Penelope a little privacy. When she leaped up and kissed him, they moved back. Her father asked, "Has something been decided?"

Penelope was so happy she was nearly in tears. "I'll go with him and we want to be married before we go."

At this David sheepishly said, "Yes, we should for your sake. When we get to my parents, I'm sure we'll have to do the same again."

"But we would want you to have a proper Greek wedding."

"I'm not Greek, sir," said David.

"To us you are. Can you swear to be a good husband in our religion?"

"Of course, but will that satisfy all your relatives?"

"We'll do the wedding right now and right here," said the father.

Alexander Paulus closed the tavern and sent his twelve-year-old son, Gregory, to round up as many of the relatives he could find. The young boy came back with almost eighty people, all aunts, uncles, cousins, grandparents, and Penelope's four brothers and three sisters.

Penelope's maternal grandmother walked up to David and introduced her nephew, George. He was a justice of the peace and empowered to issue a marriage certificate. She said to David, "We're proud to have you in our family, and George is very good at marriages. The Queen has never challenged any of them. You'll have a certificate to take with you."

She was tiny and motioned to David to bend down. When he did so, she kissed him and shouted, "Let's have a wedding. George is ready!"

The ceremony was short, the party long and boisterous. When it was over, Penelope realized she wouldn't see her parents or brothers and sisters again for a long time, if ever, but when she looked at David, she didn't care.

David took her home to Ravensport for the two weeks before they embarked on the ship. When they arrived, they found Andrew in the front hallway and David told Andrew his news. Andrew smiled. "Why weren't we invited?" He ran out to tell Henry and Anne and soon the whole household knew. After an hour, Florence and Robert and the Blairs came downstairs to greet them and wish them well.

"Oh, David. I see you're a hero to more than just me," Florence said. "Is Ravensport going to provide your honeymoon?"

Both David and Penelope were embarrassed, but Penelope soon said, "We could go to an inn or something, if this is a problem."

"A problem? Ravensport is as good as any inn," Robert said. "How about the cottage next to the pond behind the east wing? It's very private, and you'll have the pond to yourselves."

Everyone had expected some news from David, but this surprised them. Anne hugged Penelope. "Let's get you settled. Henry and I will be cooking a good old Virginia ham dinner tonight, all you can eat other than cornbread. I hope you'll like it. Virginia food isn't the same as good old London's."

CHAPTER 16

The end of March was blustery and snowy. For Sarah, James, and their contingent the voyage couldn't have been more uncomfortable. They were cold and confined to small cabins below, while the ships sailed from one rain storm to another and were tossed about like corks floating in running water.

The convoy to Virginia contained thirty ships: twenty merchant ships and ten war ships. The merchant ships were laden heavily with goods and lay low in the water, but trade winds favored them and they made good time.

The Blairs stayed on the *Brave William*, where their cabin was more comfortable and spacious. Their party included a dozen people plus crew. Sailing with them were the servants, Andrew, David, and David's new wife, Penelope.

Sarah stayed in the cabin, quite sick for most of the voyage. "When we get to Jamestown, I'd like to go to Benjamin and Elizabeth for the first few days," she told James.

James looked at his wife and knew she felt awful. She was

pale and had dark rings under the eyes. "Yes. Elizabeth can take care of you better than I. I'll be very busy with the council and the college when we get home. I'll ask Archie to look in on you."

***

After seven weeks at sea, the ships arrived at the pier in Jamestown on a sunny April Wednesday. The ships were met by the usual warehousemen, and Benjamin Harrison III, Sarah's brother, had sent his carriage. The Blairs were happy to be on dry land and in Virginia.

Andrew, David, and Penelope were met by David's parents and quickly left for Yorktown. Simon Grey stopped at Jamestown for provisioning and took the *Sweet Susan* to Charles Towne the next day.

***

When they arrived in Jamestown, not much had changed. The town had an active pier and a number of warehouses but no more than thirty buildings. The Blairs went immediately to the small plantation of Sarah's brother, Benjamin Harrison III, and Elizabeth immediately took Sarah upstairs and to bed.

Down in the parlor, Benjamin said to James, "I hope you'll stay with us here a while. You both look thin and tired."

"The voyage was wet and turbulent but we're here in just six weeks. I've much to do. We've had great success with the Board of Trade," James said.

"Yes, the council will want to hear everything. Do you know the new governor?"

"Yes, we met him and some of his friends. Mr. Nott is a favorite of many of the members of the board, and he'll be congenial to deal with. He's nothing like Nicholson."

"When can we expect him?"

"I believe he'll be on the next convoy, probably in August."

"Well, Nicholson will leave few friends, though many think he's right about building a city of Williamsburg. We have a new General Assembly Building, and the House enjoys the new establishments along Duke of Gloucester Street."

"Well, maybe we'll see a town at last. I'm pleased to hear it."

Upstairs Elizabeth asked Sarah, "Let me get you something to drink. You look poorly."

"A little tea would be good. You needn't worry too much. I'll be fine now that we're on solid land." Elizabeth knocked at the door and asked a servant to bring some tea.

Elizabeth looked at her sister-in-law and hugged her. "I've missed you very much. Benjamin IV is at the grammar school and will be back tomorrow. He missed you as well. He's turning out to be a tall, brave boy, like his father a bit."

"You've been wonderful. How do you think he'd like a brother or sister?"

Elizabeth laughed. "Do you mean it? It would be wonderful. You know your father has just about given up on me. I'd love another one, and you'll be around for everything, I hope."

"Of course, I wouldn't have it any other way."

"Tell me about the father."

"He's tall and blond and a seaman out of Carolina. He knew William and spent the last year in London doing very much what I was doing, loading ships for the voyage back. He's a very kind man but doesn't know about the baby. I thought not to worry his head about it, as we can care for the child without him being involved."

"But you'll see him again. Don't you think you should at least tell him he's the father?"

"Let's wait for the arrival. If he comes back to Jamestown now and then and I see him, I'll certainly tell him. Well, tell me the news of Virginia. How is Lucy?"

"Did you receive no news? Lucy married Mr. Edmund Berkeley two years ago, just a few months after you left for London, and the governor slit nobody's throat. She already has a new baby, Edmund. Lucy seems very happy, and our boy Benjamin is very taken with having a young little boy as a cousin. Stay with us a bit now. Lucy and Edmund will come for the weekend."

"I wouldn't miss it. I suppose Father will want a large party soon. James is delighted with how things went, and I have much to tell everyone. Daniel is a great hero you know. The Queen granted him a governorship, and he's very much the grand Englishman."

"No change there. You know, old William Byrd died last year and young William is back. He arrived just three weeks ago and seems to be serious about taking an interest in his estates. Father thinks he'll be a serious planter, although I'm sure he still has an interest in the government. He's been agent for Virginia for so long. But to meet him he seems to want to be a proper English gentleman."

Sarah laughed. "I met him at several dinners and festive occasions. When you see him next to the English, he's not English at all. Here he seems more English than anyone born here. He's very amusing and can be quite sarcastic. He can't help himself. His brain is so quick that his mouth can't keep up. When he tries to control it, he makes jokes. He needs to always express himself. Did he bring back an English wife?"

"No, but he has an eye on Lucy Parke."

"Jane will be happy, but is a Byrd good enough for the grandfather, Philip Ludwell?"

"I can't tell you everything, but Daniel has been contacted by more than one father of a potential groom. There's not only Lucy but also Frances. Do you think Daniel is solvent?"

"Governors do well, but Daniel is and always has been profligate. Nobody knows what kind of governor he'll make, but right now he's the hero of the hour."

Elizabeth heard a knock at the door. It was the maid, who

carried in some tea and then left. Elizabeth said, "Well, we can relax a bit. Do you want Archie to come over and look at you?"

"I see no problem, but I know if I get back to a normal life, I'll feel well. I trust Archie. James will never know or suspect anything. He surely won't say anything. I think I'll be ready to come to you by the end of the summer, after the crop has been harvested. You should think about an announcement in a month or two."

"We expect the new governor by the end of the summer. James and the council will be busy greeting him. They'll have many meetings at the new House of Burgesses. That would be a good time for you to come to me for the duration, don't you think?"

Both of them smiled at each other and sipped their tea.

❦

The next day, James rode over to his brother Archie and asked him to look in on Sarah. He then rode to the college to see how the grammar school had progressed. The college still had some apartments for members of the House of Burgesses but most had moved to rooms near the new General Assembly Building. Some taverns and inns had opened along Duke of Gloucester Street and Archie's general store was doing great business.

Over the next several weeks Sarah gained her strength back and saw to the unloading and resale of the merchandise from London. She also took out another lease on her small plantation from Philip Ludwell. Twice a week she rode out to the tobacco field and spoke to David's father who was helping her with the crop. In June, the Simmonses held a second wedding celebration for David and Penelope and both Sarah and James attended. Andrew wasn't there. He'd gone down to Charles Towne on Simon Grey's ship and still hadn't returned.

"Welcome and congratulations again. How are you keeping here?" Sarah asked Penelope.

"Very well, Mrs. Blair! We have our own tobacco patch, but I think I'll get David to put up a little tavern in Gloucester. I'm more used to having people come by, and people are so far apart here. What do you think?"

"Well, it's a good idea to see where the town center will be. Have you thought about coming to Williamsburg? Has Andrew decided where his forge will be? We hope we'll have a real capital city before too long."

"Well, we think we'll stay close to home just now and would want to talk to Andrew before making major decisions. Andrew's taking his time about returning. We've gotten most of his goods unloaded near where his father's forge used to be, but maybe he'd be better building a new one closer to where the stables are. Maybe he'd like to think about Williamsburg, too. Depends on Suzanne I suppose."

"Have you heard anything from Andrew? He took off in April and should be back by now."

David said, "Other sailors are back from Charles Towne and told us that the Dubois were happy to see him and that Suzanne consented to marry him. They let Andrew's mother know by sending a sloop with some seamen. Andrew's mother went down to the wedding on the sloop, along with some cousins. We've been staying at her house and expect them back very soon."

⁕

The celebration of David's marriage to Penelope was attended by several hundred people and included many Pamunkey, David's mother's relatives. David's father asked James to say a few words, and he complied, though there was no religious service. There was plenty of chanting in Pamunkey and songs and music and dancing and drinking and eating. Penelope, who was the smallest person there, looked a little anxious and held David's hand throughout the event.

In August, the new governor, Edward Nott, arrived in Williamsburg and James moved back to his apartment in the Wren Building of the college. He and the council had planned meetings with Nott and had a full agenda. Sarah went to her sister-in-law Elizabeth. Her brother Benjamin, as attorney general, stayed in Williamsburg as he had much business with the new governor as well.

Six weeks later, Sarah gave birth to a healthy baby girl. The baby was long and blond but had the Harrison high cheekbones. Though the leaders of the colony were busy in the capital with the new governor, they soon heard that Attorney General Benjamin Harrison III and his wife Elizabeth were now the parents of a new baby daughter, who'd been named Elizabeth, after her mother. Benjamin IV was delighted to have a new baby sister, but he would have preferred a brother.

The following summer Williamsburg celebrated two great weddings. On the same day in June, Lucy Parke married William Byrd II and her sister Frances married John Custis. Daniel Parke had consented to both matches, and all of the great planters, spouses, and relatives attended the enormous wedding celebration.

CHAPTER 17

The arrival of the new governor, Edward Nott, in August 1705 was a great occasion, complete with parties and fireworks and warm welcomes by the council members and the burgesses. The House of Burgesses, which had met every year under Nicholson, came out to greet the governor. They no longer met at the college's Wren Building. Since 1704 they met in a new Capitol building. Williamsburg was still only one long street stretching from the college to the assembly building, but the people imagined a great future.

Nott was a mild and benevolent person, well liked by everyone. He rented a small plantation near Williamsburg and entertained the burgesses and council members. The rancor of the Nicholson years faded away, but the weather was hot and humid, and Nott couldn't adjust to the change in food and drink. By the end of the year he took ill and took to his bed. He died in the summer of 1706. James Blair presided over his funeral service in August, and Nott was buried behind Bruton Parish

Church on Duke of Gloucester Street.

Edmund Jenings, President of the Governor's Council, became acting governor when Nott died. As acting governor, he exercised little power and wasn't highly respected by members of the council. The burgesses continued to meet every year and take whatever measures seemed necessary. As usual, they taxed and spent as little as possible.

Virginia was growing, no matter who the governor was or what the burgesses did. Immigrants were entering the colony in large numbers. Between 1700 and 1710 Virginia's population increased by half to over 80,000; almost a third of the population of all the English colonies in North America lived in Virginia. Though war between Britain and France continued, exports were up by fifty percent as well, and the planters felt rich.

In October 1707, Benjamin Harrison III invited the members of the council to his home for a birthday celebration. His father was to be sixty-two and his daughter two, a fair occasion for a large party. The house held well over two hundred people and food, drink, and games were the order of the day.

Towards evening, the two elder Benjamin Harrisons, William Byrd, Lewis Burwell, Philip Ludwell I and II, and Robert Carter sat comfortably on benches under a large maple tree that was turning bright red. Benjamin II said to his son, "Thank you for the party. At my age, one begins to count blessings, and our family is a great blessing to me."

"Don't be sad, Father," said Benjamin III, and in this he was joined by the others. Benjamin II was an older member now and held in high regard by the men. Since the death of William Byrd I two years earlier, Benjamin II, Lewis Burwell, and Philip Ludwell I had become elder statesmen to the younger generation.

"You know, we aren't that far from the starving times," Benjamin II said. "I hope the children don't forget that. Very many people died before Virginia became a place to live. Now we're

England's biggest colony, and we're growing so fast I fear we'll forget where we came from."

Burwell laughed. "Yes, but we also have to remember where we're going."

"Yes, indeed, always look forward. That's how we got here, by pushing ahead and letting anyone who wanted to help push forward with us," Ludwell I said.

James Blair moved over to the group and found a seat. "Have you heard? Queen Anne has signed onto the Act of Union. Scotland is now part of the United Kingdom. I'm as British as anyone here!"

"Welcome to the club," everyone shouted, and James received a pat on the shoulder from his father-in-law.

"Well, now you don't have to worry about being kicked off the council for birth reasons," Benjamin II said. "I suppose you'll want to be governor next." That brought a round of guffaws from everyone. Benjamin II continued, "Jenings sits as acting governor. He does little and Virginia prospers. James wouldn't want to be that kind of governor."

James worried about the college. The Wren Building, his great accomplishment of 1699, still stood in ruins from the great fire of October 1705. The fire had gutted the inside of the building but left the outer walls standing. Most of the furniture, books, and records were destroyed. The grammar school now met at small temporary structures on the college campus, and the House of Burgesses hadn't appropriated money for the rebuilding.

"I've received a note from the board in London," Benjamin II said. "They've appointed Robert Hunter, a military man, to be our next governor. Unfortunately, the French took the ship that was to carry him here. They're holding him hostage in France, demanding he be exchanged for the bishop of Quebec, who's being held someplace in London. It looks like we'll have Jenings a while longer."

"The Board of Trade gets what it asks for," Ludwell I said. "The last true governor we had was Andros, a knight and true governor general. Everyone since has been a lieutenant for the Earl of Orkney, one of the Queen's great generals. Orkney served Marlborough at the Battle of Blenheim and likely will never come to Virginia. It's as well that we can deal with the likes of Jenings. Virginia needs us."

"Virginia is us, and we are Virginia, as is the House of Burgesses," Benjamin II said. "So long as we can keep our people together and listen to their needs, we needn't fear any governor."

Philip Ludwell I reminisced. "Yes, I can remember Lady Frances, my dear departed wife's thoughts on this. She owned much land in Albemarle and Carolina, but she was a Virginian, and her husband, Sir William, was governor here for forty years, before and after Cromwell. We've had no governor of our own since. We'll have to be vigilant whatever happens. Our illustrious commissary may have to remove another one of the louts."

The group cheered James when they heard this. Everyone gave him credit for getting rid of Nicholson. He smiled and said, "Yes, and there will apparently be no bishop for Virginia either. They seem to think we don't need anyone. We'll have to be on our own. That evidently suits everyone here."

While the men conversed outside, the ladies had gathered in the parlor. Elizabeth, Sarah, Lucy Burwell Berkeley, Jane Parke, and Mrs. Custis Hill were enjoying the evening and each other's company. They all congratulated Jane on becoming a grandmother; Lucy Byrd had given birth to a baby girl just a few months earlier.

Mrs. Custis Hill asked Jane, "How do the newly-wed couples get along? I hope we'll soon be grandmothers together, but John and Fidelia seem to have nothing but shouting words for each other."

"Shouting words never stopped raising a family. I believe we'll be celebrating together soon, with John and Fidelia, within the year," Jane said. "As for Lucy and William, he talks and talks and she weeps because she thinks he makes fun of her. Then he apologizes and soon starts the talk again. It's a mysterious relationship. They care for each other but make each other very angry."

Mrs. Custis Hill wondered aloud. "Maybe they know something we don't. A good argument now and then may keep them together. I don't really understand the young people at all. We always tried to understand each other. I got along with all of my four departed husbands. We all could get along with virtually anyone, trading with Catholics in Maryland, privateers from Carolina, French Huguenots." She then said to Sarah, "Well, nearly two years in London and you're back in one piece. Did you have to shoot anyone?"

Sarah laughed and then told the tales of their arrival, the visit to Newgate Prison, the duel, and the heroics of Andrew and David. She spoke in her relaxed Virginia drawl, which had lost all connection to the clipped English speech with which she'd recently been surrounded.

Lucy asked, "Did you like London?"

"Well, I don't know what to say. It's an amazing place full of hard-working, vibrant people from many places. I loved the shopping and the camaraderie, but I can't imagine living there all the time. The aristocracy is very rich and doesn't even notice the rest of the city. The Queen and the aristocracy fight the wars and incur the debts. They have a parliament, but a few aristocrats dominate that. Not like our House of Burgesses at all. London is hardly represented in the Parliament. The city sort of goes its merry way, grows, becomes well-off from trade, and has no formal law and order at all. I suppose it's like Virginia. Most of England doesn't know we exist, either."

The women smiled and toasted Sarah. "Let's hope we can keep it that way," Mrs. Custis Hill said.

Jenings remained as acting governor, and Queen Anne designated a thousand pounds from the colony's quitrents to rebuild the college in 1709. Virginia's government did little, and the colony continued to grow and prosper. The planters started to amass vast land estates and built piers that would hold many ships. Virginia looked west when in 1710 a new lieutenant governor arrived, a military man sent by the Earl of Orkney, Alexander Spotswood.

Genealogy

SARAH HARRISON BLAIR died in 1713 at the age of forty-three. She undoubtedly could read and write, and she accompanied her husband James to London to lobby against Governor Nicholson. While in London she had her portrait painted by John Hargrave. The painting is in the collection of the Muscarelle Museum in Williamsburg, VA.

The Harrison family, one of the wealthiest in Virginia, became leaders in support of revolution.

BENJAMIN HARRISON III, Sarah's brother, became attorney general of the colony and Speaker of the House of Burgesses but died at the age of thirty-three in 1710. He bought a patent for land on the James River and moved his family estate from Surry to the Berkeley Plantation.

BENJAMIN HARRISON IV expanded the family's land holdings considerably. He built a famous plantation house, in-

stalled large dock facilities, and became one of the largest to-
bacco planters in Virginia. He owned a fleet of merchant ships.
Benjamin Harrison IV fathered ten children, the oldest being
Benjamin Harrison V.

BENJAMIN HARRISON V attended William and Mary
where he studied under law professor George Wythe and was
a classmate of Thomas Jefferson. While he was a student, the
Harrison manor house was struck by lightning, killing his father
and two sisters. Benjamin Harrison V left college and returned
home to run the estates. He eventually became actively involved
in politics and was elected to the House of Burgesses in 1764. In
1773 he was appointed delegate of Virginia to the Continental
Congress in Philadelphia and in 1776 was a Virginia signer of
the Declaration of Independence. Benjamin Harrison V served
as governor of Virginia in 1782.

His son, **WILLIAM HENRY HARRISON**, was governor
of Indiana Territory from 1801 to 1812 and was elected as the
ninth President of the United States in 1840.

BENJAMIN HARRISON VII, grandson of William Henry Harrison, was a senator from Indiana from 1881 to 1887 and
elected as the twenty-third President of the United States in
1888.

JAMES BLAIR had no natural descendants. A clergyman
and lobbyist, he amassed some personal wealth, but he was disliked for most of his life by most of the people who knew him.
His brother Archibald Blair became a leading merchant, a burgess, and was widely respected in the community. Archibald
Blair had at least five children. One of Archibald's daughters,
Elizabeth, married John Bolling Jr., a great-grandson of Poca-
hontas and John Rolfe.

Probably the most lasting legacy of James Blair is the College of William and Mary. Blair was the first president of the college and remained in that office for fifty years. For the first thirty years, the college remained primarily a grammar school.

While Blair wished to produce ministers for the Church of England, he was too avaricious to pay his faculty. Blair spent a lifetime fighting with governors, William and Mary faculty, and the Anglican ministers in Virginia. He managed to have a President's House built on the campus, but this wasn't completed until 1723.

After Blair's death in 1743 the college underwent a transformation. It housed a full faculty that taught the leading subjects of the day: natural science and mathematics, law, and moral philosophy. In 1747, the Capitol building burned, and the burgesses moved to the college buildings. During this period, the college became a distinguished law school under the guidance of George Wythe, law professor to Thomas Jefferson and Benjamin Harrison V. George Washington obtained his license to be a surveyor from William and Mary in 1747.

William and Mary trained very few ministers of religion. Its most famous graduates were statesmen: Presidents Thomas Jefferson, James Monroe, and John Tyler, Chief Justice John Marshall, Speaker of the House Henry Clay, and sixteen signers of the Declaration of Independence. Phi Beta Kappa, the academic honor society, was founded at William and Mary in 1776.

In his final years, Blair remained avaricious as ever, amassing property wherever possible. He also continued to whine and complain about all governors. Governor William Gooch described Blair as "a vile old fellow, hated abominably by all men."

FRANCIS NICHOLSON died a bachelor in London in 1728. In 1705 the Board of Trade recalled Nicholson, who rejoined the military to fight the French in Queen Anne's War.

Queen Anne's War followed the War of the Spanish Succession in North America. In 1710, the English lost Nova Scotia to the French, and Nicholson led an expedition that year that recaptured Port Royal, Nova Scotia. He returned to London with five Iroquois chiefs and petitioned the Queen to allow him to join an expedition to conquer New France. When the naval part of the expedition failed, Nicholson called off the land expedition. He was then appointed governor of Nova Scotia where he remained till 1717.

He returned to London and was knighted in 1720. In his last royal appointment, Nicholson served as royal governor of South Carolina where he remained until he returned to England in 1725. In South Carolina, Nicholson beefed up the colony's defenses against the Indians. He also interested himself in building projects and education and established new schools in the colony at his own expense. Historians regard him as one of the South Carolina's finest colonial governors.

DANIEL PARKE, governor of the Leeward Islands, died in 1710 in a riot caused by his own maladministration. His assassination surprised nobody in Virginia. In his last will and testament, he left his worldly goods to Lucy Chester, the illegitimate daughter of Katherine Chester. After her he listed as an heir Julius Caesar Parke. He remembered his daughters in Virginia, stating that if Lucy should live, he leaves property to her son and heirs provided they call themselves Parke. Following Lucy, he made the same provision for the children of Frances. He left a thousand pounds each to Lucy and Frances and fifty pounds to Julius Caesar. Daniel Parke left nothing to his legal wife, Jane Ludwell Parke, who lived until 1746.

Daniel Parke left his wife Jane saddled with substantial debts. His daughter Frances (also known as Fidelia) married John Custis and had five children. Frances's oldest son, Daniel Parke Custis, married Martha Dandridge and fathered four children, two of whom died in infancy. After the death of her first husband, Daniel Parke Custis, Martha Dandridge Custis married Col. George Washington. Martha Washington was the first First Lady of the United States.

Lucy Parke Byrd, Daniel Parke's younger legitimate daughter, and William Byrd II had six children, three of whom died in infancy. William Byrd II accepted his father-in-law's debts as his own; a burden later inherited by his son William Byrd III. William Byrd III sold off a great deal of the Byrd property to pay these debts.

Both Lucy and William II were literary figures and left detailed diaries describing life in the early eighteenth century. William was a surveyor and responsible for establishing the boundaries between Virginia and North Carolina. He published several diaries. The Byrd family of Virginia produced leading Virginia politicians through to the twentieth century.

WILLIAM ROSCOE died in 1700 of unknown causes. He died leaving a relatively large tobacco plantation and one merchant ship to his heirs. At the time of his death, he had four sons and one daughter.

THE MARQUIS OF NORTHAMPTON was a title created in 1547 and lapsed several times. Three marquises held the title during its first creation, followed by four Barons Compton and five Earls of Northampton. The Compton family descends from Baron Compton who was one of the peers at the trial of Mary, Queen of Scots. The second formal creation of the title marquis came in 1812.

JONATHAN SWIFT is best remembered as the author of *Gulliver's Travels*. Jonathan Swift was born in Ireland and studied at Trinity College in Dublin. He took all necessary requirements to become an ordained priest in the Anglican tradition and ministered to a small congregation outside Dublin.

In 1704, he anonymously published *A Tale of the Tub and the Battle of the Books*. The work became widely popular and was disapproved by the Church of England.

JOHN POLLEXFEN became very wealthy as a merchant in the peninsular trade around London. By 1677 he acquired one of the finest mansions in the city, and in 1679 he entered Parliament. He served as a gentleman of the Privy Chamber from 1678 to 1685 and commissioner for preventing the export of wool from 1689 to 1692. He served as a member of the Board of Trade from 1696 to 1707.

CPSIA information can be obtained
at www.ICGtesting.com
Printed in the USA
BVOW08s0336271016

466116BV00001B/36/P